ANNETTE K. LARSEN

Cover Art: Artbykarri.com

Character Art: Jenelle Hovde

Editing: the-writers-assistant.com

ISBN: 978-1-971677-01-9

For anyone who has ever been told it wasn't that bad.

Chapter One

LYRIELLE

I was needed.

That was the truth that dictated the circumstances of my life. I was always needed, and that need tugged on every piece of me, tearing away my dreams and ambitions piece by piece. I was so tired of being needed—never being allowed to need.

"Lyrielle, Lyrielle, let down your long hair!" a voice hollered from down below.

A smile leapt to my face, and I carefully picked up enough of my hair that I could safely cross to the balcony without dragging or damaging it. I leaned out over the banister and looked down on the grinning face of Gregor. "You're early," I pointed out, thrilled to see his friendly face.

"Yes, but I wanted to speak to you before anyone else came." He opened his worn satchel and pulled out the edge of a book.

I looked behind me to be sure that Auntie was still busy with her morning routine, then gathered all my hair and tied my special scarf to the end of my braid before slowly lowering it over the banister and down, down,

down to where he waited at the base of the tower. We'd developed this system long ago, so when the end of my braid reached him, he quickly placed the book in the large hidden pocket that I had sewn into the scarf.

I prepared to haul it back up, but Gregor held on to my hair. "While I'm here..." He held up his arm with a sheepish grin. "Aldie and I got into it this morning." His sleeve was torn, and a long scrape marred his forearm.

I shook my head, exasperated. "Why are you two always fighting? You're supposed to be friends."

He gave a shrug. "We know you'll make it all right in the end." He gave my braid a little shake. "Sing for me, Lyri."

I did so, humming a quick tune, feeling the pull of magic from my heart as it raised to my scalp, and watching my hair glow just a little, though it was barely noticeable in the bright morning sun. I'd always loved singing, making up little nonsense songs when I was only a few years old. My mother had encouraged it and often sang along with me. It had been irony of the cruelest sort that my healing magic had only manifested after my parents had died. It was a constant ache that gnawed at my insides, wondering how my life would have been different if only I'd discovered my gift in time to save them.

My healing magic flowed down through my hair, and it only took a few seconds before Gregor was moving his arm about and then grinning up at me. "What would I do without you?"

"Bleed out," I said dryly. "Suffer horrible infection. Die."

He chuckled even as he lifted the end of my braid, a reminder that I should haul my hair and the hidden book up to my balcony while Auntie was still busy.

"Thank you, Gregor!" I said as I pulled my braid up, hand over hand. It was tiring, especially since I had just healed him. My gift flowed easily, but it always took a toll.

He gave me a cocky salute. "I do what I can, Lyrielle." He turned to go, but then looked back. "Oh, I almost forgot. Baron Mabry went on a tirade again. You'll likely have more than a few of his servants stopping by." Then he ran off down the lane, toward the village of Eldmere, tossing a wave over his shoulder as he did so.

I sighed with a frown. Baron Mabry was one of the more powerful sorcerers and had influence with the High Court because of it. He also liked to use magic to hurt those who displeased him, especially those he employed. If the injuries he'd inflicted were severe, it would be an exhausting day.

I quickly hid the book Gregor had brought me in the bottom of the sewing basket beside my chair. I had a plethora of books in the tower. The walls were filled with them, but they were all books that Aunt Ethel deemed *suitable* for me—philosophical discourses, the history of the Magisterium of Branfrie and the shroud protecting it from the outside world that hated magic, and tales of morality that nearly always ended with the too-adventurous main character suffering because of their disobedience or curiosity.

Whenever he was able, Gregor would borrow a book from his master's library and bring it to me. Books about adventure and bravery. Exploratory texts about the kingdoms outside the magic shroud. Illustrated texts about animals or plants. Since being confined to this tower ten years ago, those books provided my only glimpses of the outside world aside from what I could see from this tower, and Aunt Ethel would have considered them a distraction when my life's work revolved around healing others here in this one spot—the tower of a crumbling ruin of a castle from which the royal family had once ruled. But that was before magic became a part of our land, before the High Court had taken over, when it was still the Kingdom of Branfrie instead of the Magisterium of Branfrie.

After hiding the book, I lowered my braid back over the banister and returned to my seat on the tiny balcony. The clock tower in the distance read nearly eight o'clock, and Auntie insisted I be prompt. It didn't matter if we couldn't see anyone coming; she wanted me seated on the balcony, my hair hanging within reach of the ground by the time the clock struck eight.

I couldn't wait until this afternoon when she would go on her daily walk and I could see what sort of book Gregor had given me. I cherished every single one that he lent me, knowing they were my only link to the world outside. It was getting more difficult to remember the years I'd spent outside of this tower, when I had lived with my parents—wandering the streets of the village where we'd lived, being part of the world. The dimming of those memories left me terrified that this tower was all I would ever know. But surely that wasn't the case. I was grown now, a young lady. Surely Auntie would allow me to start making my own decisions.

I shook off the heavy thoughts and reached into the sewing basket at my feet, pulling out a sleeve I was working on. Sewing clothing for myself and my aunt was a challenge that I enjoyed. Creating something whole out of parts and pieces fascinated me.

As I stitched, I sang. It was easier to simply sing the whole time I was on the balcony instead of waiting for someone below to holler up at me. The routine was mundane for the most part, only sometimes punctuated by someone pulling too hard on my hair, or by a cry of pain as someone dragged their injured body to my tower. Auntie would often supervise, peering over the edge to be sure that those who used my hair left something in return. A coin, a measure of wheat, a few pieces of fruit—whatever they could spare, whatever they thought their health was worth.

Gregor's prediction came true. Several of Baron Mabry's servants came with blackened blisters slashing across their bodies. Magic injuries were always tricky, so I leaned over the railing, concentrating on each person one by one, putting strength into my voice and singing words of compassion to encourage quick healing. When they were done, they all sagged in relief and trudged away. I could heal wounds, but there was nothing I could do about the emotional toll those injuries inflicted. After they went, I slumped down by the railing, resting my head against it while my breathing came in shallow spurts, and I wondered yet again what it would be like to just walk away from this tower.

At noon, Aunt Ethel brought me my mid-day meal and placed a few books on the table beside me. I often switched to reading in the afternoons, and it was good to break up the monotony while sitting there, looking out on all the places I was never allowed to go.

I'd grown up in a different village far from here, but after my parents died, Aunt Ethel brought me to this crumbling castle and turned this tower into our home. I didn't just long for the day she would let me leave, I craved it. I plodded through each day on the hope that one day she would tell me I'd done enough and could start making my own decisions and building my own life. There was an ache inside me, deep and throbbing, that yearned for a family of my own. I wanted the kind of comfort and security that my parents had given me. I wanted children of my own who I could love and teach and raise. And who would love me in return.

Aunt Ethel left late in the afternoon, as usual. She moved her bed aside to access the one door that led to the stairwell, then she disappeared through it and I heard the lock scrape into place. Usually that sound was ominous, but today it felt like a boon. I bent and pulled out the book Gregor had given me from the bottom of my sewing basket, running my hand over the worn leather cover before opening it.

It was a botanical guide. Names, descriptions, and illustrations of herbs, flowers, and every plant I could imagine. I wanted to devour it all. What might it be like to have a chance to see them up close, smell them, hold them in my hands? The only flowers I ever saw were the roses that climbed the tower, beautiful with their soft petals but brutal with their sharp thorns.

I was so engrossed in my study of the book that when the sound of the door being unlocked reached my ears, I had to scramble to shove the book out of sight, burying it in my sewing basket. Then I lunged to grab a different book from the little table beside me, quickly opening it and trying to look like I was engrossed in the material.

Aunt Ethel stepped inside with a bowl of cut vegetables in hand. She kept all the knives in a room below, worried I'd cut my hair. I'd tried once, when it first started growing out of control. "Hello, my dear," she said in a cheery tone.

"Hello, Auntie."

She crossed to the kitchen to set down her burden and then turned back to study me. "You look flushed."

"Do I?"

"You are not getting ill, are you?" She came over to press a hand to my forehead. "You know how important it is to take care of yourself."

"I feel perfectly fine," I assured her.

"Good." Auntie hated it when I was sick. It was difficult for me to heal others when I was not feeling well, and natural herbs and healing draughts were hard to come by, which meant that Auntie would have to purchase healing potions. I hated drinking magic. It made me feel off and I didn't trust it. If only I could heal myself.

Auntie went back to the door and disappeared through it once again, this time leaving it open. This was part of our usual routine. I sighed, envious of her ability to move about so freely. She went to retrieve a bucket of water from the well close by so that I could wash the bottom of my hair. Having so many people touch it, sometimes with blood on their hands, left it looking a bit gruesome by the time I was done each day.

I looked out at the sprawling view beyond my balcony and, seeing no one else on their way to visit me, I started pulling my braid over the railing, careful not to let it rub against the stone, lest the strands break. My hair was long enough to reach the bottom of the tower while still leaving a bit of it trailing on the floor where I sat. For a year after my gift manifested, it had grown at an unfathomable rate, reaching past my feet in the first month and growing more and more each day. Aunt Ethel wouldn't let me cut it, saying it would destroy the magic, and I'd been terrified that it would never stop growing. Fortunately, it had stopped after a year, leaving it ten times my own height.

After I'd washed the bottom portion of my hair, I arranged it on the floor in a pool of sunlight to dry before helping Aunt Ethel prepare our evening meal.

"Did I hear Gregor here early this morning?" she asked after we'd sat down to eat.

My heart jumped, wondering if she'd seen the book, but she sounded more curious than accusatory—stars be praised. “Yes, he’d gotten into a tussle with a friend and hurt his arm.” I was grateful to have that truth to tell her.

“He comes to see you often.”

I snorted. “He’s a foolish boy who thinks he’s invincible.” Just like the rest of them.

She looked me over with an intensity that made me squirm. “He’s a man now. And he likes you.”

It was an odd thing to say. Was she suggesting that someone liking me was a bad thing? “We are friends,” I said, trying not to sound like that fact was monumental in and of itself. After all, I didn’t have friends.

“Lyrielle…” Her face softened and she gave me a pitying look. It was a look I’d seen often and one that I loathed. It was the face she made when she was going to tell me a harsh reality of life that she expected me to swallow despite its biting bitterness. “You know you can never be with him, dear.”

My eyelids fluttered and widened in surprise. “Be with him?”

She tilted her head toward the little rounded balcony where my chair sat, and her pitying look turned stern. “Your life is here. Any ideas you may have about marrying that silly boy and going away should be set aside this moment. You are obligated to do what you can for the good of others.”

My mouth dropped open in confusion. I’d never once thought about Gregor in a romantic sense. He made me smile. He treated me like a whole person, not just a tool to be used. But I’d never let myself wonder if I could *marry* Gregor. Despite my yearning for a family, I refused to torture myself by pining for young men who were out of my reach.

I longed to marry someday, but I had to leave this tower first. I’d always assumed I would be allowed to grow up and have a family of my own, that I could have the sort of life my parents had lived with each other, but the way my aunt was speaking...

I spoke up, my voice tentative. "Surely I will marry some day, Auntie. Every woman should have her own family."

She leaned forward and cupped my cheek in her hand. "Not you, my darling. You must utilize your gift. *That* is your work."

My eyes stung. "But that doesn't mean I need to stay here all the time, does it?" I pleaded.

"You listen to me," she said gently. "Your magic is powerful. We are lucky we live so far from the seat of the High Court; if they knew of your abilities, they might want you for themselves. Or worse yet, they might feel threatened by you."

"But I'm no one."

She shook her head, her brow furrowed in concern. "Not to them."

"What does that mean?" She always said things like this, and I never understood what she was trying to say. Yes, she mistrusted the High Court, but didn't we all? They were the most powerful people in the magisterium. Most were power hungry and ruthless.

"Your place is here," she reiterated, each word carefully placed before me. "It will always be here. You are too valuable to throw yourself away on something as mundane as marriage." She gave me a teary smile, then turned and walked back to the kitchen.

My lungs felt empty and I could not draw breath. My limbs were numb. My one wish—to live my own life and have a family—had been instantly dismissed by the woman who called herself my family, my protector. She'd brushed it aside as if just her few words could make me forget that there was an entire world outside of this tower, one that I was desperate to be a part of. She expected me to stay. And stay, and stay.

I could not fathom what that would mean for my life. She'd called my dream of marriage and a family mundane. Was that what she believed motherhood to be? Something completely unextraordinary? I'd spent years setting my own desires aside, doing all I could to help anyone who came to me. I knew the value of helping others and I had no wish for people to suffer needlessly. But it wasn't *all* I wanted to do. Yet I'd done it, day after day, year after year. I'd kept myself in this tower. I'd protected my hair and my gift, all in the hopes that one day my wants and wishes would matter.

But that day would never come, not if Aunt Ethel had her way. And I knew in that moment, more than I'd known anything in my whole life, that I could not let Auntie have her way. I would waste away, die, go insane if I stayed in this place much longer without hope, without the promise of anything other than *this*. And if Auntie would offer me no hope, then I would have to make my own.

I had to find a way out of this tower. I had to leave—soon. As soon as I was able.

I started climbing the walls.

I'd been over it a thousand times in my head. Aunt Ethel was very careful to safeguard anything that could be used as a rope or ladder, and since my escape would necessarily have to happen in silence while she slept, I knew I had few options.

So I practiced climbing the inside walls of the tower every afternoon while she was gone. I'd spent a lot of time leaning over the banister, studying the structure of the tower, and I knew that the way the stone and mortar fit together on the outside of the tower was the same on the inside.

I had to make up excuses for why my fingers were scraped and raw when Auntie noticed, telling her it had happened while I'd scrubbed the floors or that I'd been tending the roses that climbed the tower. Despite the difficulty of getting dressed while managing my hair, I started dressing myself without her help so she wouldn't notice the inevitable scrapes and bruises on my shins and backside that resulted from my desperate endeavor.

After nearly two months, my strength and climbing abilities were improving. I was able to climb up and down the walls of our rooms, clinging to the rocks and maneuvering along them for longer and longer periods each week. Yet, the prospect of climbing over the balcony and down the entire height of the tower left me nauseous.

I started to doubt my conviction. Maybe I was being impulsive and foolhardy. Maybe Aunt Ethel hadn't truly meant it when she said what she did.

So before I took my life in my hands and left this tower, I broached the subject with her one more time.

"I know you believe that my place is here, Aunt," I said as we sat across from one another, eating our evening stew.

She paused her eating and fixed her eyes on me. "It *is* your place."

“I know how important my gift is. I know the good I’ve done, and I want to do more. But I’m grown now. I must have the freedom to live my own life.”

Her nostrils flared and her eyes narrowed. “Freedom?” The whispered word felt dangerous. “Is that what you want?”

I swallowed and felt myself start to tremble. “Yes, Aunt.”

“Freedom has a price,” she said with a cold stare. “And believe me, my dear, you are not willing to pay it.”

I shrank a little in my seat, unnerved by her hard eyes and sneering mouth. What price was she talking about? Did she think I couldn’t handle the freedom to move about in the world of my own accord? Was she just trying to scare me?

“I’m not a child anymore, Auntie,” I said, managing to keep the quiver out of my voice. “You can’t ask me to stay in this tower for my entire life. I deserve to—”

She slammed her hand down on the table with such force that I jumped. “If you continue to bring up this ridiculous notion, then you might need to spend some time in solitude.”

My lungs felt like they collapsed inside my chest at that single word—solitude. When I’d first come to live with Aunt Ethel at nine, I hadn’t understood her rules, and I’d fought her on them. I wanted to be allowed outside, so I’d pestered and whined endlessly—until she’d given me *solitude*. The rooms we currently occupied were not at the very top of the tower. No, there was another room farther up at the end of the long, winding stairwell. We used it for storage. I was never allowed to leave these rooms and go into that stairwell unless she was punishing me by giving me solitude in that upper room.

The room had no windows.

Sometimes she had left me there only for a few hours. Other times, she'd given me a "calming potion" and left me there for days with water but no food, too weak to stand and in a mental haze. I was only ever allowed one candle, and it never lasted long. The last time she'd used that punishment was after she'd taken away my precious dolls when I was thirteen, but just the mention of it left me in a cold sweat. "No," I whispered, twisting the fabric of my skirt in my hands. "I don't need that."

"You say that now, and yet I worry that in a week we will be having this same inane conversation. You know what happened to my sister. You know the tragedy that could befall countless families if you are not willing to help. Yet you insist on bringing it up time after time."

"I won't bring it up again, I promise."

"Good. But just to be sure..." She stood and crossed to my bed, tossing my pillow aside and snatching up one of Gregor's books I had hidden there. "I will be taking this." She stalked over to the fireplace and tossed the book in without hesitation. "And each time you act in an ungrateful manner, I'll burn another." She came back, grabbed both of our half-eaten bowls of stew, and threw them in the wash tub. Stew splattered the walls and ground, but she ignored it and left the kitchen.

My breathing was pained and shallow, my eyes stinging with unshed tears, but I forced myself to breathe past the horrific panic that consumed my chest, then stood and cleaned up the mess she'd just made.

Aunt Ethel was asleep—and had been for some time—yet I waited a few moments more, gathering my courage before slipping from my bed. I didn't have time to delay. I had to dress, gather the few things I would take with me, and then...go.

Climb down the tower. Leave my entire life behind.

Gain some semblance of freedom—I hoped.

I quickly dressed, taking the time to grab the back hem of my skirt and pull it forward through my legs, stuffing as much as I could into the sash at my waist so it wouldn't be in the way as I climbed. I grabbed the necklace my mother had gifted me from my bedside table and secured it around my neck. Then I pulled out one of the long scarves that I used to bind my hair and placed a change of clothes, my aunt's shoes, some food, and a water pouch in the middle. I tied it in a bundle, then crossed to the balcony, grabbing Auntie's cloak as I went. I held the cloak as far out over the railing as I could and then let it go, watching as it plummeted and then slumped onto the ground. My heart leapt to my throat. I was used to being up high; it was all I'd known for the past ten years, but watching that cloak fall made me realize just how high it was. If I lost my grip and fell...

No, I wouldn't fall. I'd been practicing. I was good at clinging to the rocks. My grip was strong. My toes knew how to find the right holds.

I took my bundle of belongings and tied it to the back of my belt. This was it. I was going. There had only been two visitors to my tower today, both with small injuries, so I still had my strength. I glanced over my shoulder, at the shadowed figure of Aunt Ethel still sleeping soundly in her bed that blocked the door that only she was allowed to pass through. She'd been my only comfort and companion since my parents died, and I would miss her. I knew that much, but it wasn't enough to make me want to stay, not when she would never allow me to have anything more than this set of rooms. My life was so small, and the world outside was so big. I wanted the chance to discover at least a portion of it, to meet new people, to make a family—to make my own choices.

"Goodbye, Auntie," I whispered, feeling as though there should have been more to say, but unable to find any more words.

I threw my leg over the banister, got a good toehold, and then let my other leg follow.

I was going, and I couldn't hesitate. I was strong, but the longer it took for me to scale the tower, the more my strength would wane. So I settled my weight on my feet and extended my arms to lower my body. I moved my feet down to new holds, then gathered my courage, my heart beating out of my chest, and released one hand from the banister. I found a grip on the rocks easily, then did the same with my other hand. It felt familiar and secure. I'd been right to think it would be much the same as climbing the walls inside. I could do this. My body was strong.

I lowered myself again and again. Foot, foot, hand, hand. My hair tugged gently at my scalp as more of my hair was pulled over the ledge of the balcony. I was making steady progress, and I wasn't worn out. This would work.

I moved down again, and there was a sudden rushing beside me. Glancing over, I saw that instead of my hair being pulled over the ledge a little at a time, it was falling like water, tumbling toward me all at once. I had the shortest moment of realizing my mistake, and I gripped the wall tighter, hoping that when the full weight of my hair pulled at my neck, I'd be strong enough to hold on.

The weight came, my head was viciously jerked back, and my fingers failed me, losing their grip on the stones. Nothing to hold on to. Nothing but air around me. In all my practice climbing, I'd never climbed with the full weight of my hair pulling on me.

And I was going to die for that mistake.

Chapter Two

TAVRIC

I leaned my forearms on the railing of the ship and looked out over the swells as the moonlight glinted off the water. We'd been out all day, inspecting coastal fortifications. Most of the watchtowers had been well maintained, but there were a few repairs needed, as well as a lax garrison commander who would need to be disciplined.

It was a beautiful night for sailing, but Harlan had shaken his head at me when we'd finished our inspection and I'd told him to steer us farther out to sea. My crew found my propensity for sailing at night odd, but it was where I found the most calm. And since we were already out on the water, I didn't feel bad about taking a few extra hours to clear my mind and look for telltale signs of life in the water.

We'd been sailing out in open water for more than an hour, and the crew had left me alone for the most part, knowing my preference for solitude. But now Harlan was approaching, a spyglass in hand. "I assume you'll want this," he said as he held it out to me.

"Thank you." I was quick to hold it to my eye and scan the water.

"Any chance you'll tell me what you're searching for?"

I gave a shrug. "Nothing in particular."

He scoffed.

I cut my eyes over to him and raised a brow, silently waiting for him to speak his mind.

He ran a hand through his ruffled hair and over his beard that had just a few strands of gray in it. He was ten years my senior and had been the one to teach me how to sail. As my first mate and my friend, I trusted him, but I didn't tell him everything. "You've been searching for something ever since your birthday."

I looked away. He was right, of course.

"You ever going to tell me what it is so I can help you find it?"

I tapped the spyglass against my palm, debating for several moments. "Not *it*," I finally confided. "*Who*."

His brow shot up. "You're looking for someone?"

I nodded. "When I went overboard on my birthday, I didn't make it to shore on my own."

He faced me more fully. "What does that mean?" There was an edge to his tone, and I couldn't blame him. I'd given everyone the scare of their lives that night. Having the crown prince disappear overboard on his twenty-fourth birthday wasn't on anyone's to-do list.

"You remember how inebriated I was." I stared at my hands, remembering how I'd sailed off on this ship, seeking the oblivion of salt spray and drink after my father had told me about his condition.

"Of course I do. I also remember seeing you fall into the ocean when you got in the way of that yardarm."

I fingered the raised scar at my hairline, still embarrassed that I'd been worse than useless when the storm had come up. "I didn't lose consciousness, but it was dark and I was disoriented." It had been terrifying, and for just a few moments, I thought I might drown. But then a set of arms had looped around my chest and started towing me to shore, and I'd let them. "I didn't make it to shore on my own. Someone helped me."

He looked baffled. "Who?"

I shook my head. "I don't know her name." I'd started calling her Melody in my head because she'd sung to me. That was how I'd known it was a woman even before I saw her face. The sound of her voice had entranced me. "But I want to find her, to thank her at the very least." She'd brought me close to shore and pushed me forward so I could drag myself onto the sandy beach. When I'd turned back, I'd been shocked to see the woman still half submerged, fire-red hair dancing in the water around her. She'd sung a few more notes, the tune sounding like a farewell, and in the few seconds it took to rub the water from my eyes, she'd disappeared.

"And you think we'll find her in the ocean?" Harlan looked both confused and awed. "Are you saying..."

I shrugged, unwilling to say it out loud. None of us had ever seen one with our own eyes, but the rumors were rampant.

And how else could Melody have disappeared so completely unless she was a—

"Mermaid!" The shout rang out from the crow's nest.

I looked up to see Jenkins pointing out at the ocean, and my heart shot into my throat.

I ran.

LYRIELLE

There was a loud noise. Blackness surrounded me. Cold enveloped me. Water shot up my nose.

Water? What was happening? I kicked against the wetness around me, shocked and terrified and unable to breathe. How was I in *water*?

I clawed at the wetness, trying to remember what my father had taught me about swimming. When I finally broke the surface and gulped in air, my lungs constricted in spasms as I coughed and tried to breathe despite the freezing water. I pushed down, hoping to keep myself up. I'd only tried to swim once, and that had been nearly ten years ago. Lifting my chin to keep my nose further from the water, I strained to see around me, but there was nothing except waves of inky blackness, tipped by ribbons of moonlight that reflected off the water.

But *what* water? Why was I in water? I'd been falling and there had been nothing but hard ground below me. I looked around for land, but there was none. Was this what death looked like? Cold, endless water? What if—

My head was tugged back, and I gasped one deep breath before the weight of my hair and the rolling waves pulled me under the surface again.

I was going to die. Auntie had been right. Freedom did have a price.

The water tugged at my braid, pulling me deeper.

Just as my lungs screamed and I felt I couldn't keep myself from trying to breathe any longer, something caught under my arm. A branch? A rope? A hand? Was there someone else in the water with me? I was now being dragged through the water. But dragged where? Up? Or down?

Air hit my face again and I gasped for breath, flailing around until my hands latched on to the shoulders of a man who was in the water with me, his face stunned but determined.

"I've got you," he shouted as he secured me to his side. "Don't fight or you'll pull us both under."

I coughed and sputtered, desperate for more air, but tried to do as he asked. As I clung to his neck and did my best to convince myself that I was not on the verge of death anymore, I could feel him kicking and using one arm to pull us through the water. My eyes darted around, trying to make sense of this impossible situation. My whole body shook with terror and with cold, but the warmth of the man I clung to anchored me just enough that I was able to focus. A large shadow loomed above us, and after several moments, the shadow took the shape of a ship; that must have been where the man had come from.

I looked up at the railing , where several faces peered over the edge.

"Do you need assistance, Highness?" one man hollered down at us.

"No. Stand by," the man holding me yelled back.

"It's a mermaid, it is!" another shouted from above. "Tritan has blessed us with one of his daughters."

A ladder made of rope hung down the side of the ship, and the man reached out with his left hand to take hold of the first rung, his right arm still firmly anchored around my waist.

I continued to cling to him, shaking and frantic.

"Grab hold of the ladder, miss." I looked at him, frightened and unsure, but his eyes were kind and encouraging. "You can do it."

I nodded and, with great effort, managed to release him with my right hand and latch onto the closest rung.

"Well done. Now pull."

Working together, we were able to pull our upper bodies out of the water. My arm shook with the effort, even though I was certain that he did most of the work.

While his right forearm kept me anchored to his side, he reached out with his right hand so he could hold the ladder while his left hand moved up to the next rung. "Now you. Move your hand up. Good. Pull."

The sea swelled and the current pulled on my hair, weighing on my neck. I cried out, afraid I'd be sucked back into the sea. "Don't let me go," I begged.

He looked back over his shoulder at the length of my hair trailing down my back and into the depths. "Poseiden's hoard, maybe you truly are a mermaid," he muttered in astonishment.

Before I could reply, the waves heaved again and the pull on my hair was so strong that I lost my grip on the ladder. The man tried to keep a hold of me, but his grasp broke and I was swallowed by the waves once more.

As I sank into the blackness that stole my air, I wondered if perhaps the man and the sea had just been one last vivid daydream before the plummet from my tower ended my life.

It had been nice to think that someone had been willing to care for me. Perhaps that was the best I could hope for in my last moments in this world.

A strong hand circled my arm and pulled, forcing me to acknowledge that I was not quite dead and should try to keep it that way.

I kicked my legs and grabbed at the water until my head broke the surface. I latched onto his neck again, pulling close, desperate to keep my head above water. My hair was going to kill me.

"Calm down," he insisted, his voice tight as he reached behind me. "This hair is going to drown you."

I felt him tugging on it and wondered why he wasn't taking me back to the ship. But all I could do was hold on to him as he kicked his legs, keeping us above water while he pulled and tugged my hair. What was he doing? My hair wasn't any good to him unless I sang.

"Forgive me, but if you want to live..."

"I'm coming down to help," a voice shouted from the deck above.

"Don't!" the man said, still pulling on my hair. "You'll only make it worse."

"Is it a mermaid?" The shout came from a different voice above us.

The man's eyes cut to me, a question in his gaze. What did he expect me to say? I lived in the only magic kingdom known to man, and even we knew that mermaids were nothing but a myth or a bedtime story.

He went back to his task and I finally realized what he was doing.

Sparks and fire. He's cutting my hair. I could see some of the strands reflecting the moonlight as they floated away.

A wave of horror washed over me, an instinctual bristling. Cutting my hair was the ultimate betrayal of everything I'd been taught. All of my worth, all the good that I had ever done, had been because of my hair.

Yet, with each cut, it became easier to hold my head above the water.

So I closed my eyes and I let it happen. This was what I'd wanted. This was why I'd run away—to be free of the life my hair tethered me to.

"There," he said and immediately grabbed my waist and swam us both back to the ship. "Shall we try again?"

I stared, slack-jawed over his shoulder as the last of my hair slipped beneath the inky surface. Gone. My hair was gone. The way my head rested on my neck felt wobbly and strange.

This time, he put me in front of him and encouraged me to climb while he caged me from behind. I discovered that my months of training to climb the tower made it fairly easy to scale the ladder now that my hair was gone, though a ladder that swung precariously from a rocking ship was certainly different from a solid stone wall, and the man kept having to pull my skirt out of my way when it would tangle around my feet.

Hand over hand, I climbed toward the railing above and the men who waited there.

So many faces peered down on us. All men. Some young, some old. Some grizzled and rough, some fresh-faced.

"Has King Tritan sent us one of his daughters, Highness?" one of the younger men yelled.

Highness? Was this man royalty, then? And the King Tritan they spoke of, perhaps he was a ruler of another land. One who regularly threw his daughters into the sea? That didn't seem right. Then again, nothing about this was right.

Those strange thoughts swirled in my head, distracting me from the strain of pulling myself up the ladder. The man—prince?—who'd saved me stayed one rung below me the whole time, anchoring the ladder and telling me I could do it.

When we reached the top, several sets of hands took hold of me and dragged me over the railing.

As soon as my feet met the wooden planks, I collapsed onto the deck, catching myself with my hands. My chest heaved with labored breathing, and my eyes darted around, tired and confused. I was on a ship in the middle of the sea, and the tower from which I'd fallen was nowhere in sight.

I looked up, acutely aware of all the eyes staring at me in the lamplight as unease crept up my spine.

The wet, wooden planks beneath my hands testified to the fact that this truly was a ship, and I truly was surrounded by men, one of whom had just saved me from certain death.

Chapter Three

LYRIELLE

The ship dipped and bobbed as the men stared down at me.

"She's a mermaid, she has to be," one whispered.

"She's a beauty. A gift from the sea gods?" another hissed.

I curled in on myself, trying to hide, to be small.

Then a pair of bare feet landed on the deck. "Give her some room, men. She's had enough fright for a lifetime, I'm sure."

They shuffled back, immediately deferring to his authority. A prince, indeed. I looked up at him as he stood there, dripping wet, his blue trousers and loose white shirt clinging to his body.

"Maybe she'll sing for us," said an old man with a weathered face.

My muscles tensed, terrified that they somehow knew of my gift and would insist on using it.

But then—I glanced down at my cut hair, which barely brushed my elbow—I didn't have my gift anymore. I blinked heavily as that fact sank in.

A man with a neat beard and dignified bearing shook his head. "She's got legs, lads. She's not a mermaid."

My eyes darted to my legs, hoping they were not too exposed. Thankfully, the hem of my dress clung just below my knees. Not quite respectable, but considering I'd been fished from the sea, I wasn't going to quibble over the modesty of my calves.

"But her hair!" the old sailor protested. "I've never seen such a thing."

"Miss," the prince said, ignoring the comments of the crowd of men and crouching in front of me. His dark, dripping hair clung to his forehead and his clothing was finer than the other sailors. "Miss, are you all right?" His brow furrowed in grim concern.

"I...I don't know." My voice shook. All of me shook.

"I'm sorry about your hair, but there really was no other option."

I nodded mutely. Yes, I'd planned to cut my hair once I got away from my tower, but the actual loss of my hair was more than a little frightening. However, on the heels of that feeling, a huge, coursing surge of joy washed through me. Looking down at my remaining hair, seeing the choppy, uneven cuts, was such a...*relief*. Without my hair, I no longer had the ability to heal, and without that ability, I wouldn't be obligated to help everyone around me. I wouldn't be sapped of my energy day in and day out. It was what I'd longed for, the ability to decide what I wanted, what I *needed*. I would have the opportunity—finally—to have some say in the course of my life. I'd be able to *move*—unencumbered by my hair.

Startled tears rushed down my cheeks as I breathed freely in a way that had been impossible for too many years.

The man's eyes traced my face, concern etching the corners of his eyes. "Are you hurt, miss?"

I gave a tiny shake of my head. "No, sir. It doesn't hurt at all."

"Then why are you crying, little mermaid?"

The silly nickname made me chuckle just a bit. "Um...relief? I think?"

He studied me for a moment and then nodded. "I suppose that's as good as can be expected. I don't know how you could have lived your life with the burden of all that hair weighing you down."

"It was a challenge," I whispered, the words completely inadequate.

"How did you end up out here?" he asked.

His question brought back all my confusion, and I searched for any sort of logical answer I could give. "I don't know."

He paused and narrowed his eyes at me, almost suspicious. "You don't know?"

My eyes swept my surroundings once more, but beyond the ship's deck, I could only see the dark night and hear the splash of water. "I...I shouldn't be here. It shouldn't be possible for me to be here."

He frowned but didn't respond. Instead he focused again on my hair, reaching out to gather it all at the nape of my neck.

I stiffened. His closeness, his gruff kindness, the feel of his fingers brushing my neck, this whole situation was too much, and my silent tears increased. "What are you doing?"

He gentled his stoic expression, curving his mouth in what I supposed was meant to be an encouraging smile. "I just need to be certain I didn't cut your shoulders or back while I was cutting your hair." He lifted my wet hair and inspected my neck, back, and shoulders, then allowed my hair to flop back into place.

He stood and reached out both hands. "Come along. You need to get warm."

I stared at those hands. For the last ten years, I'd only ever been touched by my aunt. It was such a strange thing to have this stranger reaching out to me, offering help and even comfort. I didn't know if I could trust it, but I longed to, so I put my hands in his. When he pulled me to my feet, I became dizzy.

He held tight to my hands while I steadied myself. "It will take a while to get your sea legs."

I studied the ship, with all its wood and rigging, watching as it swayed not quite with the waves, but in contrast to them. I'd only ever seen depictions of ships in books that Gregor had snuck to me. How strange and marvelous to be on one myself. "It's not the ship." I looked back at the sea, where my hair had all disappeared. "It's strange to stand without my hair pulling on me. My neck feels unstable." I let out a breathy laugh, then more tears leaked from my eyes.

"You are overcome." He released my hands and picked up a vest and coat that had been discarded on the deck, then carefully maneuvered to my side so he could put a firm arm around my waist. "Harlan, find her a place to rest."

"Where, Highness?" the dignified man with the neat beard asked in low tones. "Among the crew?"

The prince let out a grumbling sigh. "I suppose that won't work."

"Pardon," Harlan said, "but the only private space is—"

"Yes, I know. Thank you, Harlan." He tugged me through the crowd of men. "Come, miss."

A nod was the best I could do as the feeling of his warm hand shot through me.

"And all of you, get back to work," he shouted at the milling crew.

I looked back over my shoulders at the men, the ship, and the sea. Was this all a dream? A hallucination? Perhaps it was a strange afterlife, but I didn't think so. The water dripping from my clothing, the chill of the wind against my wet skin, the gentle pressure of this man's arm around my waist—it all felt too real to be imagined. I grabbed onto the hand that rested on my waist, my throat tight with emotion as the simple comfort of human interaction washed over me. Auntie's hugs and touches of affection had always felt cheap, or disingenuous, and sometimes even dangerous. But this man, who knew me not at all, simply seemed to *care*, and that brought even more tears to my eyes.

Despite the insanity of the situation, despite the men staring at me with awe, and despite the confusion of not knowing how I came to be on the water, I was *happy* to be here.

The prince guided me toward the back of the ship, to a door that was nestled between two sets of stairs leading up to a higher portion of the deck, which I couldn't remember the name of because I'd had to return the ship book to Gregor before I could adequately study it.

He opened the door, and my brow jumped as I took in the opulence of the small room. Silk drapery and fancy carved wood adorned the space. A bed occupied one corner, a desk in another. A trunk sat to my right.

"What's this?" I asked, fascinated by the difference in this space compared to the main deck.

The prince cleared his throat. "It's the captain's quarters."

I turned to look at him, my head seeming to move too fast. “Are you the captain?”

“Yes.”

“Are you also a prince?” I was curious due to having no experience with royalty since the royal family of Branfrie had been ousted by the High Court more than three generations ago, after magic had manifested in our land.

The captain prince was slower to answer this time. “Yes.” He guided me to a chair, and after I’d sat, he gave me a very fine bow.

No one had ever bowed to me before.

“I am Prince Tavric of Islewyn.”

“Hello.” That probably wasn’t the right thing to say. He was a prince, so maybe I should have said something more formal, but I was wet and getting colder by the minute. Also, I’d never heard of Islewyn. Some of Gregor’s books had spoken of kingdoms outside the shroud, but Islewyn hadn’t been one of them.

Prince Tavric grabbed a coverlet from the bed and wrapped it around me. Then he pulled a cloth from a cabinet and placed it in my hands. “For your hair.”

“Thank you.” I did my best to squeeze my hair with the cloth, fascinated by the way my short hair moved. I stared at the blunt and unevenly cut ends hanging to my waist.

“I’m sorry about your hair,” he said, using another cloth to scrub the water from his own hair.

His brow seemed to be perpetually furrowed, though I wouldn’t call his expression angry. Just…pensive. Perhaps moody, though I was smart enough to know I shouldn’t say that to him. “Don’t be. This is better. Different, but better.”

I looked to the door of his cabin, which had been left open. Several curious sailors lingered just outside. I thought perhaps the open door was supposed to be reassuring, but it wasn't. The prince was the only one who looked at me without either awe or suspicion. At least half of the crew seemed to believe I was a mermaid who'd miraculously procured legs.

"Your name?" the prince asked.

I returned my attention to him, noting for the first time that I liked his face. "Lyrielle."

"It's a pleasure to meet you, Lyrielle. And where are you from?"

Should I tell him? I'd escaped and didn't want to return, but now that my hair and my gift of healing were gone, perhaps going home would not be so terrible. As fear and discomfort surged within me, I immediately dismissed that idea, however. I didn't want to return. Yet, no lie came to mind. I had to say something, but I knew very little about any other kingdom or land, and lying was not in my nature.

"From Eldmere," I confessed.

His brow scrunched even more. "I've never heard of Eldmere."

"No? It's a village in Branfrie," I said, curious if that name was still known to the outside world. The shroud that had been erected around Branfrie was for the express purpose of hiding it and its existence from anyone but its inhabitants, but before the shroud had been erected, Branfrie had been a kingdom similar to any other.

His eyebrows pinched together. "I don't know that name."

That was best. The world outside of Branfrie hated magic, and I had no wish for them to suspect that I had magic—or rather, that I *used* to have magic.

"And I am well versed in the geography of this area," he pointed out. His stern expression seemed to suggest that he thought I was hiding something, but I was just as lost as he was.

“Then perhaps you can tell me where I am.” I kept squeezing my hair, the strangeness of the situation coming to the forefront of my mind and beginning to bring panic with it.

“You don’t know where you are?”

“I know I’m on a ship, in the...sea.” Squeeze and wring, squeeze and wring.

His eyes studied me for several moments, then he went to the door, closed it, and returned to me. “What ship were you on before?”

“I wasn’t.” My hands fisted around my hair, trying to hold on to something.

His eyes narrowed. “Pardon?”

“I wasn’t on a ship,” I reiterated.

“Did you swim?”

I threw the cloth on the ground and the blanket slipped from my shoulders. “I don’t know how to swim.”

“Well then how—”

“I don’t know,” I snapped as all the questions, insanity, fear, and unknown rose up to drown me. “It’s madness. I shouldn’t be here. I’ve never even seen the sea before, much less touched it.” My voice rose with each declaration as my eyes darted about, trying to find anything around me that would make sense. I wanted to see something familiar, something that felt real, but I was unmoored, so I kept rambling as he moved closer. “It shouldn’t be possible. I was in my room. I was finally leaving my room. Leaving that tower. But then I fell and...”

“You fell from a ship?” he interrupted, his voice loud to match the volume of my own even as he pulled the blanket back over my shoulders.

“There was no ship!”

"There had to have been a ship," he insisted. "Perhaps you just don't remember."

"I remember it perfectly." I burst to my feet, and he had to step back as I ranted, trying to put into words something that I still couldn't fathom. "I fell from my tower, and instead of falling to my death, I was dropped in the sea. I told you, it's madness. Impossible. I don't understand it, but I'm here, and I'm wet, and you're real, and this room is solid, and I don't know how that could be when a few minutes ago, I was just trying to get out. I was just trying to get away." I covered my eyes with the heels of my hands and dug my fingers into the front of my hair, breathing hard.

TAVRIC

She was trying to get away...from who? Despite all her answers to my questions, which truly weren't answers at all, that was the one detail I was stuck on. It shouldn't have surprised me. A young lady would not end up swimming—or rather drowning—in the middle of the Lantis Ocean without some sort of trouble putting her there.

Despite the fact that I'd been looking for a mermaid, I hadn't actually expected to jump into the ocean and save one from drowning.

She's not a mermaid, my mind reminded me. *Yes, I know, but she's very pretty*, my heart responded. It was a constant battle between those two.

My heart, of course, was correct. She was extraordinarily pretty. Porcelain skin, fine features, lovely curves, which I happened to know all about thanks to her drenched condition. Her dress was not a fashion I was familiar with; it was light purple, laced up the front, and had small puffed sleeves, one of which had slid off her shoulder along with her blanket when she'd burst to her feet, ranting about her strange predicament.

I would have loved to say that she was simply confused from her fall, and surely she'd just gone overboard from another ship. But few ships traveled at night, and I had a fine lookout up in the crow's nest. I knew very well that there had been no ships in sight for more than an hour, and the coast of Islewyn was only barely visible on the horizon. Lyrielle claimed she couldn't swim, and I was prone to believe her. Her situation did not make sense, but logic failed to provide me with the answers I sought. Magic? I immediately rejected the thought. Though sailors still liked to believe in the existence of mermaids, there was no evidence of real magic.

The length of her hair still astounded me. I'd seen some of it floating on the waves, glistening in the moonlight as it stretched out endlessly. Why would anyone have hair that long? And how? It didn't seem natural.

"Well," I said in what I hoped was a calming tone, though I'd been told many times that my presence was less than soothing. "You got away."

My statement of the obvious made her go still, and her breathing became less panicked. When she looked out from behind her hands, her eyes were a little less wild.

She sat abruptly in the chair once again, bringing her down almost to my eye level as I knelt in front of her. She stared at me, her green eyes deep, fathomless, and glistening.

Then her tears welled, her breathing raced anew, and she fell apart in front of me, curling over with her hands fisted in her hair, sobbing.

Suddenly, the how of her arrival on my ship no longer seemed to matter. I was just glad that she was alive, and that she was here instead of wherever she'd come from.

Chapter Four

TAVRIC

Lyrielle was asleep in my bed.

When she'd nodded off, I'd grabbed a dry set of clothes and left the cabin to change. I couldn't feel okay about stripping down with her in the room, even if she was asleep, but the discomfort of the wet fabric against my skin wasn't something I could put up with for long. I'd offered her dry clothing as well, but she'd shaken her head and pulled the blanket more tightly around herself.

After I'd changed, I spoke with the crew, ordering them to take us directly back to shore since we couldn't very well go gallivanting on the ocean with an innocent and naive passenger on board. Especially a female passenger.

When I'd returned to my cabin, it was to find her curled up on the foot of my bed where I'd left her, her damp, uneven hair splayed over the coverlet, her fist curled under her chin, and her dark lashes resting in stark contrast against her pale cheek. In light of her comment about finally getting out of her tower, the paleness of her skin made my heart lurch. Had the sun ever touched her skin?

Though I made a habit of hiding away in my library when I was at home, I couldn't imagine not having the ability to escape on my ship, to have the salt spray in my face, the wind in my hair, and the sun warm on my shoulders. What if this girl had never been allowed outside?

I shook my head, chastising myself for letting my imagination get away from me. *No reason to invent horror stories.*

Sitting at my desk, I attempted to organize my maps, but my eyes kept wandering back to her face, hungry for another glimpse. It felt wrong, like I was betraying the woman who had saved me, the one I'd been searching for for the past month.

After all, she was the reason I'd come running when Jenkins had shouted "mermaid." While Lyrielle was clearly not a mermaid, I felt in my bones that Melody was. But whether Melody was a true mermaid or not, I had to find her—to thank her for saving my life at the very least.

Shaking thoughts of mermaids from my mind, I returned to my maps, grateful that we would be back in port before too long. Sleeping in this chair was not on my list of wants, and I wouldn't dishonor Lyrielle, myself, or my parents by sleeping in the same bed with her.

Despite my determination to study nothing but my maps, the young woman curled up on my bed kept snagging my attention. A young lady, who was obviously running from something or someone, had been unceremoniously dropped in my ocean. What was I to do about that? My eyes slid over her dress, which was obviously homespun. Was she from a far kingdom? Had she escaped from pirates or been held prisoner? I couldn't wait for her to wake so that I could start asking her some of my many questions. Hopefully she would be more receptive to them this time around.

LYRIELLE

I startled awake, my eyes darting around, looking for the familiar shapes of my tower.

I blinked.

And blinked again as my breathing came in shallow gasps.

It hadn't been a dream. I was in the quarters of the ship's captain prince who had fished me from the water after I'd fallen to what should have been my death.

Relief and panic warred within me as I told myself that this was what I'd wanted. Freedom from Aunt Ethel, from that tower, and from that life.

I wrapped my hands around my still damp hair, feeling the bizarrely short strands, so foreign in my hands.

"I imagine that will take some getting used to."

I lifted my eyes to see Prince Tavric sitting in the chair I'd been in earlier, leaning forward with his elbows resting on his knees. I wondered if he always looked so stern and serious, or if it was just my presence that made him frown.

My own mouth turned down as I tried to figure out what he referred to.

He nodded toward my hands, and I looked down at the jagged ends of my hair. "Yes," I admitted. "I still can't believe it's gone." I was glad for it, and maybe if I kept telling myself that, the guilt would eventually subside. Or perhaps not. Perhaps I'd always feel guilty because my decision had been entirely selfish and I really was squandering the gift I'd been given.

I divided my hair into three sections, pulling on the tangled strands that were gritty with salt water, and working it into a braid. The ease of the task was startling. My remaining hair was so very manageable, and my eyes stung from the strangeness of it.

As I pulled my hair off my neck, I suddenly realized how bare it was. I dropped my hair and put both hands to my neck, feeling for my necklace, then started looking around me on the bed and on the floor.

"What are you looking for?" the prince asked.

"My necklace. It must have fallen off." Tears burned my eyes.

"Was it special to you?"

I nodded. "It was a gift from my mother. She wore it every day until she gave it to me on my eighth birthday."

He grimaced in commiseration. "I'm sorry you lost it."

I shook my head, devastated but trying not to show it. I was alive, after all.

"Lyrielle," he said rather abruptly. "Are you running away from something?"

My chest tightened as I thought of my tower, my aunt, and the fierce anger she'd be feeling the moment she discovered me missing. If I was sent back, what would she do to me? I opened my mouth to try to answer, but there weren't words, not ones I could say. I refused to speak of magic or healing, and I was too tired to think of any safe truth to speak, so I just gaped as my face heated and an ache grew in my throat.

The prince's expression turned startled and concerned. "I'm sorry. Forgive me," he said, leaning back and pulling a hand down his face. "You needn't... It's fine. You don't need to speak of it."

I'd made him uncomfortable, but at least he'd let me off the hook.

Getting up, he paced in front of me to the other side of the room, where he looked through a porthole. "We will arrive at shore soon. Then I suppose I'll have to decide what to do with you."

"You needn't take care of me. I'm certain that I can take care of...myself." The last word came out as a quiet question as the realization hit me that NO, I certainly could *not* take care of myself. I had not even the slightest inkling about how to make my way in the world, because I'd never been in it. My goal had been to escape, and the likelihood of succeeding in that plan had been so minuscule that I'd never thought to consider what would happen next. My only plan had been to find something sharp so that I could cut my hair, which would have allowed me to flee Eldmere. But actually living in the world...I looked up at him, my eyes unnaturally wide as the precariousness of my predicament washed over me.

The prince allowed a small, reassuring smile to curve his mouth. "My mother would likely adopt you. I have three brothers and no sisters, so she always longs for more female company. Perhaps she can help you find a position."

I nodded, swallowing down my terror as I latched on to his reassurance. His mother might help me find a position. I believed that was what they called it when someone was a servant. I could do that. I could cook and clean for someone. I could even sew. If someone would pay me to do those things, then perhaps I was not so useless after all.

"You'll need to tell people that you fell off another ship."

My eyes were pulled back to him and my brow furrowed. "Why?"

"Neither you nor I understand how you came to be here, and that could make people wary. It's best to give them an easy explanation."

I agreed, frighteningly aware of how little I knew about anything, especially in this foreign land. The people in this kingdom likely feared the unexplainable because it could mean magic. I supposed it was lucky that I could honestly say I no longer had any.

A few minutes later, a knock came at the door and a crewman informed the prince that we were nearing land. Prince Tavric encouraged me to follow him to the deck and stand at the railing so I could watch as the land came closer. "The transition from ocean to land will be easier if you see the solid land for a while before you step onto it."

I did as he suggested, wishing with all my might that it was daylight so that I could take in this new view and perspective. I wanted to see it all, to see if it was completely different from Branfrie or if there were similarities, but all I could see were shadowy shapes lit by the moon and a smattering of lanterns.

Once the ship was properly docked, Prince Tavric offered me one arm and gestured toward the plank that led from the ship to the dock. "Can I assist you down the gangplank?"

I nodded, took his arm, and then reached behind me to pick up my hair, only to remember that it wasn't there. My mind and body froze for just a moment, confused by all the strangeness that now surrounded me.

"Miss Lyrielle?"

I shook off my momentary stiffness and allowed him to lead me from the ship. When we stepped off the plank and onto the dirt, I was surprised at the sharp rocks that poked the bottoms of my feet.

"Hmm." Tavric must have noticed my wince. "I'm certain my mother will be able to find some shoes for you. Fortunately, the carriage will not hurt your feet." He gestured toward the conveyance, and a footman quickly stepped forward to open the door and fold out a step.

I got inside with only a little difficulty—it was more wobbly than I had anticipated—and we were soon off, the carriage rocking and jostling as it made its way up a winding road. I looked out the window and had to assume we were aiming for the large castle that sat atop a small hill. I couldn't see its details, only that it was large and many of its windows were still lit from within. "Do you usually come home in the middle of the night?"

"No, I had planned to be gone until morning," he said, his words stiff.

"I'm sorry you had to change your plans because of me."

"I'm not. My plans to amuse myself are hardly worth your life." He sat back and folded his arms over his chest, closing his eyes as he leaned his head against the seat.

I couldn't remember the last time I'd ridden in a carriage. I knew my parents had one, and I'd often gone with them, but those memories were dim.

It took only a few minutes to arrive at the castle, which was much larger than I had anticipated. When the government of Branfrie had shifted from the rule of royalty to those with magic, most of the royal and noble residences had fallen into disrepair as those families lost both their influence and their affluence. The only castle I'd ever seen was the one where I'd resided. My corner tower had not offered a view of the rest of the castle, however, and I had moved there so many years ago that I could not even say how large it had been.

The carriage rolled to a stop in front of a set of huge, carved wooden doors. Prince Tavric got out of the carriage first and then urged me to follow. The cobblestones of the drive were smooth under my feet, and as I looked up and gaped at all the shadowed majesty, Tavric pulled me along until we entered the enormous grand hall inside the castle.

And then I gaped some more. Even with only a few torches to light the hallway, it was spectacular, and I wondered what it would look like in full daylight.

"Tavric, really?" a woman called from down the corridor. She was wrapped in a dressing gown but had a regal bearing and the look of a mother. "The middle of the night? You come wandering in in the middle of the night! You should have returned from your inspection well before sunset. It's bad enough that you take off without warning on these little adventures of yours, but it's the height of discourtesy to wander in at all hours and expect—"

Her Majesty had finally looked away from her son long enough to catch sight of me. She fell silent, and I watched her eyes go just about as wide as I'd ever seen before an enormous grin curled her mouth and lit up her entire face.

Tavric leaned down to murmur in my ear. "I told you she'd be happy to see you."

"My darling, what have we here?" Tavric's mother rushed forward, reaching her hands out toward me as she addressed him.

"Mama, this is Lyrielle. Lyrielle, this is my mother, Queen Ondyra."

"A pleasure, Your Majesty." I did my best to sink into a curtsey but utterly failed. I'd never had a reason to curtsey to anyone before.

"And you," the queen said as she grasped my hands and gave them a squeeze. "But tell me, how did you come to be here?"

"I fished her from the ocean, if you'll believe it," Prince Tavric explained.

The queen's look indicated that she didn't know if she should take him seriously or not. "You did what?" she asked, her eyes bouncing from her son to me and back again.

"It was quite terrifying, to tell the truth. We spotted her in the water, nearly drowning, and I jumped in to retrieve her." He made it sound simple, and yet there was something in his tone suggesting that he truly had been terrified.

The queen's eyes fixed on my face, compassion tugging on her features. "You poor dear," she said, wrapping a protective arm around my shoulders and anchoring me to her side before guiding me further into the castle.

TAVRIC

As my mother pulled Lyrielle along at her side, the confused little mermaid looked over her shoulder, unsure but not frightened. I gave her an encouraging nod, knowing full well that my mother would slather her with an excess of love. Could one be drowned by love? Hopefully not.

I just hoped that my mother didn't get it into her head that Lyrielle should be a permanent guest. Mama was a matchmaker at heart, and I had a feeling that if she became attached to our mysterious guest who seemed in need of a home, she might get it into her head that I should be her home. And aside from the fact that Lyrielle and I didn't know each other, or that I felt no need to rush to the altar, there was still Melody to consider.

I sounded like a fool, like I'd had my head addled by a siren, which was why I never said any of it out loud. I would continue my search for Melody and hope that the ocean gifted me the chance to at least see her, just once. Just to say thank you. Just to assure myself that she was real.

I was a fool, indeed.

I should have been dead tired and ready to retire myself, but the mystery of Lyrielle's origins swirled fiercely in my head, so I turned to the library.

The rows of books were a comfort, and the desks gave me room to work. I lit several lanterns before going in search of answers, pulling out atlases and histories, hunting for any reference to a place called Branfrie. I pulled out maps, digging out the oldest ones I could find and looking over each one carefully, hoping I'd find it somewhere.

I turned pages and scoured maps until my eyes were dry and gritty and I couldn't keep them open. But I never found any references to Branfrie. It was like it didn't exist.

Despite my failure, the mystery ate at me and I couldn't leave it alone. It was the same sort of fixation I'd felt after Melody had saved me, and I fell asleep in a chair in front of the fire, a giant book open on my chest.

I jerked awake when someone shook my shoulder.

"Hello, Brother, I come bearing good news," Dorian said without preamble as he stood over me. He was less than two years younger than me, with hair as fair as mine was dark.

I blinked and tried to shake the sleep from my head, but also smiled at Dorian's greeting. "Glad to see you made it back safely." I stood to embrace him.

He pounded on my back. "I was back last night, but you were off galavanting on your ship again." He pulled back and squeezed my shoulder with a frown. "How's Father?"

I opened my mouth but couldn't find the words. "You'll have to go see him for yourself."

His expression turned grim. "Right." He went to sit in a chair by the fireplace, slouching into it and looking exhausted. "I hear you brought home a stray."

My muscles tensed and I sucked a breath through my nose. "Don't call her that. She's been through enough," I chastised as I sank into the chair opposite him.

He lifted a brow. "You better not have developed feelings for her."

I scoffed. "I met her less than twelve hours ago, Dorian. Don't be daft."

"Glad to hear it. Now ask me how my diplomatic mission went."

The corner of my mouth twitched. "Tell me."

"We will soon have a guest." His tone tried and failed to sound enthusiastic.

I frowned. "Are the Ravencairn royalty coming for a visit?" It wasn't good timing, not at all.

"Not all of them. Just one. Princess Saria is coming here, Tav."

"Congratulations," I said, confused by his stormy countenance. Dorian and my parents had been hoping to make a marriage alliance with Ravencairn, and it looked like they were close to succeeding.

"Not for me, you idiot. She doesn't want me. Why would she when the crown prince of Islewyn is as yet unwed?"

There was a bitterness to his tone, but I couldn't focus on it.

"Excuse me?" Surely I'd misheard; he wasn't really suggesting—

"Brace yourself, Tav." He pulled a flask from his boot. "You're about to be betrothed." He raised it and then took a swig of whatever spirits were in the flask.

I was dumbfounded. "That's...that's not funny."

"It's really not," he said as he leaned his elbows on his knees. "The stupid thing is that I actually thought she and I would make a good match." He tried to look nonchalant about it, but I could tell that he was wounded.

Perhaps stating the obvious would help. "I'm not going to marry her."

"Of course you are." His tone was resigned, almost bored.

"Give me one good reason why."

He sat forward, his eyes snapping with fire. "I'll give you three. Princess Saria is delightful. Ravencairn is a powerful ally, and you will be king much sooner than any of us wish."

My shock turned to pure anger. "You can't drag a girl home with you and assume I'll marry her. *Are you mad?*"

"Believe me, this wasn't *my* first choice—it's hers. But, by all means, if you don't want to give a beautiful, cultured woman a chance, then go ahead, tell the Princess of Ravencairn to turn her ship around and go home. I'm certain that will end stupendously." He took another harsh swig from his flask. "You'll undo all the goodwill I've accrued by going on this pathetic, diplomatic mission."

"I was not the one to invite her here," I pointed out, my clothes feeling suddenly itchy and the room too warm.

He just shrugged.

I pinched the bridge of my nose. "When is she coming?"

"A fortnight."

It was both more time than I had feared and far less than I needed.

"I will treat her with respect and dignity. However," I said as I looked up and fixed him with a stern glare, "if you somehow gave her the idea that I would jump at the chance to marry her, that's your fault, not mine."

"I don't know why you're acting like this is some great imposition," he grumbled. "I'm basically hand delivering you the perfect queen. Just say thank you, Tav."

I bit my tongue, too uncomfortable to keep fighting and too aware of how dejected my brother looked. "We'll talk of this later. I have to check on Father, and you should too."

Leaving the library, I traversed the castle corridors in the early morning light as I tried to breathe through the shock of what Dorian had told me. Surely Princess Saria would not truly expect a proposal. The very idea made my chest tighten, and the sound of my own feet hitting the stone floor echoed in my head.

Chapter Five

LYRIELLE

When I woke in the morning, I went immediately to the window. It was large and offered a brilliant view of vegetation-covered mountains rising to my left and the sea stretching out to my right. My mind was overwhelmed as I started cataloging all of the differences between this view and the one from my tower. The sea was a beautiful teal blue, and there were islands off in the distance. The little houses that populated the village below were some sort of white stucco with red tile roofs, so different from the drab coloring of Eldmere.

Unfortunately, my appraisal was cut short when a young girl walked into the room and bobbed a curtsey with a "Good morning, miss. I'm here to help you dress."

It seemed strange to lend me a helper since I certainly wouldn't be staying here for long, but I tried to accept with grace. Aunt Ethel had often helped me dress while avoiding my hair, so accepting this girl's assistance wasn't too awkward, although as she opened the wardrobe, which was somehow filled with dresses, she didn't look particularly happy to be helping me.

Once I was dressed, with my short hair braided and coiled around my head, I followed the girl through the labyrinth of halls, looking longingly out each window that we passed, until we reached a large but cozy room where breakfast was set out. The young girl turned to me and curtsied before leaving the room, which was utterly baffling. Why would anyone curtsey to me? Was it simply because I'd been taken in by the royal family?

My stomach turned over at that thought. I was staying in a castle—with a royal family. But for how long? I needed to look ahead and decide what my next move would be.

I turned back to the room, which had appeared empty at first, but then a chair scraped across the floor and I saw Prince Tavric rise to his feet at the far end of the table. "Good morning, Lyrielle." He gave a solemn nod.

"Good morning," I responded, my hands clasped with nerves.

"Please." He gestured to a long, skinny table pushed up against one wall that held an assortment of food. "Help yourself to anything you'd like."

Certainly, I thought to myself. *No problem. I'll just fix a plate and sit down to breakfast in a beautiful, elegant room with a prince.*

And then, tomorrow, I might fly amongst the clouds and train a chipmunk to dance.

"Perhaps I've gone insane," I whispered to myself as I crossed to the table of food. "This could all be in my mind."

After sitting with my plate of food, breakfast was a quiet affair. Prince Tavric had a stack of what must have been correspondence that he was reading or reviewing at one end of the table, and I was sitting about halfway down, wishing to give him his privacy.

I finished my food but was still hungry. Perhaps falling from a tower into a different world will do that to a person. I looked from my plate to the still heaping table of food, wondering if it was acceptable to go get more and realizing once again how little I knew of etiquette in this situation—or any situation.

I sat there, undecided, staring at Prince Tavric and willing him to look at me so that I could just ask. But he didn't look up.

I huffed a sigh and gave an awkward clearing of my throat.

He lifted his eyes to me.

"I'm sorry. Forgive me. I was just"—I gestured to the food—"Is it all right if… I didn't know if it was appropriate for me to perhaps get more, or…"

"Yes, of course. Please help yourself." He returned his focus to the papers in front of him. "My mother would be mortified if I allowed a guest to leave the table unsated."

"Thank you." I liked the queen. She'd been just as Prince Tavric had told me—gushing and effusive, and clearly happy to have someone to take care of.

My second plate of food was gone just as quickly as the first, and I was nearly finished when Tavric gathered his papers and stood. "Would you like to see the library?"

I shook my head.

His face crunched in confusion. "No?"

Perhaps my honest answer had been rude. "I'm sorry. That's a kind offer, but…I have spent too much of my life surrounded by books."

His head tilted. "What would you like to do, then?"

I froze at the question. No one had asked me that since my parents had died. I'd spent the last ten years being told what I *must* do, not being asked what I *wanted*.

Did he truly wish to know? It was hard to imagine that my frivolous wants were something a busy prince would be interested in.

"Come now," he prompted after several quiet moments, sounding a bit impatient, though not unkind. "You're in a brand new place. Surely you'd like to see something."

"Of course," I sputtered as all the possibilities rolled through my mind.

"Then what would you like to see?"

"Everything."

The corners of his mouth twitched, but he only gave a stiff nod. "I'm not sure we can see everything in one day, but we could try. Where shall we start?"

I licked my lips and swallowed, nervous to ask for anything. "Outside?"

"Very good. And what should we see outside?"

"Flowers? The ocean? Trees? I saw lots of trees out my window this morning. I'd never seen so many trees before, and I'd like to walk among them, perhaps."

He studied me.

"If that's all right," I hedged, terrified that he'd tell me no.

He grunted. "If a walk in the trees is all it takes to make you happy, then it would be pitiful for me to deny you."

Tears sprang to my eyes. He acted as though giving me a dream was easy, and yet for years, I'd begged my aunt to grant me that privilege, and every time she'd acted as if I were selfish for even wanting it, much less *asking*.

He noticed my struggle and his face drew down in concern. "Have I said something wrong?"

I gave a sharp shake of my head. "Not at all. I'm just thankful."

"It is only a walk."

I tried to nod like I understood, but I didn't, not really. How could a prince want to help me get what I wanted?

He cleared his throat and nodded toward the door. "Let's go, then. I'll show you some of the grounds."

I followed after him, wringing my hands with nervousness. Last night we'd come straight from the dock to the front door of the castle. I still hadn't truly had the chance to feel the earth beneath my feet yet.

I looked down at the shoes that were carefully tied onto my feet, wondering if it would be terribly rude of me to tear them off and go barefoot. I would resist for now. Instead, as we crossed the great hall, I fixed my eyes on the large doors ahead. Prince Tavric motioned to the guards standing by, and they both stepped forward to open the doors for us.

Sunlight flooded in and I blinked my eyes against the brightness, my feet hurrying ahead, anxious to cross that threshold and go beyond.

I heard Prince Tavric chuckle from behind me, but I ignored it. The area just outside the doors was mostly pebbled walkways and cobblestone carriageways, but beyond that was a broad expanse of curated gardens, then a large stone wall. Past that, there were trees in every shade of green, and rolling hills dotted with sheep and other animals before those hills turned into towering mountains.

"Where would you like to go?" Tavric asked from beside me.

I chewed my lip for a moment, then decided to be brave. "Are we allowed to go beyond the wall?"

His brow pinched together. "Of course."

A thrill surged in my chest. It was one thing to be wandering outside of a building at all, but to be let beyond the stone walls that were meant to keep this castle and the royal family safe...

"Can we walk up that hill?" I asked, pointing to the nearest one.

The prince tried to hide a smile and cleared his throat. "I do believe that is within our power."

I grinned and started in that direction.

"One moment. That hill is farther than it looks. Let me get my horse."

"We're going to ride a horse?"

"Yes, if that's all right with you."

"Yes, that's...yes. Fine." What a terrifying and wonderful prospect. I had ridden with my father occasionally, and I still remembered the freedom of racing across a meadow, feeling the wind tugging at my hair and clothing.

The grooms made quick work of preparing the horse, saddling the large stallion with a special something called a pillion. It added an additional padded seat behind the normal saddle so we could both mount. "Will this overtax the horse?" I asked.

"Brutus is plenty strong, and we won't be going far," Prince Tavric assured me, patting the horse's neck before mounting. The groom encouraged me to step up on a mounting block, and after I'd situated myself on the little seat, the prince told me to hold on. I circled his waist with my arms, immediately aware of the warm breadth of his back. I hadn't been in such close proximity to a man since I was a child, and I certainly wasn't a child now.

I clasped my hands together over his chest and told myself not to be a ninny. A very kind prince was going to show me some of the world, and I would do well to focus on that world instead of the way his body heat made me feel. But, stars above, it was becoming painfully obvious that I was starved for human interaction and touch.

Luckily, I was well and truly distracted once he urged the horse into motion. My head was on a constant swivel, trying to take in everything all at once as we trotted through the grounds, passed under the gate, and then continued down the road, taking in the views of trees in full bloom, fields of flowers and animals, and even a waterfall sluicing down the hillside.

"Whoa," he called to the horse, slowing him to a walk as we veered off the road and into a copse of trees and vegetation. "This seems like a good spot," he said as he pulled the horse to a stop. "Now, take my arm with both hands."

He held his right arm away from his body, and I did as he instructed and latched onto it.

"And swing yourself down."

Right. Easy. I didn't give myself time to second guess his direction, just trusted that he could support my weight as I slid, swung my legs, and fumbled my way off the horse.

He leaned down and held on to me until I'd gained my balance again. "I probably could have given you better direction," he admitted with a bit of self-recrimination in his tone.

"It's fine," I said, not bothering to look back at him. I was too preoccupied with the way the mossy earth felt soft beneath the soles of my shoes as I took a few steps. The air was thicker and cooler than it was in Eldmere, and the way the sunlight filtered down through the leaves overhead, dappling the ground with spots of light, created a kind of beauty I'd either never known or forgotten.

I walked several steps and then fell to my knees, pressing my hands into the earth, appreciating the way the soil molded to my palms. This wasn't stone. It was vegetation. It was living things, thriving plants, and I could have sworn that I felt a vibrant, living energy penetrate my palms, weaving up my arms and into my whole body. I leaned forward until my forehead rested against the earth, wanting to be closer to it, close enough that I could take it in and remember it forever. I breathed deeply, in and out, over and over as silent tears slid from my eyes and into the foliage beneath me. I'd missed so much, longed for so many things over the last ten years, and this was one of them.

The scent of the ground was heady and calming. I'd been able to smell a fair number of things from my tower balcony, but it had been nothing compared to the experience of having my nose pressed into the soil as its aroma saturated my lungs. I sank down further until I was lying on the ground completely, my stomach, chest, and the full length of my legs flush with the ground.

TAVRIC

I didn't know what to think of this creature—this maiden I'd pulled from the ocean, this young woman who so clearly longed for freedom but was terrified it would be snatched away at any moment, this girl who now lay snuggled against the earth as if she had been deprived of living things for a long time.

Who was she, and why was she here? And what was it about her sudden presence that I found comforting? Perhaps it was her lack of pretense. Maybe it was just that I wanted to shield her from whatever she'd run from.

Whatever it was, I was grateful she was here. After hearing the news of Princess Saria's impending visit, I'd jumped at the chance to leave the castle, especially since the days I was able to do so were becoming fewer and fewer.

I spent a good portion of my life trying to avoid crowds, noise, and all the other things that grated on me. Often I felt desperate to simply be left alone. Yet as I sat on the ground with a tree supporting my back, I had no wish to run from this odd little mermaid. Instead, I wanted to know more.

Eventually, she rolled over onto her back with her arms splayed out to her sides as she looked up at the canopy of leaves above. She looked small, here under the large trees and expansive sky. There was no reason I should have invited her to stay at the palace, but something about the smallness of her and the loneliness of finding her abandoned in the middle of the ocean had caused a fierce protectiveness to rear up inside me.

"Miss Lyrielle?"

She looked over at me, a bright smile lighting up her whole face. "You can call me Lyri."

The sweet innocence of the invitation made my heart lurch a bit. "Very well. May I ask you a question, Lyri?"

"Of course." She rolled to her side and pushed up so that she sat facing me, her thick hair falling out of its braid.

"Where did you come from?"

Her smile dipped and her eyes dimmed. "I told you. Eldmere."

"Where is that?"

"It's a village in Branfrie, near enough to the sea that I could smell it but not see it. The capital was a half-day's journey."

"What sea?" I knew it wasn't the Lantis Ocean. I could understand how she might confuse an ocean with a sea if she didn't know the geography, but I knew every kingdom and village that bordered the Lantis, and Eldmere was not one of them. Neither was Branfrie.

"Lockmere."

I shook my head. "I've never heard of it." I scrubbed at my forehead and blew out a frustrated breath. "Tell me again. How did you end up in Lantis?"

She looked off, distress tugging on the edges of her face. "I don't know."

"What happened right before I found you in the water?"

She looked back at me and took an unsteady breath. "I fell from the tower."

I blinked several times, stunned by the answer. "You fell from a tower?" She'd mentioned a tower last night, but I thought I'd misheard her or that she'd been babbling nonsense.

"Yes."

All right. Perhaps she had hit her head. Maybe she was knocked unconscious from the fall. "But...what were you doing in a tower?"

"It's where I lived."

Odd. "How did you fall?"

She shook her head and looked down, but I could still see the way her cheeks paled. "It was foolish of me. I'd practiced climbing the stone walls inside the tower many times. I was good at it, but I'd never done it with the full weight of my hair pulling on me, so when I climbed down the tower—"

"Wait," I said, holding up a hand and trying to wrap my mind around what she was saying. "You were climbing down the outside of the tower?"

"Yes, to get down."

"Why didn't you just walk down?"

Lyrielle blinked up at me, as if confused that I would question her circumstances. She tilted her head as she looked up at me, like my reaction was new and unexpected. After several moments of hesitation, she said slowly, "The tower was where I lived all the time."

"Right..." I prompted, still not understanding what that had to do with her apparent need to scale the outside of a tower in order to leave it.

"What I mean is...I never left," she clarified. "I stayed in that tower all day of every day of every year since I was nine years old." There was a hollowness to her voice as she said it that sent a chill through my bones.

My mouth gaped and my face went slack as confusion morphed into doubt and then settled on utter horror. My jaw flapped uselessly several times before I got one word out. "Why?"

She gave a small shrug. "Those were my aunt's rules. She was trying to protect me."

"From what?" I asked.

"From everything and everyone." Lyrielle looked down and plucked a few tiny flowers from the ground.

Last night when I'd pulled her from the ocean and she said she was trying to get away, I thought she'd encountered ruffians of some sort. I thought it had only been a temporary danger that she'd fled from. Never would I have imagined that this maiden had been imprisoned by her own family member. And though the way she said it made it clear that she had resigned herself to her aunt's reasoning long ago, I could also tell that it had never been all right with her.

"How old are you now?"

"Nineteen."

My fist clenched. Ten years. "You never left?" I had to ask, hoping she'd give me a different answer this time.

"Never."

"What of your aunt, did *she* leave?"

She gave a little nod, chin tilted up in defiance even as her jaw tensed and the remnants of pain and betrayal made her eyes glisten. "There was one door. She would lock it from the outside when she left."

I tried to hide my disgust, but I was certain I failed. "And when she was there? Could you not leave when she slept?"

"She would move her bed in front of the door. Every night, I hoped she'd somehow forget, but of course that never happened. She would move it into place, always with a smile and a placating word about how I must be protected."

Fresh indignation rose up, but I shoved it down. "Did you feel protected?"

It took her several moments to respond. Her face was slack now; the only indicator of distress was when she swallowed. "Sometimes," she finally replied, then looked off into the trees, her hands pressing harder into the earth below her as her fingers curled.

That movement combined with her desperate need to feel the earth beneath her suddenly made horrible sense. She'd been held captive in a tower for ten years, surrounded by stone, cut off from nature. Cut off from people and freedom and choice. I gave myself several moments to compose myself before returning to my questions. "So you climbed down the tower to escape?"

She nodded but didn't look at me. "I was doing well with the climbing, but then the rest of my hair came over the balcony, and the weight of it..." Her gaze stared into the trees, but I didn't think she actually saw her surroundings. “I lost my grip. I fully expected to meet my death at the bottom of that tower. Instead I was in water.” Finally, she turned to look at me, utterly perplexed. “How is that possible?”

I opened my mouth, but of course I had no answer. It wasn’t possible.

Lyrielle watched me flounder for words, and the longer I kept silent, the more her mouth fell into a frown and her shoulders rounded in. She broke her gaze and looked away. “You don’t believe me.” Her tone was devastated.

“I don’t know what to believe. My rational brain would love to label you as insane or a liar, but the truth is that I was there in the middle of that ocean. I know we were too far from land for you to have come from shore, and I know there were no ships nearby when we found you.”

She looked over at me, a bit of hope shining in her face.

“So if you’re insane, then so am I.” I gave her a grim smile.

“Hopefully, neither of us are.” She stood, a bundle of flowers in her hand as she turned slowly in a circle. The breeze kicked up just a little and she closed her eyes for several moments. When she opened them again, she let the wildflowers drop to the ground and raised a hand to shade her eyes, looking off into the distance with an awe that I envied. What would it be like to see the world with such unabashed wonder? She stood there, comfortable in the silence and stillness while the wind fluttered her golden hair.

Then she ran.

It took me several seconds of watching her retreat for my brain to comprehend it. Then I scrambled to my feet and went chasing after her. She must have seen something that frightened her or...something. I didn’t know why she was running, only that I was terrified of letting her out of my sight.

"Lyrielle!" I yelled.

And she laughed. *Laughed.*

"Lyrielle, stop!"

She came to an abrupt stop and whirled to face me, her face ashen and her hands pressed to her stomach as I skidded to a halt in front of her. "I'm so sorry. I shouldn't have done that," she babbled. "Please forgive me, I only—"

"There's nothing to forgive," I assured her, holding out a placating hand. Her darting eyes suggested that she thought I was angry with her, and that frightened her. "You didn't do anything wrong, I just worried you might lose your way."

"Yes." She nodded, pinching her eyes shut. "Of course. I should have been more careful. It was foolish of me." She swallowed hard.

"I just..." I began carefully, determined not to frighten her again. "I just wondered where you were going." I tried to make my face curious instead of stern, though I knew I was terrible at softening my features.

She gave a sharp shake of her head. "Nowhere." Her breathing was still uneven after her abrupt sprint. "I was...I'd forgotten what it's like to run."

"You..." She'd forgotten because she'd been imprisoned for a decade. I swallowed. "And what do you think of it?"

A small smile peeked through. "It's rather exhilarating."

I nodded, wanting to assure her that I understood her meaning. "Yes, I can see how it could be exhilarating."

She tilted her head and studied me. "But you think me odd for it?" The fear had left her eyes, leaving her expression curious but not offended.

"I didn't say that."

"But did you think it?" she asked with a tiny teasing smile tugging on her lips.

"For a moment, yes."

She put her hands on her hips and looked out over the valley, brushing a piece of hair out of her eyes when the wind pulled it loose. "I imagine that's bound to happen more than once as I get reacquainted with the world. I'm sorry if it embarrasses you."

"You don't embarrass me."

She turned back to me with a smile. "Good." She bit her lip, obviously debating something before she said, "Then race me back," and took off running yet again.

A breathy laugh escaped me before I chased after her, grateful she'd gone back in the direction of the horse. Grateful that my father had been feeling well enough today that he didn't need me to stand in for him and I could be here in this moment with this woman.

Chapter Six

LYRIELLE

The maid who had helped me dress seemed surprised that I was still in the castle the next day, and maybe even...annoyed by it? Perhaps it wasn't normal for the royal family to have guests, especially guests like me who held no important position or title.

Still, when I asked for some scissors, she obliged and went to find some. She even offered to help me cut it, but I declined, not liking the idea of this discontent young lady taking scissors to my hair. I spent quite a while cutting it, trying to even out the sections that had been so hastily cut by Tavric. Learning to use the scissors was a little tricky, but the overall result was at least better than it had been.

The maid braided and pinned up my newly-cut hair, then offered to show me the way to the dining hall again, but I just smiled and assured her I could find it on my own. I looked forward to meeting Tavric there again, expecting that it would be a repeat of the quiet meal we'd shared the day before.

I was very wrong.

When I entered, it was to find the prince surrounded by several people. Advisors or nobles, I didn't know which—maybe both. Each seemed to have important questions or favors to ask or papers to be signed, and new ones kept coming in, replacing the ones who were sent on their way.

I was worried that I would be an inconvenient presence, but since I chose a seat at the other end of the table, no one paid me any mind, and the swirl of activity was fascinating. I watched Tavric and the way he responded to everyone vying for his attention. At first, he seemed cold and intimidating, which was so different from the way he'd treated me that I couldn't resist staying to study him further.

Then I noticed the way his fist would clench when someone spoke especially loudly, or how he clutched at his plate and sent away the servant who tried to remove his food, which he hadn't really had time to touch.

At one point he looked up and caught my eye, and all I could do was give him an encouraging smile. It seemed clear that he was uncomfortable, and I wondered how often this was part of his daily life. It was then, just after I'd smiled at him, that one of the nobles looked in my direction, his eyes raking up and down my frame as his brow furrowed in disapproval. He was older, stiff and stuffy, and the way he looked down his nose at me made me wonder if I had done something wrong.

When it was evident the chaos would not let up any time soon, I got up to leave, a little disappointed that I hadn't been able to speak with the prince. After all, he and his mother were really the only two people I knew.

I chewed on my lip as I left the dining hall, wondering where I could or should go. Was I allowed to go anywhere I wanted? And if so, where would I start? The possibilities were endless, yet terrifying, especially if I didn't have someone like Prince Tavric to show me the way. I was all too aware that in addition to being unfamiliar with this land, I also had no knowledge of how to comport myself in any social situation.

Only a few steps outside the dining hall, I was waylaid by a man with a neatly trimmed beard.

"Miss Lyrielle," he said with a bow.

"Oh." I didn't know how to respond to a bow. "Hello."

"My name is Harlan, miss."

"You were on the ship." I recognized him as one of the more rational crew members.

"I was. I act as His Highness's first mate when he sails." He studied me for an extra moment, then gestured down the hall, encouraging me to walk with him. "His Highness was asked by his father, King Valtren, to fill in for him today, so he regrets that he won't be able to show you more of our kingdom."

"I didn't expect him to," I assured him. I had hoped for it, but not expected it. "I don't expect anything, I'm just—"

"I know, miss. His Highness has a protective streak though, and he asked that I make some suggestions for how you might spend your day."

"Is he in there, Harlan?" someone asked from behind me. I turned to see a man with dark eyes and blond hair approaching. He had a distinct air of authority and privilege.

Harlan bowed to him. "He is, Your Highness."

"Why isn't he in my father's study?"

"You'll have to ask him, Your Highness."

The prince—he must have been one if Harlan was calling him *Your Highness*—let out a frustrated sigh. He spared me a glance, giving me a head nod and saying only,

"Miss," before turning toward the dining hall and leaving us behind.

"That was Prince Dorian," Harlan said. "Next time, you really should curtsey."

My cheeks burned. "Of course. I just wasn't expecting..."

"No harm. Now let's find something for you to do."

Ultimately, I ended up going to the village. I felt bold and brave exploring the streets. There were so many people, so many shops to see and vendors to speak with. I talked with merchants and bakers and cobblers. Some people were kind, some were abrupt, and some ignored me. I just soaked it all in. Many people smiled at me without wanting anything in return. No one was telling me what to do or demanding that I give them anything.

Harlan had arranged for a young boy to tag along with me and make sure I didn't lose my way. He'd even provided me with a small number of coins that I was able to use to buy fresh rolls and fruits that I'd never encountered in Eldmere. A small part of me felt guilty, knowing full well the gift I was being given, but the larger part of me was so desperate and excited to just be *out* that I was determined to take advantage of this boon while it lasted. I would need to seek a position and start providing for myself, but just for today, I was going to experience as much of the world as I could.

When the sun started to dip in the sky, I returned to the castle and was shocked when I was invited to dine with Queen Ondyra in her private sitting room. Part of me was illogically disappointed that I wouldn't be able to spend time with Tavric, while the other part of me was deeply flattered.

"This is so kind of you," I said as I nervously cut a bite of meat.

"The pleasure is all mine, my dear. I'm surrounded by far too many men in my life, and to be frank, your lack of pretense is most appealing." She gave me a conspiratorial smile over the rim of her wine goblet.

"I...am not sure what that means."

"Precisely," she said with a wink.

Her obvious comfort quickly put me at ease, and she told me stories about her life and family. She asked me a little about myself, and I told her that my parents had died and that I had lived with my aunt. She must have seen my discomfort concerning the topic and didn't press me further, which was a relief. I didn't want to lie and say I'd fallen off some unknown ship, but I couldn't tell her the truth either.

Since the queen had other responsibilities, I left as soon as the meal was done, but as I returned to my room, I wondered at the fact that underneath her kindness, she'd seemed melancholy or distracted.

The next morning was more of the same. Tavric was again surrounded by people clamoring for his attention or approval, and I had to stuff down my disappointment at not having the chance to speak with him. Since the last thing I wanted to be was an added burden on his time, I instead dove into another glorious day of freedom with Harlan's help.

When I suggested I wanted to explore the countryside, a horse was provided for me. When I told them I had very little experience riding, they assured me that my horse would simply follow along behind a groom who would ride just ahead of me. It was extraordinary. The hills and fields kept going, on and on. Whenever I wanted to stop, the groom would help me down and hold both of the horses while I picked flowers or waded through a stream.

The backs of my legs were quite sore the next morning from all the riding, so I decided to content myself with an exploration of the castle grounds.

The servants gave me curious looks, no doubt confused by my sudden and unexplained presence, but they weren't exactly unkind, just...obviously too busy to bother with me. The only exception I encountered was a laundress by the name of Amilee. She was younger than I, perhaps only fifteen, and when I offered to help her hang laundry, she accepted gladly. It eased my anxiety after so many of the castle's inhabitants had ignored me. I wished to explore the world of people just as much as I wished to explore nature, but that was difficult when no one would speak with me. Thankfully, Amilee loved to talk; she told me all sorts of interesting facts about Islewyn, its people, and yes, its monarchs.

"They are benevolent rulers?" I asked. I couldn't imagine Tavric being anything other than kind, and yet all my experience with the High Court of my own country had led me to believe that in the end, greed and cruelty usually ruled the day.

"I'd say so," she answered as she shook out another piece of clothing. "They always try to be fair. But when Prince Tavric becomes king, that will be the real test."

"How so?" I asked, handing her another piece of clothing.

"You never really know what a ruler is going to be like until they actually get the crown. If they have a greedy heart, they aren't going to bother hiding it once there's no one in their way."

It was an astute but disheartening observation. "You think Prince Tavric will be that way?"

She shrugged. "What do I know? He's a quiet one, though. Always likes to be by himself. Not like his younger brothers."

"Where are the other princes? I've only seen Prince Dorian."

"Yes, he returned from a diplomatic mission to Ravencairn the same night you arrived—and has been in a mood ever since. Prince Kavian is at university and Caelmir went on a voyage, but no one knows where." She tilted her head in a conspiratorial way. "Rumor is the queen asked him to go."

"Why?"

"Might be in search of a wife. Might be looking to make diplomatic relations. Might be searching for buried treasure, for all I know." She laughed at her own joke.

Strange. I wondered if Prince Tavric would answer me if I asked him about Prince Caelmir's voyage. Not that it mattered. If his schedule ever slowed down, there were plenty of more important things I'd like to discuss with him. As it was, I had continued to breakfast in the dining hall the past few days despite all the commotion and knowing we would not likely have a chance to speak. I did my best to catch his eye and give him a smile as often as possible, because for some reason, no one ever seemed to smile at him despite the fact that he was clearly uncomfortable.

Unfortunately, with each passing day, the amount of sideways looks I received from staff and nobility alike increased. All the important people who milled around the prince did not like my presence, but they never said anything about it; they just wrinkled their noses and looked away.

I fully expected someone to tell me to leave. Or ask when I was leaving. Or insinuate in any way that I *should* be leaving. But none of those things happened, and I realized it was time. Tavric had been so welcoming, and Queen Ondyra was a delight, but I couldn't continue to rely on their hospitality. I wasn't afraid of hard work, and when I'd climbed from my tower, I had never imagined living in luxury and being waited on day in and day out. I'd planned to work, and there was no better time than now to do something about it.

So I returned to the village the next day, dressed in my own dress instead of the very fine ones that the queen had lent me, and instead of exploring and looking for ways to spend a few coins, I inquired about work. But the tailor said he didn't need any help, and the way he looked at my homemade dress—which was admittedly a different style than most wore—made me think he wouldn't have hired me even if he were desperate.

I spoke with the owner of a tavern, but he just waved me off with a brusque, "Can't afford to pay no one else."

The result was the same at the bakery and the dress shop, which left me standing in the middle of the town square, chewing on the side of my thumb, feeling small and inconsequential and wondering what to do next. I couldn't think of anything else that I would be good at. I was happy to learn a new skill, but if no one would even give me a chance...

I let out a sigh and turned to the young boy who was playing the role of my tiny escort. "What am I doing wrong?" I asked, not expecting an answer.

He squinted as he looked up at me, which made his nose wrinkle. "You come from the castle."

My brow lifted. "What?"

"You're a guest at the castle. No one is going to disrespect the royal family by hiring you."

"But I need work."

He shrugged. "They don't know you. They only know you come from the castle."

To the castle I returned, disheartened and frightened as the uncertainty of my future weighed heavily on me. The nobility continued to snub me and the servants disapproved of my presence, but the queen and Prince Tavric continued to act as if I were welcome. I wondered what I should do. At some point, one of them was bound to realize that I could not continue to stay here indefinitely, and when that time came, I had no confidence that I'd be able to find work to support myself in the village.

When I found Amilee the next morning, she told me about her position as laundress, as well as some of the other positions held by the myriad of servants in the castle, and that gave me an idea. What if the prince could help me to find a suitable position here in the castle?

So on my sixth day in Islewyn, I walked to the dining hall, expecting another chaotic breakfast scene but determined to stick around until I could have a word with Prince Tavric. Instead, I found only the prince, sitting in silence by himself.

He looked up at me and smiled in a way that I hadn't seen for days. "Good morning, Lyri," he said.

"Good morning, Your Highness." That was the appropriate way to address him. I'd called him Prince Tavric for the first day, but after noticing the odd looks people would give me, I realized that everyone else called him Your Highness. I crossed to the narrow table, which I now knew was called a sideboard, and filled my plate. As soon as I sat, I launched into my speech, worried that at any moment, someone would rush in demanding his attention. "Might I speak with you about something?"

He looked over at me, apparently startled by the conversation starter, but then offered a soft smile. "Of course," he answered.

"I cannot thank you enough for your hospitality. You've been truly gracious, but I do not feel right about imposing on you any longer. I think I must find a way to earn my keep elsewhere."

He seemed to freeze, as if both his face and his voice were stuck. Had I surprised him? Offended him? I was suddenly horribly aware of how little I knew about etiquette and socially acceptable interactions. "Do you not agree?" I asked tentatively.

"I—" He stopped and cleared his throat. "I know I have been busy, but I had still wanted to show you around a bit more."

"That's very kind of you, and I have been so grateful for the use of your horses and your suggestions for where I should go, but I do not want to impose."

He frowned. "You are not an imposition."

"That's kind of you to say." I looked down for a moment, remembering all too well the countless times people had looked at me as though I were nothing *but* an imposition.

"And you do not owe me anything," he said, fidgeting with his napkin. "I hope you know that. You are not in my debt."

"I know, but...I can't stay here as your guest forever. I need to do something to support myself."

"If you are looking for ways to feel useful or productive, there is plenty here you could do."

"Oh?" It was a relief to hear him say so.

"You're practically doing it already. I've seen you helping the laundress, and I'm certain she's glad for the help."

I wrung my hands in my lap, realizing he wasn't talking about an official job. "I can sew. In fact, I enjoy it."

He looked almost relieved. “There is always plenty of work for someone who knows their way around a needle.” He stood and walked closer to my end of the table, pulling out the chair beside me and sinking into it so that he was facing me. “I understand your need to support yourself. If you need a reliable position, I’m certain that can be arranged, but please don’t feel like you need to be in a rush to start. From what you’ve told me, you’ve more than earned the right to just be in the world and see what it holds.” One corner of his mouth twitched up. “I’d like to give you that opportunity, at least for a time. Please stay,” he said with quiet earnestness, reaching out to cover my hands with one of his. “As my guest. As my friend.”

A sweet warmth filled my chest. “Are we friends?”

His lips only curved up the slightest bit, but his eyes were warm. “Yes, Lyri, we’re friends. There is plenty more of the kingdom for you to see, and I’ll find the time to show you—I promise.”

Nothing would thrill me more, and it was sorely tempting, but I worried that if I stayed as a guest for too long, I might want to stay forever. However, the prospect of having Tavric show me more of his land wasn’t something I had the strength to reject, nor did I want to. I bit my lip to lessen my grin.

When I nodded, he squeezed my hands once more and then went on his way, leaving me to marvel at his words.

Prince Tavric was my friend, and he wanted me to stay. Even without my gift, he thought my presence was worthwhile—and that was an odd thing to accept. Odd, but wonderful.

Chapter Seven

TAVRIC

Are we friends? She'd seemed so surprised and delighted by the idea of a friend that I had to wonder...had this girl never had a friend? I thought the answer to that was...perhaps not, because the way she had smiled, with her entire face brightening, you would have thought I'd presented her with a thousand rainbow butterflies. I'd felt foolish at first, asking her to stay, but that smile assured me I'd done the right thing.

I wasn't certain what had come over me, but everything inside of me shied away from the idea of her leaving, even if it was only as far as the village. Lyri was...a comfort. Something about being in her presence soothed my anguished soul, and with the uncertainty of my father's health clawing at my back day after day, I needed her here. I needed her steadying presence each morning, and I needed the distraction of watching her roam the grounds. But when she'd brought up her desire to earn her keep, I also understood that all too well. My own need to feel capable was almost compulsive, so I'd suggested she continue helping the laundress in an effort to give her that feeling of competence while keeping her here.

Why was it so important to me that she stay? Yes, I'd fished her from the ocean like a wayward water sprite, but though I felt protective of her, keeping her here long term was not practical, and I knew that.

Yet, if she went away, where would she go? She was so unfamiliar with the world, and I was terrified that she'd be consumed by the chaos and I'd never see her again. Like Melody.

I was on my way to speak with my father when a steward stepped up. "Your Highness," he said with a bow.

"Yes?"

"One of your shipmen is in my office. He says he needs to speak with you."

My curiosity was instantly piqued. I went sailing nearly every day, so it was strange that a shipman would feel the need to seek me out instead of waiting to speak with me the next time I was at the docks.

As soon as I entered the steward's office, I saw a young man waiting in a chair. Martin jumped to his feet, looking nervous as he clutched his cap with both hands.

I smiled to put him at ease. "What can I do for you, lad?"

"Begging your pardon, Your Highness, but I just thought—" He stepped forward and thrust a fist toward me, fingers down, like he meant to give me something.

I held out my hand, allowing him to drop a necklace on my palm.

He immediately stepped back. "I found it. I was swabbing the deck and I found it, caught between two planks." He looked up at me, eyes wide and excited. "Thought it could only belong to the siren, Captain."

"She's not a siren," I corrected as I closed my hand around the pendant. "Thank you. I will give it to Miss Lyrielle." Obviously this was the necklace she'd spoken of.

Martin hesitated a moment, clearly wanting to talk more about Lyrielle, but instead he bowed and left.

I thanked the steward and left his office, grateful that I would be able to return such a precious keepsake to Lyrielle. As I hurried down the corridor, I glanced down at the necklace and nearly tripped over my feet. I stepped closer to a patch of sunlight streaming down through a window, taking a good look at the piece of jewelry. It was a flat, round piece of silver stamped with a family crest. A crest I recognized, and yet…didn't.

The image depicted a castle turret, circled by a crown. It was, of course, the crown that gave me pause. *Royalty*? Was there any other explanation? The only family crests that incorporated crowns were those of royal families. My own family crest was a ship's helm circled by a crown. Having been educated and raised to be a diplomat, I was familiar with many such crests as I had to be able to identify the royal crests of all the surrounding kingdoms. This one, though, I did not recognize.

Who was this girl, and where had she actually come from?

Instead of going to speak with my father, I went to my library and found every book I could think of that described or illustrated royal crests. I hadn't found any mention of Branfrie when I searched before, but if I could find this crest, that would mean that Lyri was much more than she appeared.

It was foolish of me. I knew that. Hoping that Lyri was royalty wasn't going to change the fact that Princess Saria would show up here in barely more than a week, hoping to make a match. But there was a strangely strong part of me that thought, perhaps, if Lyri were royalty…

I shook myself and returned to my investigation, studying hundreds of crests, hoping to find the one from

Lyri's necklace. Alas, the results were the same as when I'd searched for the name of her home. It wasn't there. I looked at each page multiple times, frustrated that I could not confirm my suspicion.

She'd lived in a tower. That tower was likely part of a castle, and yet she'd lived alone with her aunt, completely isolated.

I slammed the book shut and got to my feet, pushing my hands into my hair as I walked to the large window that overlooked the garden. Instead of going on a fruitless search, I should have been trying to center myself and soak in the quiet peace of my library in preparation for this afternoon, which would be filled with diplomatic meetings that my father was too ill to attend. It had been a gift that he'd felt well enough to receive his advisors this morning.

I hated holding court. The room always felt too small and too loud, and while I'd always been uncomfortable around crowds of people, it was so much worse now that my discomfort was coupled with worry for my father.

As I looked out at the garden, reaching for the calm that the library usually provided, I was met with the sight of Lyri, and my body instantly relaxed. I'd appreciated her presence each morning at breakfast. She likely had no idea how much it helped for me simply to see her there, unruffled and undemanding. If only I knew who she was.

Now she was in the gardens, conversing with the gardener, and seeming to ask questions about the different flowers he was tending to. He, in turn, looked thrilled to have an attentive listener.

I lost track of time as I watched her, but eventually I heard the library door open. Instinctively, I stiffened, worried someone was about to destroy my peace, but when my mother came into view, my tension slipped away and I turned back to the window.

She joined me, letting the silence rest for several moments before speaking. "You told her she could stay?"

"Were you eavesdropping on our breakfast conversation?"

"Yes."

I smiled at her candor. "Is her presence here a problem?"

"Not a problem, but shouldn't you be looking for a way to get her home?" she asked gently.

I gestured to Lyri, who looked up to where the gardener pointed at the branches of a tree, probably looking for a bird. Her smile was so wide, I could not imagine it getting any bigger. "Does she look like someone who is missing her home?"

"That does not mean no one is missing her."

The thought of her aunt filled my chest with hot anger. "They are not my concern. She is. And until she gives me some indication that she wishes to return to wherever she came from, I certainly won't be the one to push her away."

"You like her."

"I do."

My mother rested her hand on my arm, pulling my gaze to meet hers. "Is it more than that?"

"What? Of course not. I haven't even had time to get to know her." I'd been too busy trying to find Melody. Each evening, I'd taken my small boat and gone out on the water, hoping to catch a glimpse of her, just like I'd been doing for the past several weeks. With my father's failing health, the mystery of the mermaid who'd saved my life was the best distraction I could think of. Though, as I watched Lyri trying to coax a bird closer, I had to admit that she was a close second. "There is nothing more, I assure you."

"Then why are you staring at her?"

I sighed. "She fascinates me," I admitted, knowing I couldn't lie to my mother. "I won't pretend otherwise, but that doesn't mean I truly know her." I stopped speaking, my own words slapping me in the face. Was I talking about Lyri? Or was I talking about Melody?

"She's a sweet girl, Tav, and I see the appeal, but if you are going to spend time with a young woman, she should at least be a suitable one."

I swallowed, uncomfortable with the mere suggestion of not spending time with her, which was disconcerting in and of itself. "I thought you would enjoy having Lyri here. You're always lamenting your lack of a daughter."

"Yes, but what I and this kingdom need is an *actual* daughter."

I bit my tongue, hoping she wasn't going to say what I suspected she would.

"Someone like Princess Saria."

A frustrated sigh burst past my teeth. "Not you too. I am not on the hunt for a wife."

"I know it's not ideal, but you must take this visit seriously. Promise me that you will honestly consider Princess Saria as an option."

"I can't think about entertaining a young lady right now."

"Then stop giving the entire kingdom reason to think that you are."

The undertone of accusation gave me pause. "What are you talking about? I'm not the one who invited Her Highness here."

"I'm not speaking of Princess Saria." She lifted her brow and then looked pointedly toward the window.

"You're talking about Lyrielle?"

"Of course I am." Her voice snapped with impatience. "People talk, Tavric, especially about you. And having a young woman here as your guest, a woman whose origins we don't even know, is—"

"I know her origins," I blurted, interrupting her.

She raised one elegant brow in a challenge. "Do tell."

I cursed myself, realizing there was no going back now. If I wanted Lyri to stay, I had to give my mother a reason to continue welcoming her, so I reached into my pocket and pulled out the necklace Martin had given me. "This belongs to her," I told my mother as I handed it over.

Her face showed confusion, which quickly turned to curiosity, as she took the pendant in hand and studied it. Then her eyes widened and a short gasp sounded between us. "Is this what I think it is?"

I swallowed, unprepared for this conversation even though I'd dangled the bait like an impulsive fool. "What do you think it is?"

She narrowed her eyes at me. "Do not act ignorant, Tavric. I can see by your face that you know exactly what I mean." She was silent, waiting for me to speak, but I didn't. She lifted the hand that held the necklace and let it sway in front of my face. "She's royalty?"

I sighed. "I don't know, Mama. I don't recognize the crest. Do you? Perhaps it's from an old family who died out, and that necklace is just an antiquated relic now."

"Do you truly believe that?"

I blew out a frustrated breath. "I don't know what to think. I don't know where Lyri came from. She has no memory of being anywhere near the ocean before I pulled her from it, and I don't recognize the name of her home."

"What's it called?"

"Branfrie. A village called Eldmere."

Her lips pressed, clearly annoyed. "I've never heard of it."

I resisted the urge to smile. She'd probably been hoping to one-up me. "Neither have I, and Lyri has said nothing to indicate that she is royalty. The way she speaks of her life...it's hard to believe a princess would have lived the way she did."

"Perhaps she's a princess who doesn't know she's a princess?"

A chuckle escaped my nose. "You'd like that, wouldn't you?"

She tilted her head as she looked at me. "No, but I think you would."

I chose not to acknowledge her comment. She didn't know what she was talking about. Just because I'd befriended Lyri didn't mean I was scheming to marry her. *If anyone is scheming to marry me off, it's my brother*, I thought bitterly.

Mama looked at the necklace again. "It looks like pure silver, Tavric. It must mean something."

I shrugged, not knowing what she expected me to say. I'd been mulling over the mystery of Lyrielle's origins for a week and had no answers.

"Perhaps you should make the time to get to know her." She turned to look down at the same scene that had captured my attention as Lyri flitted about the garden.

I breathed a sigh of relief, confused by how grateful I felt to have that permission.

"Hopefully, she's the answer to our little dilemma."

My back tensed. This was the price I paid, I suppose. As much as I wanted a chance to get to know Lyri more, I did not appreciate my mother trying to foist her on me as a marriage prospect, especially when there were far more important matters pulling on my attention. "My lack of a wife is not a dilemma."

"But it could be. I know Saria's visit is not what you hoped for, but you must know that if you ascend to the throne, the entire council will be after you to produce a queen, and quickly."

"Produce a queen?" I stepped away from the window, needing to separate Lyrielle from this conversation. "Do you know how maniacal that sounds? As if I could magic an entire person into existence."

She followed me over to my desk and stood across from me. "It looks to me like you have two candidates right on your doorstep, and the council isn't wrong. Your father is not doing well."

"Papa will rally."

"Will he?"

I clenched my jaw, hating the raw truth that shone from her red-rimmed eyes. She hadn't been sleeping well, not for months, and my father's health had been deteriorating too rapidly over the past two weeks.

"Caelmir has yet to return, and when he does, he might not have anything to show for his search." She crossed her arms and looked away as she sniffed. Then she gave her head a stiff shake and looked back at me. "If you like this girl, then why not give her a chance? Stop running off and get to know her. If she truly is royalty—"

"Stop, Mama." The idea of chasing after Lyri only because she could be royalty felt wrong.

She reached across the desk and put her hand over mine, her gaze filled with heavy grief. "I don't know if your father is going to recover. And if he doesn't, you will need to start considering who you might want for a wife."

I looked away, my eyes burning. "Don't say that."

"Say what? That your father might not make it? What else should I say?" The warble in her voice tore at me.

"Caelmir will return."

"We cannot place all of our hopes and expectations in your brother bringing back a cure. I refuse to ignore the reality that is knocking on our door." Her lips trembled and her eyes were glassy. "Of course I hope for a miracle, but I have to be practical too, and I hate it. I hate that my position forces me to do anything other than hope, but it does." She straightened, clearly agitated. "And if this girl is royalty, and if you care about her as much as you obviously do, then why should I not put some hope into that?"

"And if I fall in love with her and she isn't royalty?"

She looked at me as if I were daft. "I have every faith that you have the ability to ask her questions and figure out for yourself if she is royalty or not before you fall in love with her. It's called communication, Son."

I huffed in annoyance.

"Return the necklace. See what she says about it and go from there. If Saria comes and you truly cannot get along with her, then of course I want better for you. Ruling is difficult enough, and if you can find a lovely partner to rule at your side, it will be one less burden on my heart. So please, don't ignore the option that is right in front of you."

My mother's grief washed over her features. Was I adding to her broken heart by refusing to face the future? "Yes, Mama," I conceded, wanting more than anything to ease some of her worry.

Chapter Eight

TAVRIC

My mother's words sat heavy on my heart. I hated that she had no confidence in my ability to rule on my own. The idea that my family needed to parade young women in front of me in the hopes that they could help me rule was humiliating. I'd get used to ruling. I didn't have a choice.

So the very next day, I told myself that I would buckle down and accept my obligations with more grace and less trepidation. I could do this. I didn't need to rope a young woman into marriage to hide my weaknesses.

But it didn't matter how long I sat there, listening to advisors and trying to tell myself I was born for this—I didn't get used to it. It didn't get easier. My panic and discomfort never ebbed, and instead I felt as if I were crawling out of my own skin, needing to escape the constant chaos and energy of so many people. I wanted to be out on the water by myself, searching for Melody. Or... Was that what I wanted? Yes, I wanted to escape, but was searching for Melody just an excuse?

Once all the petitioning nobles and clerics had been heard, I left the grand hall and retreated to my room, where I took off the stuffy formal robes and sat down. My elbows dug into my knees as I pressed my hands to my face, trying to regain my composure as I forced myself to be honest about Melody. I was immeasurably grateful that my life had been saved that night on the water. I believed a mermaid had been the one to save it, and I would have appreciated the chance to thank her.

But did I actually need to find her?

No.

Did I even *want* to find her? There was a time when I had, but now I wasn't certain. I wanted to sate my curiosity, and I wanted to get away from all the noise and people, but there were so many more important things I should be doing.

Either way, I had to do something, something other than sitting with the council like I was supposed to this afternoon. The council would have to wait for another day, another time, and if my lack of tolerance for people and chaos was going to prevent me from being competent at my own duties, then I could at least fulfill a promise to Lyri and make my mother happy. I'd promised Lyrielle I would show her more of the kingdom, and Mama wanted me to get to know her. If I were honest, the idea of escaping out on the water with Lyri was not only strangely welcome, but it would also give me a chance to return her necklace. Was she royalty as I suspected?

I supposed I would find out. Yet even the idea of discovering she was royalty didn't sound as exciting as simply watching her experience the ocean in daylight.

Less than an hour later, I found her helping a laundress hang clothes on a line, her braid draped over one shoulder. She noticed me approaching and gave a small wave, which was all the encouragement I needed. I walked up to her, nervous energy coursing through me, and blurted the words before I could think better of it.

"Come sailing with me."

Her mouth fell open into a little O and her eyes widened.

"You want to see the ocean, don't you?" It was one of the things she'd named that first day when I asked her what she wanted to do and where she wanted to go.

"I..." She looked over at her friend.

The laundress shook her head with a chuckle. "Don't let me keep you. It's a fine day for sailing, I'd imagine."

"Very well." She finished draping the fabric in her hands over the line and then turned to me.

"Wait," the laundress called. She grabbed a finely woven shawl from a different line and tossed it to Lyri. "Take that. It's windy on the water."

Lyri caught it with a smile and wrapped it around her shoulders as she joined me.

Since I'd sent Harlan ahead to ready and stock my boat, it was only a matter of leaving the palace grounds and walking down the hill on the backside of the palace. A narrow path bent this way and that down the hill, and I had to slow my hurried steps to be certain that Lyri could keep up with me.

I stepped out onto the small dock and leapt onto my one-man skiff, my body adjusting easily to the swaying boat. It was the only vessel I kept in this bay. My other ships, including the galleon I'd been on when I found Lyri, were safely anchored in port. Relieved to finally be free, I reached back a hand to Lyrielle with a pleased smile. I was rarely happier than when I was on the water.

Unfortunately, Lyri didn't seem to share my enthusiasm. She hadn't even stepped onto the dock, but still stood on shore, as though uncertain she wanted to get close to the water. Both of her hands were wrapped around her braid, twisting it in agitation.

Fool, I berated myself. She'd nearly drowned last time she was near water. "I'm sorry," I said, immediately returning to the dock and carefully approaching her. "I wasn't thinking. You probably have no wish to be on another boat."

Her nervous eyes darted to me. "No, I do."

The sincere response surprised me. "You do?"

"Yes, but I just wasn't expecting...this kind of unease. I don't know why..."

I snorted. "I know why. It's completely natural to be wary of water when it's nearly killed you." Even I had avoided the ocean for a few days after Melody had dragged me from its depths, and the water and I were longtime friends.

I watched her swallow before looking up at me with curiosity in her eyes. "Do you speak from experience?"

"I do." I looked at her and then back at the boat, wondering what to do. Now that we were away from the bustle of the castle, the humming panic in my chest had eased and my urgent need to be out on the water had abated. "We could stay here if you prefer. It would afford us a lovely view of the ocean."

She cast her eyes out at the horizon instead of fixing them on the water that lapped at the shore, and I watched the tension in her shoulders ease. "It's enormous...unfathomable."

"That's what I love about it."

After several moments, her eyes returned to the skiff. "Is it safe?"

"Perfectly. I promise you won't fall overboard. Not on my watch."

She took a deep breath, then nodded and reached for my hand. "Just don't let me fall in."

I took hold of her hand, surprised by how small it was compared to my own, and carefully led her down the dock until we came alongside the boat. "Stay right there," I said before releasing her hand and once again boarding my skiff. Lyri still looked unsure, so instead of asking her to take the one precarious step into the boat, I simply reached out, wrapped my arm around her waist, and lifted her into the boat.

Her fingers dug into my arms and her breath caught. I looked at her face and realized just how close I'd brought her. As soon as her feet found purchase, I loosened my hold, my heart pounding strangely. There was something undeniably pleasant about having her pressed close to me.

When I encouraged her to sit on the bench at the front of the boat, she did so and was able to let go of my arms. She was a brave little thing, I'd give her that.

I looked around the little boat as it rocked in the shallows, the smell of pitch rising from the planks, and noted the supplies Harlan had left. Then I took up my position at the stern and gave Lyri an encouraging smile. "Are you ready for a little sailing adventure?"

She nodded, her face a wonderful combination of nerves and excitement. My own shot of nerves ran through my chest as I waited to see if she would love this as much as I did. Would she understand the draw of the ocean swells and the joy of feeling a salt breeze in her face? It shocked me how viscerally I wanted just that.

I shoved the mast into its socket, then hauled the square of linen upward. "Hold tight," I said, just before the sail caught the afternoon breeze with a snap.

Lyri made a little noise of alarm as she grabbed at the sides of the skiff. "You're certain I won't fall overboard?"

"I promise," I reassured her. "I'm very good at this, and I would never do anything to put you in danger."

As the wind pulled us along, I aimed for a tiny island close by, a spot where Lyri could look for seashells and play in the waves. It was amazing how calm I felt in this tiny boat with her sitting across from me. Usually, a day like today would have driven me to seek complete isolation, but something about Lyri made her presence comfortable. Being around her didn't feel like work.

"Why did you invite me to come with you?" she asked, raising her voice to be heard over the sound of the wind and waves.

"You haven't seen much of the world, and this is something everyone should get a chance to experience," I said, keeping my eyes on the horizon.

"But you'd rather be by yourself."

That pronouncement forced me to look at her. She said it with such conviction. "Why do you say that?"

"You have a lot of places where you go to be alone."

I chuckled. "Yes, I do."

She shook her head, turning to look out at the water with a little smile on her lips. "I don't understand that."

"Understand what?"

"Wanting to be alone."

The wistful expression layered over her melancholy sobered me. "I suppose you wouldn't. You've been denied company and companionship for so long. It makes sense that you would resist solitude now."

"I hate solitude." There was a dark ferocity in her voice that surprised me, and my imagination once again reached for an explanation of what her life had been before she fell into my ocean.

"Was there no one who knew you were being kept in that tower?" I asked.

Her chin pulled back and her brow lowered in confusion as she looked back at me. "Everyone knew."

A startled breath hissed through my lips. Each time I believed I could not be more surprised, I was proven wrong. "What do you mean *everyone*?"

"The whole village. They knew where I lived. They came to see me...sometimes." She looked away. "No one was ever upset by it." There was a resignation and numbness to her tone that ate at my nerves.

The captivity of a young girl had not been cause for concern? "No one ever tried to help you?"

"Help me what? I wasn't being mistreated. I just—"

"Being kept against your will *is* mistreatment," I snapped.

She looked at me, her lips pinched and her eyes boring into mine as heavy emotion tugged on her features. For several seconds, she held my gaze, the only sounds those made by the skiff and the water. "It is?" she finally asked.

"Yes, Lyri. It is."

She cut her eyes to the side, then nodded as a single tear slipped down her cheek. She looked...relieved?

The current pulled on the hull and I adjusted the steering oar.

I waited several moments, giving both of us time to collect ourselves. My temper was rising, and I had no wish to take it out on her. Though I was impressed she hadn't cowered at my snapping. Most people did.

"What made you leave?" I finally asked. "What made you risk climbing down that tower?"

She swallowed and seemed to have gained her composure when she spoke again, though she was still turned so I could only see her profile.

"I had always believed that once I was old enough, my aunt would let me make my own decisions. I told myself over and over that once I had done enough, helped enough, obeyed her rules enough, that she would let me go. I believed that when I was old enough she would let me have a life, have a *family*." Her eyes filled immediately with tears at the mention of family, and she turned to look at me as raw vulnerability swam in her eyes. "I've wanted nothing more than to be a mother for as long as I can remember. My dolls were my most precious possessions when my parents were living. I cherished them above all after I went to live with my aunt. Even at thirteen, I still loved to care for those dolls and dream of having babies of my own one day." She swiped at her tears and turned to face into the breeze again. "But I turned seventeen, and nothing changed. Eighteen, and nothing changed. After I turned nineteen, I finally told her. I said I wanted a family, and I dared to suggest that I would leave the tower and live my own life." She looked down at her hands. "The very notion incensed her. She called me selfish and ungrateful."

I swallowed down all my indignation and tried to speak calmly. "What a backward notion."

"What?" she asked, turning to look at me with hurt crimping her face, and I realized she might believe I was calling her want of a family backwards. But that wasn't it at all.

"The idea that motherhood is selfish. That might be the biggest lie your aunt ever told you."

LYRIELLE

I stared at his profile as he turned his face into the wind like I had been doing. He'd responded so confidently, and it was a relief to have that bit of evidence telling me that what I wanted might not have been unreasonable. In fact, it may have been Aunt Ethel who was unreasonable. And perhaps the villagers too.

"I'm sorry you didn't have anyone to protect you," he said suddenly, but it was quiet enough that I almost didn't hear it over the wind and the snapping of the sail.

I didn't respond, too emotional to talk and unable to think of what to say as my heart filled with liquid warmth. Was this what it was like to have a real friend? Gregor had been my friend, but my aunt's strict rules had dictated the depth of our friendship, and Tavric was making me realize how little I knew of genuine friendship. I'd had friends when I was a child, but I couldn't skip rope or climb trees now that I was older, could I?

A sudden gust of wind tugged on the boat, and my attention was drawn to the vastness of ocean surrounding us. Trying to explain my life's circumstances had distracted me from my nervousness, and now that we'd been bobbing on the water for several minutes, my fear had eased. The sound of gentle waves lapping against the side of the boat was soothing, and there was something thrilling about being out here with Tavric.

When he'd hooked his arm around my waist to bring me onto the boat, a strange bundle of nerves had knotted in my stomach. I liked being close to him, and yet the pleasure was almost uncomfortable because of how wild it felt. Were these the sort of feelings that came with true friendship? Or was it more? I couldn't tell because I had nothing to compare it to. The upheaval inside of me could simply be caused by my complete lack of experience with courting—or even just human interaction.

Still, his protectiveness certainly added to that pleasant knot of nerves.

I looked ahead of us, raising a hand to shield my eyes against the sun. "Are we going to that little island?" I asked, turning back to him.

"Yes, we are." A grin split his face, and I was so startled by its sudden appearance that I stared. I'd never seen Tavric grin before. He often had a kind smile for me, but he could also come across as gruff and serious. "It's one of my favorite places to run off to when I want to be alone," he admitted.

I wanted to ask him again why he had brought me with him, but instead, I spread my arms wide and reveled in the feeling of my shawl whipping around my arms and fluttering at my back.

As we neared the island, Tavric lowered the sail and used the oar to row us right up to shore, where we came to a soft stop on the sand.

Tavric discarded his shoes and encouraged me to do the same. As I removed my own footwear, I watched as he rolled his trousers nearly to his knees, looking more relaxed and content than I'd ever seen him. He jumped from the boat into the surf, then turned back, that same grin curving his mouth as he reached for me, sweeping me into his arms and lifting me from the boat as if it were the most natural thing in the world. His feet splashed through the lapping waves as he walked several feet and deposited me on sand. I think he was trying to help me avoid touching the water, which was so thoughtful that it confused me. He was constantly guessing at my wants and needs and then fulfilling them as best he could.

His kindness was disconcerting, and I suspected I didn't deserve it.

As I admired the beauty of the island, I was half-aware of Tavric pulling a small box of supplies from the boat and placing it far out of reach of the water before stringing a rope from the boat to a tree trunk. Then he pulled a blanket from the box, spread it out and flopped himself onto it.

That was all the permission I needed to sit on the blanket and bury my toes in the sand. I dug my fingers in as well, loving the soft scrape of sand against my skin. I closed my eyes, once more drawn into communing with the earth. I couldn't help myself. After being surrounded by nothing but stone for so many years, the opportunity to feel all different kinds of soil was not something I could pass up.

"I have something for you," Tavric said suddenly.

I turned to face him, surprised both by his words and by the look of unease on his face. "What is it?"

He reached into his pocket and pulled out his closed fist, holding it toward me.

I held out my hand, curious, and when he opened his fist, my necklace fell onto my palm. I sucked in a breath and blinked back the tears. "You found it," I said in awe as I drew it close to my heart.

"One of my men did," he said. "He brought it to me yesterday."

"Thank you," I whispered while my trembling fingers fought to open the clasp.

"Here," he said, placing a calming hand over my own. "Let me."

He gently took the necklace back and got up on his knees so he could loop the chain around my neck. I fought a shudder as his fingers brushed my neck. As the pendant settled into place, I covered it with my fingers, comforted by its familiar weight. It was the only thing I still had from my parents.

"I'm sorry I didn't give it to you yesterday. I've been...distracted." Tavric sat back on the blanket, resting his elbows on his knees. His expression was subdued but steady. He nodded toward the necklace. "What does the symbol mean?"

My brow scrunched in confusion. "It doesn't mean anything."

His eyes narrowed. "Are you certain?"

I nodded. "It was my mother's. It was the only thing I was able to bring with me when I left the tower."

"Hmm." He seemed dissatisfied with my answer, but it was the truth, so I just sat back and let the sensation of the wind on my face and the sand on my feet seep into me.

Tavric and I rested in silence until he sat up and pointed down the beach. "Do you see those?"

"See what?"

"Watch the sand carefully and you'll see them move."

I did as he asked, and sure enough, the small shells that littered the beach were moving. "What are they?"

"Hermit crabs. They find shells to crawl into and then they scuttle around the beach."

I got up for a closer look and found that when I was moving, the crabs would move less, but if I stayed still, they would suddenly come to life, hauling their tiny houses on their backs as they went here and there. Two of them bumped into one another and then circled around each other. "These two seem to be doing a dance," I commented.

"Which one?" he asked from behind me.

"What do you mean?"

"Which dance are they doing?"

I looked over my shoulder at Tavric. "I don't know the names."

"Were you not taught how to dance?"

I tilted my head as I looked at him. "Not only does dancing require a partner, but do you remember how long my hair was?"

"Oh, right." He rubbed at his forehead. "Sorry."

I shrugged. "Nothing to be sorry for. I've never danced. I've never done a great many things. Before today, I had not sailed on the sea with the wind in my hair. I'd never felt sand under my feet, and I'd never lounged on a small island with a prince. So, as I said, *you* have nothing to be sorry for. You've been a true friend." I looked away from him to prevent myself from gushing out all of my thanks. Instead I took a few steps toward the water until I was on damp, firm sand. I admired the light reflecting off the water, the bright white clouds against the blue sky, and the way the trees swayed in the wind.

I heard Tavric moving behind me but was surprised when he circled around to face me and swept into a deep bow, holding one hand out. "My lady, might I have this dance?"

A chuckle escaped me. "I told you I don't know how."

"Then I'll show you." He stepped forward so his toes nearly touched mine and reached behind me to press a hand into the center of my back. *Sparks and fire.* I could hardly breathe. This did not feel healthy. I was suddenly overheated and I couldn't feel my fingers. I also couldn't move, so I just stared up at him.

He raised his right hand up at his side. "Take my hand."

I obeyed immediately.

He nodded toward his left shoulder. "Now place your other hand there."

I did so. "Do you have a secret fondness for dancing, Your Highness?" I asked, trying to dispel the thickness in the air.

"Under the right circumstances, yes. Now, you will take two steps back, starting with your left foot. One, two."

I stepped back as he counted, and he stepped forward to match me.

"Now we'll do a quick turn to switch places. One and two."

I stumbled a bit, but we made the turn and I better understood what he meant.

"Now it's my turn to go back and you'll come toward me with your right foot. One, two, turn a-round."

This time, the turn came easier because I understood the rhythm.

"Very good. Now we just repeat that over and over. Ready?"

I nodded, excited both by the prospect of continued close proximity with Tavric and with the idea of having the ability to dance now that my hair was gone.

"Step, step, turn around. Step, step, turn around." He trailed off as I easily caught the rhythm and we traveled our way down the beach.

I couldn't help the elated smile that curled over my face, and a laugh burst from my mouth as our pace sped up.

"You're doing great," he assured me, but then our course took us far enough up the beach that the sand had dried and become soft and pliant under our feet. We both tripped and toppled to the ground. I landed half on top of him but immediately rolled into a sitting position, breathless and chuckling.

"Is this how you dance with the ladies at court?" I asked.

"No. This is how I dance during the summer festivals, when the whole kingdom comes out to celebrate."

"You topple your subjects to the ground during festivals?"

A laugh burst from his mouth, but he didn't bother sitting up. "No. I just meant that's the sort of dance we do at festivals. That wasn't a court dance."

"Ah. I suppose it wouldn't make sense to teach me any courtly dances. I certainly won't ever attend."

He rolled his head to look over at me. "Why do you say that?"

My brow scrunched. "I thought courtly things were only meant for royalty and nobility. Am I remembering that wrong?" I thought I'd read that in more than one book. "Perhaps that's not the same in all kingdoms."

"You're right, that's the norm. But you could still come." He closed his eyes. "Friends of the prince are always welcome."

The threat of tears burned my eyes as his kindness washed over me. He gave it so effortlessly, and it continued to surprise me. He didn't see me as a burden, and he didn't seem to want anything from me.

As he lay back with his eyes closed, I admired his dark hair and short-trimmed beard. His hair was windblown, and he'd set aside his vest, lounging in his linen shirt and trousers. The word that came to mind as I looked at him was *scrumptious*, though why I would attach that word to a man was beyond me. My fluttery heart had some very strange ideas.

He cracked one eye open and caught me staring at him. "What?"

"You're a different person here."

He snorted. “I’m not a prince here.” He covered his eyes with his arm. “I’m just a man on a beach beside a pretty girl.”

The knot of nerves in my stomach liked that pronouncement *very* much.

Chapter Nine

TAVRIC

"I need to get out of here again," I said without preamble, walking into the dining hall.

Lyri was having lunch and I was interrupting. She took a cautious sip of her tea and then looked at me. "What happened?"

"My father was unable to hold court this morning, so I did so in his absence." I dug my short fingernails into my palms, trying to focus on that so I could ignore the rolling discomfort in the rest of my body.

Her face was immediately draped in concern. "Is your father all right?"

"Just feeling a little unwell," I lied. "But I don't have much practice with such things, and it was nearly five straight hours of a loud, crowded room, and everyone wanted me to solve all their problems. I just...want quiet; I need quiet."

"I thought you usually went to your library for quiet."

"They'll find me there."

She looked up at me with a mix of concern and anticipation. "Where did you have in mind?"

I looked at her plate, which was nearly empty. "Have you had enough?"

She sat back and rested her hands on her stomach in a way that no noblewoman ever would. It was a sharp reminder that she wasn't royalty, and that I shouldn't be seeking her out. Yet, she was the one person who felt safe at the moment. "Likely too much," she admitted. "There are always so many wonderful things to choose from. I can tell my maid is not lacing my dresses as tightly as when I first came, and it's been barely more than a week."

"Good. You deserve to be well fed." I held a hand out to her. "Please, can we go before the council decides they need my attention too?"

She stood, slipping her hand into mine, and something in my chest loosened.

Instead of taking the winding footpath down to my boat, I had a horse saddled with the padded pillion seat for Lyri and pulled her up behind me. The feeling of her arms banded tightly around my chest calmed me perhaps better than anything else I had tried. I placed my palm over her hands where they rested just below my sternum, hoping she would keep them there. I was rewarded by the feeling of her arms tightening further, and more of my tension melted away.

We rode through the village and down to the part of the shoreline that stretched out with sandy beaches until they ran into the black cliffs on the south tip of the island. There were tide pools here, but my aim was the caves tucked away under the cliffs.

I tied my horse in a copse of trees lining the shore and ran after Lyri when she headed toward the water, sand kicking up behind her, shoes tossed casually in the sand. She stopped well before she reached the water and then just stood, letting the wind pull on her skirts and knot the loose tendrils of her hair, her eyes closed and her face tipped to the sky.

Escaping the palace had been for my own benefit, but seeing the way Lyri soaked in all the freedom and adventure that I was able to give her was a different kind of pleasure. I wanted to ask her to dance with me again—to see her smile, yes, but mostly as an excuse to touch her. I was so used to the comfort of being by myself that it was a strange thing to crave her proximity.

I walked slowly to where she stood but resisted the urge to rest a hand on her lower back. "Have I converted you to my love of the ocean?"

She laughed. "No, I'm fairly certain the ocean managed that without your princely help."

I grinned, loving that she wasn't intimidated by my princely ways. "Wait until you see the caves."

She looked off toward the craggy cliffs. "Are they there?"

"Yes."

"Then what are we waiting for?" she asked, taking off at a run again. I loved watching the joy she found in movement and I tried imagining what it had been like with all that hair. It would have ruled her life. I was certain that the reason she ran and spun and dashed here and there was because that simple freedom was new to her.

Naturally, I chased after her like a lovesick fool, trying to tell myself it was only an innocent attraction.

I was a liar.

I'd nearly caught up with her when she came to an abrupt stop, turning around to look at something on the ground that she'd passed. I came to an ungraceful halt and joined her as she stooped to pick up a sanderling and cradle it in her palms.

She ran her fingers over its wings. “Hey, little one, what’s wrong?”

“What have you got there?” I asked as she held it gently to her chest and stroked its back.

“Just a bird.”

“Is it injured?” I asked, not seeing anything obviously wrong with the sanderling.

“I’m hoping it’s only stunned.” She stroked its little head and back and made little clucking noises at it, then looked up at me with a grin. “He can come with us,” she declared, and then started heading toward the caves again, this time at a sedate walk.

I smiled to myself as I followed after her, catching up so I could lead her to the opening in the cliffs. Once we stepped through, there were only a few feet of dry sand inside the cave before the water was lapping at the little beach inside.

The cave was a deep crevice that ran from this side of the cliff all the way to the other side, where it opened out to the ocean. The waves rushed in from the far side and gently tumbled their way toward us, petering out not far from where we stood. Sunlight poured in from both sides, lighting the dim space enough that we could appreciate how wide the cave had become from the constant onslaught of waves beating away on its inner walls.

“This would be the perfect hideout for mermaids,” Lyri commented, one hand pressed to the rock wall at the entrance while the other still held the bird.

“Yes, it would.” I studied her bright eyes and the braided gold crown of hair ringing her head. “You know, my men believed you were a mermaid when we pulled you from the ocean.”

“I remember. I thought it was very strange. Mermaids are the stuff of legend, not reality.”

I blinked as I considered her words. It was just another example of how she'd come from somewhere completely foreign to me. "You don't think mermaids are real?"

She froze and fixed me with a stare, then blinked and asked, "Are they?"

"Well, now I feel foolish admitting to my belief."

She let out a laugh. "I've spent the past ten years isolated in a tower. Believe me, I don't think I am an authority on anything happening in the world. If you say there are mermaids, then I believe you. It's actually a relief to know that something so fantastical could exist in this world." She looked down at the sanderling in her hands and stroked its head. "Have you ever seen one?"

I bit my lips together for a moment before deciding to confide in her. "Once. In fact, I think she saved my life."

She looked up at me, her eyes wide with awe. "Truly?"

I nodded. "I was foolish and I should have drowned in that ocean, but she brought me to shore...and then she disappeared."

"How extraordinary." She looked off at the crashing waves and then turned back to me. "Shall we thank them?"

"What?" I asked with a chuckle, expecting to find that teasing spark in her eyes, but she looked sincere.

"They communicate through song, do they not? I think I read that in a book." Then she turned to face the deeper recesses of the cave and sang out, "*Thank you, mermaids, for saving the prince.*"

I sucked a breath through my nose, completely captivated.

Spellbinding. That's what her voice was. Beautiful, soothing, angelic, and devoid of pretense. She sang out with confidence and wild abandon, yet there wasn't even a hint of pride in her voice or bearing.

When Melody had saved me, her song had been just as magical, but it had a haunting quality, and there had been a haughtiness to it, as if she knew all too well the effect her voice had on me.

Suddenly, the bird Lyri had been cradling stood up and fluttered its wings.

"Oh!" Lyri jumped in surprise and let out a delighted laugh. "Had enough rest, have you?" she asked the bird.

The sanderling hopped once, fluffed its wings again, and took flight, disappearing into the bright sunlight outside the cave.

Lyri's face was shadowed by the dim cave interior, yet her smile was so bright, I had to wonder how someone who'd spent years as little better than a prisoner could have retained such effervescence and hope. I envied her ability to move about the world with such optimism.

So much of the time, I felt strangled by the world and the people in it. Maybe that was why I'd chased after Melody for so long. The idea of living in the quiet of the ocean was appealing. And yet, I'd thought of Melody less and less since I'd pulled Lyri from the same ocean. The dark allure and mystery of Melody couldn't hold a candle to the bright openness and steady calm that Lyri brought with her.

She stepped a little closer to the water and reached up to wrap a hand around her necklace. She did that often. It was clear that she valued the necklace for its attachment to her mother and nothing else. I'd been around plenty of foreign royalty, often with them vying for my attention, and it had always made me uncomfortable. Perhaps that was why I'd pushed back so much when my mother had gotten excited at the prospect of her being royalty. I didn't want to pursue and marry someone who made me feel uncomfortable.

But Lyri...

A larger wave rolled into the cave and rushed around our feet. I jumped forward to be sure she didn't lose her balance, but she let out a startled yelp, followed by a delighted laugh as she clung to my arm to keep her balance. "Perhaps your mermaid friend is trying to get you back in the water," she teased.

I just shook my head. "I'm happy where I am."

Chapter Ten

LYRIELLE

"Tav!" someone shouted.

I looked up to see a gentleman stride into the dining hall. His arms were open as he approached Tavric, who immediately stood. This must have been one of his brothers, another prince of Islewyn.

"You're home," Tavric said as he embraced the man in a crushing hug.

"Of course," the man said as he pulled back and squeezed Tavric's shoulder. "It was time."

"It's good to see you," Tavric said, and I could hear the lump in his throat. "Oh." He suddenly turned and gestured to me. "Lyrielle, this is my brother, Kavian."

Caught off guard, I only nodded, and then had to wonder if I should have stood and curtsied. Probably.

"Ah, yes," Prince Kavian said as he raised his brow and swept his eyes over me. "Mama said we had a...guest."

He didn't like me. I didn't know how I knew that, but it was perfectly clear, just like it was clear that much of the castle staff didn't like me.

Kavian gave me one last narrow-eyed look, then turned back to Tavric, effectively cutting me out of the conversation altogether. “Collecting trinkets from the ocean again, are you?”

Before I could shrink down into my chair, Tavric’s hand shot out and smacked his brother high on his chest. “Apologize,” he said in a dark tone.

I was speechless. Was he angry at his brother on my behalf?

Kavian shrugged away from him. “For what? I didn’t say anything.”

“Lyrielle is a guest in our home, and calling her a trinket is insulting.”

My eyes burned with sudden emotion.

Kavian put his hands up in surrender. “I didn’t mean it that way,” he said, and yet he still didn’t bother to apologize or acknowledge my presence further.

Tavric gave him a look of disgust and pushed past him. “Never mind.” He walked over to me and held out a hand. “Let’s go.”

I hadn’t quite finished eating, but I grabbed the remaining half of my biscuit and let him pull me to my feet and hurry us toward the door.

“Tav, come on, I didn’t mean anything by it,” Kavian said as we passed.

Tavric ignored him, and we’d almost made it to the door when the queen appeared and blocked our way.

“There you all are,” she said with a satisfied smile. “Kavian, I see you’ve met Lyrielle.”

“Yes, a pleasure,” Prince Kavian said in a much more polite tone than he had afforded me before.

“It’s been such a treat to have her. And did she show you her necklace? It’s a fascinating piece.”

Tavric looked at the ceiling with a huff, but both the prince and I regarded her in confusion. What did my necklace have to do with anything?

Prince Kavian looked at me, curious and expectant. I didn't know if he actually wanted to know or if he was just humoring his mother.

"I..." All the attention was uncomfortable and I felt my shoulders roll forward. "It's nothing special. Just..." I pulled it out from my bodice with my free hand and took one step closer to the younger prince so he could see. Might as well get this over with and get out of here. This was my first time meeting Kavian, and his hostility toward me was making my stomach clench.

Prince Kavian stepped forward and gave my necklace a polite glance, but then his eyes widened and he gave the queen a very meaningful look before turning and giving Tavric that same look.

My eyes jumped from one family member to another. Tavric looked annoyed, the queen smug, and his brother incredulous.

"It was a gift from my mother," I said to fill the silence.

"We're going now," Tavric said and towed me from the room.

I hurried at his side, wildly curious, but I waited until we'd rounded the corner into another corridor before I spoke. "That was very strange."

"I'm sorry he was so rude."

I looked down at our still-linked hands and then slowed my step. Instead of letting my hand drop or dragging me along, he slowed and came to a stop with a resigned sigh.

Once he looked at me, I asked, "Are you going to tell me *why* it was strange?"

His jaw tensed.

"Why is your mother interested in my necklace? I didn't even know she'd seen it."

He groaned and dragged a hand down his face. "Because family crests with crowns in the design always mean royalty."

The idea was so startling that I stepped back and pulled my hand away. "I beg your pardon?"

He gave a little shrug. "My mother has come up with some fanciful ideas about you being some sort of lost princess." One corner of his mouth tugged up just a bit.

I rubbed at my forehead with one hand and clutched at my pendant with the other. "It's supposed to mean royalty?" That didn't make sense.

He nodded. "Here, I'll show you." He gestured for me to follow him and I did, unsurprised when we ended up outside the library.

I'd passed it on a number of occasions but had never wanted to go inside. The shelves and shelves of books reminded me too much of my tower home. But I ignored that apprehension and followed him through the rows until we reached a back corner near a fireplace with a long desk strewn with maps and books, some stacked and some lying open.

He pulled one forward and pointed to a spread of pages covered with illustrations of family crests.

"I started searching through these right after I first saw your necklace. But look." He gestured to the crests that all included crowns in their designs, then flipped to another page of the same. "There is nothing like the crest you wear." He flipped page after page. "I've studied all of them, and the one from your necklace isn't here." He flicked one last page over and then stepped back, his hands on his hips, his brow tugging down with the corners of his mouth.

I moved forward, my eyes taking in the wide variety of crests illustrated in the book.

"I even studied all the noble houses," he said, turning to another page that illustrated crests without crowns. "Just to be sure yours wasn't some sort of variation."

I fingered the page of the book, wondering if I should be bothered that he hadn't mentioned this before now. Then again, what would I have said? Even now, I wasn't sure if I was disappointed or relieved that he hadn't found the crest. I turned and leaned back against the edge of the desk, looking up at him. "Tavric—"

His brow shot up.

My face heated. "I mean, Your Highness."

His chin tilted down a bit, but his eyes remained fixed on my own. "You can call me Tavric, or even Tav."

My cheeks warmed further, but I ignored them. "I was just going to say...there is no royalty in my land."

His chin pulled back. "What do you mean?"

"Branfrie is not ruled by a king. Not anymore. And even if it were, I do not think you'd find evidence of it in one of your books."

"Why not?"

"Because the royal family was ousted more than seventy-five years ago. It's ruled by a High Court now, and any evidence of royalty has been destroyed or fallen to ruin." I bit my lip, but then plowed on. "My tower—the tower I was kept in—was just one corner of a crumbling castle where the royal family resided more than three generations ago."

Tavric stepped back and laced his hands behind his head as he paced, his eyes darting about, no doubt trying to make sense of this information. Then he abruptly came forward again. "Fine." He flicked the book closed and leaned one hand on the table so we were eye level with one another. "Why were you kept in that tower?" His mouth was stern as he asked it. "I don't care about the crest, or even your land's form of government. What I want to know is what happened to *you*." His eyes delved into mine, begging for answers. "Was it punishment? Did they fear you? Was your aunt just a terrible person who wanted your misery?"

"She was protecting me."

His brow furrowed even more, like he sensed the partial truth. "I know that's what she said, but...you also told me that people visited you regularly and were not concerned by the fact that you were locked away. Tell me why."

I shook my head, not ready to admit to my magic and expose myself to his suspicion or censure.

His face fell. "Why won't you tell me?"

How could I explain it? "You won't like it."

"Of course I won't. Whatever excuse your aunt came up with will—"

"Not her. Me."

Two parallel creases appeared between his brows as they squished together. "*You* what?"

"I don't want you to think less of me," I admitted, realizing just how much I'd grown to cherish and depend on his friendship. "I'm afraid you won't trust me."

He went a bit pale. "Lyri, you're making me think the worst. Please just tell me."

"What would be the worst?" Would he say magic?

His lips pressed in frustration. "Did you hurt people?"

I almost laughed at that. "No."

"Are you here to hurt or manipulate me or my family?"

"Of course not."

He lifted his hands from his sides. "Then I can't think of anything else."

I studied him, confused that he hadn't thought to mention magic. Every story I'd been told about the world outside of Branfrie was that they feared and hated magic and anyone who wielded it. Had that been lies? Or maybe things had changed over the years. He'd spoken of the mermaids without fear, and surely mermaids were synonymous with magic.

The sincerity in his eyes tugged at me, begging me to let him in, to give him the chance to actually know me. I took a deep breath—and told him the truth. "My aunt was protecting my gift."

I could see his surprise. "What gift?"

There was no going back now, but even though I wanted him to know, my voice still trembled. "I could heal people." The confession was barely a whisper as fear coiled tighter inside me.

He seemed bewildered by my confession, like it was of no consequence. "You had a talent for healing?"

I chewed on my lip a bit, frustrated that he wasn't getting it. "It was more than that. I didn't heal with herbs and knowledge."

"Then what did you use?"

I licked my lips and tilted my chin up, gathering my courage. "Magic."

A small breath hissed through his lips and I held my breath. "Magic?" He blinked, his mouth hanging open, looking at me with both skepticism and awe. "You have experience with real magic?"

His lack of anger or fear was a comfort, and I nodded.

He opened his mouth, but I'd left him speechless, apparently.

I hurried to explain, hoping that the more he knew, the more he'd understand. "When I was nine, I gained the ability to heal, but only through my hair, and only if it was never cut."

"You can heal?"

"I *could*." I looked down at my hair that hung only to my elbows and then back at him. "Not anymore."

His eyes grazed over what remained of my hair. "I took your magic from you?" he asked in a raw whisper.

I nodded.

I thought perhaps this piece would make him feel better. Yes, I'd had magic, but I didn't anymore. If he feared magic, that should have been a comfort. Instead he looked devastated as he said, "I'm so sorry."

Tears of relief pricked my eyes and I shook my head. "Don't be. It's better this way," I assured him as guilt marred his face.

"How can it be better?"

His utter confusion made me certain that I'd been wrong. "Isn't magic a bad thing?" I asked.

"I don't know, " he said, his eyes darting about, obviously trying to work out all the implications of my revelation. "I've no experience with it."

I wrung my hands as my world reordered itself and a knot of fear eased.

Finally, Tavric's eyes settled back on me, questions written all over his face. "Why is it better that you lost your magic? Being able to heal..."

"Is an extraordinary gift, yes. So extraordinary that it was coveted and envied." I lifted my chin again, feeling just a little defiant for telling him this truth. "And well used."

He narrowed his eyes. "Well used?"

"You asked why my aunt kept me in that tower. That's why. She believed it was my responsibility to use my gift to its fullest because if I'd had my gift when my parents fell ill, I could have saved them. She always resented me for not being able to save her sister, and she wanted to keep others from suffering that grief. If I was always in the tower, then the sick and injured always knew where to find me, so my magic could always be used. And anyone who wished me harm couldn't reach me."

His eyes darted around as he tried to make sense of it all. "Who wished you harm?" he finally asked.

I shrugged. "I had powerful magic, and powerful magic was coveted in my land. The High Court liked to have people like me under their control."

He stood straight, his jaw working, forming words that never escaped, until finally he looked to me. "Here." He gestured toward two chairs that sat in front of a nearby fireplace. "Come sit."

I did so, and he sat on the edge of his own chair, leaning forward. "How did it work?"

I let out a little breath of relief, grateful that he was curious instead of suspicious. "As long as I was singing, someone needed only touch my hair and they would be healed."

"Cuts? Bruises?"

"Yes."

"Broken bones?"

"Yes."

"Fever? Infection?"

"All of it."

"Astounding."

My eyes stung and I blinked. "All these years, I thought—I was told—that everyone outside of Branfrie hated magic. That they feared it."

He let out a bewildered little chuckle, shoving his hands into his hair. "There are enough records and rumors of magic that I think we all know it's out there somewhere. We assume the mermaids in these waters have magic, though our only understanding of their existence consists of mere rumors and rare sightings." He studied me, almost like he was seeing me for the first time. "There is an entire land filled with magic?"

I nodded. "It wasn't always that way. Magic first presented itself in our land seventy-five years ago. It was strong and random. Not many had it, and those who did found themselves in a position of power. A few strong sorcerers thought the land would be better ruled by a High Court of those with magic instead of by a royal family without."

He shook his head in disbelief. "Why have I never heard of this land?"

"It's shrouded. No one but the inhabitants know it's there. I've always known it remained invisible to the outside world, but the fact that you don't even recognize the name of it... I hadn't expected that."

He studied me for several moments, looking like he wanted to say something but was holding back. I waited him out, and finally he spoke. "Do you want to return?"

A deep, visceral reaction crashed through my whole body. The answer was a resounding and unequivocal *no*, but I worried that if I said that, Tavric would feel obligated to take care of me, and the last thing I wanted to be was a burden.

But I also couldn't lie.

"Do you think I should?" I asked, terrified that he might say yes.

"It's not up to me."

"But you have an opinion?" I asked, suddenly impatient for him to just answer.

"Of course."

"Which is?"

"Don't go back," he said, almost begged. His eyes were deep with worry and want as he said it, and I knew he meant it.

I drew in a tight breath. "Why?"

"That place wasn't good for you."

I wanted to ask if there was any other reason. Did he want me to stay for my own good, or for his? But I wasn't that brave. Not yet. "How do you know that?"

He let out a gentle scoff. "You hadn't touched land for ten years. You'd been turned into a slave. You were so miserable that you risked scaling the side of a castle turret to escape that life. You hadn't interacted with anyone but your aunt for a decade."

"I interacted with people." I didn't know why I was arguing with him. Perhaps I just wanted to believe that it hadn't been *that bad.*

"Face to face?" he challenged.

"Well...I was up in the tower, and they were on the ground, but yes, I could see their faces. I could talk to them."

"But did you have any friends?"

"One."

"What was her name?"

"His name was Gregor."

He paused as some sort of puzzled look crossed his face. "And he would visit you?"

I nodded, grateful for this one piece of brightness that was part of my story. "He would always speak to me when he came by, asking about my day. He was kind and funny and brought me books that we knew Aunt Ethel wouldn't approve of."

His smile was small but genuine, though there was a sadness behind it that pulled on the threads of sadness in my own heart. "I'm glad you had someone who cared for you."

"Me too. He was always gentle when he used my hair."

Tavric's brow furrowed and his eyes took on that stormy quality. "Would he do that often?"

"Do what?"

"Use your hair?"

"Of course. That's why he would come. That's why everyone came."

His jaw tensed and he looked away for several seconds. "That sounds lonely."

I gave a small shrug. "It was less lonely when they came. At least the ones who spoke to me. And it was comforting to know that I was helping."

His lips pressed together and his eyes narrowed, like something about my answer frustrated him. "But they were always there to use you. Did that not bother you?"

Yes, but... "They needed my help."

"Did they?"

I huffed. He was always challenging my answers this way. This time I kept my mouth shut, certain he had something to say.

"When people sought your help, were they gravely ill?"

"Sometimes. Most often, they didn't let it get that far. They came to me right away. Wounds rarely got infected because I could heal them when it first happened."

"People mostly came to you for small things?"

"Yes. Scratches and bruises. Congestion, headache. Though some of the lads would make a game out of seeing how long they could wait before coming to me."

Concern cloaked his features. "What do you mean?"

"They would each give themselves a cut with a dirty knife, all at the same time, and then the person who lasted the longest before coming to be healed would be the winner."

He looked horrified, staring at me for several long moments before turning to look away, rolling his shoulders in agitation. "Those boys didn't need your help."

"I assure you they did. Waiting that long caused awful infections."

He pressed his lips together, his nostrils flaring. "I've lived my whole life without someone to instantly heal me," he pointed out. "I've had more injuries than I can count, and far more than my mother would prefer. I've dealt with each one. I've taken care of myself. I've used the herbs given to me for healing. You weren't their only option."

"They weren't the only ones I healed," I defended myself, even though in the hidden parts of my soul I'd thought all the things he was saying. "Some people came to me gravely injured by no fault of their own."

"And the gift you gave them was a true miracle. I'm glad for their sakes that you were there for them. But it sounds like most people came to you because they were careless or lazy or just didn't know that there was another way."

"Yes," I conceded.

"You've been used, Lyrielle. For your entire life."

"I haven't had the gift my entire life," I pointed out with another stubborn lift of my chin, unwilling to think too hard about what he'd just said.

He stood and paced more, agitated. "Fine then. You've been used every day for the past ten years."

He was right, but it sounded so much worse when someone else said it out loud.

"They needed help," I said quietly, mostly out of habit.

Tavric nodded. "Some did. Most just *wanted* it. But what do you want? More importantly, what do you need?"

I bristled at the question. "Aunt Ethel always said it was selfish to want things when I'd already been given so much."

His eyes narrowed with curiosity. "And what had you been given?"

Questions, questions, so many questions. "My gift," I answered, exasperated.

"Healing?" Another question. "Could you heal yourself?"

I shook my head. "No, that's one of the reasons Aunt Ethel was so protective of me. I could heal everyone but myself."

His lips pressed together and he took a deep breath before huffing it out in a frustrated sigh. "So your aunt said wanting anything else was selfish because you had the gift of healing others?"

I nodded.

"Lyri...how can a gift that can never be used for yourself possibly make you selfish?"

I knew all the answers to his questions, and yet I had the feeling that he wouldn't be satisfied by them—probably because I'd never been fully satisfied by them. "My gift gave me power." I shrugged.

"But did it? Did you feel powerful when you were locked in that tower?"

My eyes burned as all the helplessness and desperation for freedom that I'd held on to all those years suddenly filled my chest again. "No."

His expression softened. "I know a little something about power. I've watched my father wield the power of a king, knowing that power would one day be mine. I've seen the way people envy, fear, or respect him. I've seen the way it *burdens* him. And I've felt a little of that burden recently." He swallowed with difficulty. "Power is a burden to those who wield it responsibly. And I'll take it on. I'll take on that burden when I have to, but there is no part of me that *wants* that power. Did you *ever* want yours?"

I couldn't bring myself to shake my head. Instead my gaze dropped to my lap and my mouth trembled. "No. And I don't want to go back. I *don't*."

He let out a giant sigh at my firm pronouncement.

"But..." I closed my eyes and toyed with the ends of my hair, finding it impossible to silence the voice of my aunt that rang in my head. "Be grateful," I murmured to myself.

"Pardon?"

"It's what she always said to me. Anytime I complained about people pulling on my hair. Any time I asked to go out, she would say 'be grateful.' And I tried." I spoke past the knot in my throat. "I tried for so long. But I almost always failed. I wasn't grateful, except on a very few occasions." Tears dripped onto my hands that looked blurry as they fidgeted in my lap. "Last year, a baby was brought to me. The mother came running to the tower, the limp infant clutched in her arms, screaming, wailing my name, begging for help. When my hair brought that baby back from the brink of death, I was grateful. When that mother sobbed with joy, clutching her pink-cheeked and crying child, I was grateful. When she looked up at me with so much gratitude and relief, I was more grateful than I'd ever been."

He curled a finger under my chin and nudged it up until I was looking at him. "It's incredible that you could save that child. You are a wonder, Lyri. How did a soul as beautiful as yours come out of that place?"

Tears pushed at my eyes. "My soul isn't beautiful."

"It is," he insisted, keeping a finger under my chin so I couldn't look down. "One of the most beautiful I've ever seen." His thumb moved back and forth over my jaw in a light caress.

Warmth shot from my stomach up into my lungs, and I had a sudden need for his arms to be around me so I could feel his strength and his warmth. I wanted to fall forward until my head rested on his shoulder. But I held back, too terrified to act.

Instead, I dashed the tears from my cheeks and gave him a forced smile. "Now you know my secret. Tell me one of yours."

His eyes immediately pinched as if he was in pain and he took an unsteady breath. "My father is dying." He breathed out the words as grief crashed over his features. "And there is *nothing* I can do about it."

"Oh, Tavric." Waves of compassion washed over me as the pieces slotted together. The reason he'd been so busy lately, the king's lack of public appearances. I'd known he was ill, but I'd had no idea it was so dire.

"It's why I'm suddenly expected to hold court. It's why the council demands so much of my time. For a while, he was having good days and bad days, but now... He's too sick to rule, Lyri."

"Is there no hope?"

"Only Caelmir."

"Your brother?"

He nodded. "My mother sent him off in search of a cure or a doctor or anything at all that might help."

I bit my lips together, hating that I couldn't go to the king right then and give him his life back. "Do you think he will find something?"

"I've tried not to hope, but I can't help it. Because if I don't hope...then all that's left is that he's dying, and I don't know how to make that truth fit into my brain when everything about it is wrong."

My heart shattered for him. Not only did I remember exactly what it felt like to be so helpless in the face of a parent dying, but there was also a wave of guilt that rose up to strangle me. If I still had my gift, I would have the power to heal his father, and yet the moment that gift had been taken from me, the most prominent feeling I'd experienced had been relief. “I'm so sorry,” I said, knowing the words were inadequate. Knowing I meant them in more ways than one.

Chapter Eleven

TAVRIC

We'd ridden down by the cliffs again, and this time we were seated on the sand, watching the sunset. I'd had nearly two days to ruminate on the fact that magic was real and that Lyri had once had it. It was still difficult for me to comprehend the sort of culture she came from. I wanted to know more about it, about her. I wanted her to know that she could confide in me.

"Do you ever miss your gift?" I asked.

Her chest rose as she took a deep breath. "Yes. I missed it the moment you told me your father was dying." She looked over at me with utter sadness. "I'm sorry I can't give him back to you, Tavric."

It took several tries for me to swallow. "Me too. You must have saved so many," I said, trying to calculate just how much good she would have done, how much pain and suffering she'd prevented.

But my comment made her face crease with regret. "Not as many as I could have."

I searched her face, wanting to understand. "Why do you say that?"

"Because some of the most ill, the most gravely injured, were so poor that they had no wagon or horse to convey them to my tower. Their loved ones would come anyway, begging me to go with them, to go to their dying relative and save them, but I couldn't."

It took a moment for her meaning to sink in. "Your aunt wouldn't let you leave."

She shook her head.

"Not even to save a life?"

She just stared at me, the truth swimming in her wet eyes.

"Why not?" I asked, incredulous.

She turned her face to the setting sun and the light caressed her face. "Aunt Ethel always said they could purchase a draught or potion if they truly needed it, but I knew they couldn't. Healing potions were rare and expensive, and only available in other villages. No one bothered making or selling them in our village because they didn't need to. *They had me.*" Bitterness coated each word.

I reached out, fingering the golden strands of her hair before pushing it behind her shoulder. "Power is a burden."

She nodded, clearly trying to push away the regret. "I wonder how the village is faring without me," she mused as she looked over at me.

A grim smile pulled at my mouth. "Hopefully word of your departure got out before another group of intrepid youth decided to hurt themselves for sport." I was still horrified at the idea.

"I hope so." She sniffed and then let a watery smile lift her lips. "And maybe with my absence, the masters will stop hurting their servants so much."

She sounded hopeful, and yet her words washed me in revulsion. I could feel the blood drain from my face as I stared at her for several swollen moments. "That's barbaric," I finally choked out.

Lyri's face fell. "What is? Did I say something wrong?"

"No, not you, Lyri. I just..." How could she think *she* was the thing that was wrong? I got to my feet, pinching the bridge of my nose as I tried to calm my ire. "Let me make certain I'm understanding correctly." I held the side of my fist to my mouth for a moment. "You were given the gift to heal anyone of anything. And because of that *miraculous* gift, the people of your village not only hurt themselves for sport, but those in power used your gift as an excuse to torture their servants over and over again. Is that correct?" I asked, trying desperately to keep my anger at bay.

She was wide-eyed and looked unsure of how to respond. But finally, she asked in a small voice, "Is that not the way it is here?"

"No!" I nearly exploded. "No, Lyri, that is not the way it is here. That's not the way it should be in any civilized society."

"I'm sorry," she whispered.

"Why are you apologizing to me?" I shouted, annoyed that I hadn't controlled my reaction, and upset that she would think for one moment that I expected *her* to apologize.

"Because you're angry."

"Not at you," I assured her. "At them! At those people who made you believe that holding a young girl captive for *years* and torturing servants repeatedly was just the normal course of life. I'm angry at them, Lyri, and you should be too." I searched her eyes, looking for the anger and indignation that she had every right to feel, but all

I saw was vulnerability. I fell to my knees in front of her and cradled her cheeks in my hands. “I'm baffled by the idea that the people of your village have been blessed beyond their wildest dreams, and yet they take their lives for granted and treat their health and the health of others with contempt.”

She frowned and her chin quivered, but she closed her eyes and nodded.

My thumb traced the curve of her cheek and I wished I had the right to press a kiss to her trembling mouth. But I didn't, so I released her and sat back on my heels. “Perhaps your land knew you deserved better, and that's why the magic brought you here.”

She opened her eyes and gave me a soft smile with tears balancing on her lashes. “It's certainly better here.”

“Good.” I sat down beside her again, focusing on the sunset as it colored the sky in purples and pinks, while my mind chewed on the grim life she'd led. Her aunt was a conundrum that I couldn't unwind. The contradiction of a woman who forced her niece to be at the beck and call of everyone—all day, every day—to prevent death and yet wouldn't allow her the simple freedom to step outside her tower, even when it would mean saving a life, was confounding. If we had that here in Islewyn...would we recognize it for the gift it was? I knew we would in the beginning, but would we then fall into the same ungrateful patterns that Eldmere had?

If only I could answer that question with confidence.

“How long have you known your father was ill?” Lyri asked from her spot on the sand, effectively pulling me from my thoughts.

I turned to her, admiring the way her loose hair blew back from her face, the golden strands catching the red sunlight. "He kept it from me, from all of us, for a long time. He told me on my twenty-fourth birthday."

She grimaced. "Happy birthday?"

Her attempt at humor pulled a smile from me. "It's my own fault. I wanted him to go sailing with me. It was my birthday, and I thought he would make the effort, but my mother came to me, making excuses for why he couldn't come. I went and found him, ready to berate him for not caring enough about me." I picked up a handful of sand and let it run through my fingers. "And instead, I was confronted by the truth. I walked in on him when a doctor was treating him, so he finally told me. He'd hoped it would get better on its own, that there would be no reason to worry his children." I brushed my hands off on my trousers, then rested my arms on my knees.

"What did you do?"

"I ran like the coward I am."

"You're not."

She was sweet, but wrong. "I'm a seasoned sailor, and I drank enough that when a storm came up, I ended up in the ocean," I confessed, the words bitter on my tongue as I fingered the scar on my forehead. "Believe me, a coward is exactly what I am."

"Grief isn't cowardice."

My scalp suddenly felt hot and a weight settled on my chest. "Grief... Is that what this is?" I whispered as I stared at the waves washing a little closer to our bare feet. "Can you grieve someone when they're not dead?"

"I grieved my parents every day of their illness."

I turned to her. "What was it that took them?"

It was her turn to stare out at the ocean and nod. "A wasting illness tore through our village when I was nine."

I frowned, confused. "I thought you said you had your gift when you were nine."

"Not yet..." She took a stuttering breath, mashed her lips together and pinched her eyes shut, preparing to say something that I intuitively knew would break my heart. "My magic manifested the day after they died."

And break it did. "Oh, Lyri," I breathed out as the implications rolled over me.

Her chin trembled. "Aunt Ethel said my magic was likely triggered by my grief."

"I'm so sorry," I said, wrapping her in my arms. She immediately tumbled toward me as tears watered her cheeks. I slid my hand around the back of her neck and threaded my fingers into her hair, tucking her under my chin.

"One day," she choked out. "They would be alive if it had manifested just one day earlier. Instead, I was weeping over their coffins, and when I decided to sing them one last song before they were put into the earth, my hair got brighter, almost like it was glowing. We probably wouldn't have noticed it if the day had been sunny, but it was raining and dark. People saw it and knew it must mean I had some sort of magic, though we didn't know what kind." Her hand fisted into the fabric of my sleeve. "They started congratulating me. While I wept over my parents' graves, they congratulated me and pawed at my hair."

I wanted to flog every last one of them.

"Aunt Ethel shooed them away and took me home. She didn't rush me. She didn't ask me to sing. In our grief, neither of us thought it mattered what my magic was for. It took me nearly two weeks to discover that I could heal. I don't know who was more angry, my aunt or me. I think she blamed me for not discovering my gift sooner, because if I had..." Her breath hitched and she crumpled even further. "She made it sound like I could have controlled it. Like it was my fault it hadn't manifested earlier. She would go on and on about how her sister was dead. It was always 'my sister' and never 'your mother.' And she never even mentioned my father—like his death didn't matter. She rarely acknowledged my pain because she was too consumed with her own."

I held her tighter and kissed the top of her head, knowing that words were meaningless in moments such as this. And she let me. She let me hold and comfort her, and there was a large part of me that thought perhaps I always wanted to be this person for her.

I berated myself for letting my feelings get this far. My mother had warned me not to fall for her, but here I was, tumbling down a cliff.

LYRIELLE

We returned to the castle on horseback after sunset, our pace slow with only the moon to light our path. My arms banded tightly around Tavric's chest in the way that I knew calmed him and comforted me. Despite the tumult of telling him more about my powers, the time I'd spent with him had been rejuvenating. It always was, because Tavric always saw me, always listened to me.

After dismounting the horse at the stables, I expected he would have to go his own way and return to his duties, but he looked hesitant, like he wasn't quite ready to return. He stared at me for several long moments, and I waited to see what he would say.

"I want you to meet my father," he finally blurted out.

My whole chest flooded with warmth. "I would love to meet him," I whispered, gratified that his desire to introduce me to him had nothing to do with healing.

He nodded and swallowed, his lips and eyes tense with emotion, then gestured toward the castle.

We walked side by side—not touching, but almost—as we wound through the castle corridors. We passed the room I was staying in and turned down another hallway. At the end of the corridor, two guards were stationed on either side of an elaborate set of carved doors. They reached out and opened them as we approached, and I held my breath as we entered the king's bedchamber.

The weight of sickness and despair sat heavy in the air.

Tavric led me to the side of the bed, and I was immediately overwhelmed by just how ill the king was. He was wasting away, practically only skin and bones under the coverlet—just like my parents had been. He was pale, the skin of his face wrinkled as it hung loose from the lack of healthy tissue beneath. I hadn't seen sickness like this since before I'd had my gift. Aunt Ethel had moved us away from the village I'd grown up in, the one ravaged by sickness, only days after we'd discovered what my magic could do. She'd taken us to Eldmere, to the tower.

Tavric bent down, leaning close to his father. "Papa," he whispered, and the king's eyes fluttered, a weak smile briefly dashing across his lips. "This is Lyri. She's a...good friend, and she wanted to meet you." He reached out a hand and drew me forward, urging me to sit on the chair that was pulled up close to the king's side. "You can talk to him if you'd like," he said, then turned and crossed to a nurse who stood in the corner.

I reached for the king's hand, and he gave mine a tiny squeeze but kept his eyes closed. Seeing illness up close this way...I wasn't used to it. "I'm glad to meet you, Your Majesty," I managed to whisper. "You have a remarkable son, and a tremendous wife."

He let out a little puff of air, perhaps in agreement. In that moment, I missed my gift terribly. I wanted nothing more than to be able to heal this man, but I didn't even know how to comfort him, so I did what I'd always done with those who were suffering: I started to sing, wishing I could take away his pain.

I'd only sung a few phrases before I felt the familiar, awful pull that started at my heart. But instead of rising to my scalp, it pulsed down my arms and into my hands, warming the space where my palm pressed to his.

Suddenly, the king took in a breath that was less labored than it had been only moments before.

I pulled my hands away and sat back, my pulse thrumming and my breathing quick. My eyes darted around, expecting the nurse and Tavric to rush over to investigate, but they were still in quiet conversation. I pulled my hair forward to look at it, expecting to find the dim glow that typically lingered in the strands after I'd healed someone. But it was just its normal shade.

Then my hands caught my eye. It was barely noticeable, but I was almost certain that my palms looked warmer and lighter than usual. I fisted them closed.

My heart pounded and my breathing sped up even more. I could still heal? I'd hoped for that only moments ago, but the reality of it...

My throat worked to swallow down my unease as my stomach rolled.

This was...this was...what was it? Good? Terrible? A relief? A gift? A curse?

I could help the king. I could make the sadness in Tavric's eyes go away.

And then what? Would I be confined again and forced to give all of myself for the good of others?

My thoughts raced and churned, not knowing how to accept being thrown back into my old reality—the reality where I had to give and give. Always give.

But as my eyes settled back on King Valtren, whose brow was pale and damp with a sheen of sweat, I realized I might not know what I would do tomorrow, but I knew that right now, I could help. I *wanted* to help.

I cut my eyes over to be sure Tavric and the nurse were not watching, then I moved to perch on the edge of the king's bed, blocking my hands from view as I picked up his hands again and started singing softly. My gift flowed easily, just like it always had. The only difference was that it was channeled through my hands, which surprisingly felt better, more natural than when it had manifested through my hair.

My gift had always felt out of my control before. I had sung, and healing went to the person holding my hair, but I'd had very little control over how that happened. Having the healing in my hands made it intentional, and as I concentrated, I could locate where my attention needed to go. The illness was seated deep in his lungs; I could sense it and focused my effort there.

It was immediately clear that there was a stark difference between trying to heal the king's illness and all the healings I'd done in the past several years. I had only healed this sort of devastating illness in the first year of having my gift, because after that everyone in Eldmere knew to come to me right away. Repairing fresh cuts and bruises, wiping out small infections, and taming fevers were all quickly done. That kind of healing sapped my energy, but not the way I knew this would. This illness was different. It had been breaking down the king's body for months, maybe even years, and I knew it would not go quickly or easily.

The weight of a hand settled on my shoulder. "Lyri?"

I pulled away from the king, my breathing already labored, and crossed my arms, tucking my hands against my sides to hide the glow, terrified my gift would be discovered and I'd end up locked away and used again. I wanted to help the king, but I couldn't let anyone know—not even Tavric. The fear of being caged was all too real.

"Your singing has soothed him," he said. "You're good at that."

"Good at what?"

"Comforting people."

I knew the king was far from well, but I had felt enough of the infection burn off that I thought perhaps he was no longer in immediate danger. Unfortunately, that wouldn't last long.

"I'll give you some time with him," I said, hoping to escape quickly.

"That's not necess—"

"I will see you tomorrow," I interrupted and then hurried from the room.

I was desperate to be alone, to sort through what this all meant, so as soon as I was out of sight of the guards who stood outside the king's chamber door, I ran back to my own quarters.

I had just healed the king. How could that be? Tavric had cut my hair. My ability to heal had been gone. Hadn't it?

As years of using my healing gift flashed through my mind, I realized that I'd never tried to heal in any way other than through my hair. Aunt Ethel had isolated me in that tower so soon after I'd discovered my power that even if I'd thought to heal with my hands, those who needed help were always out of reach. And anytime Auntie needed healing, she would just grab my hair like everyone else.

Shutting myself in the beautiful room that I'd been allowed to stay in, I sank down on the bed and stared at my hands cradled in my lap, shaking violently as the implications washed over me and the usual fatigue of healing settled over me.

I didn't want this. I didn't want my gift back, because it hadn't been a gift. It had been a curse, a weight around my neck that held me back and dragged me down. But I'd never had a choice. I hadn't had a choice when my magic manifested. I hadn't had a choice when Tavric cut my hair and took it away, and now I didn't have a choice in it coming back. Would I ever have a say in my life?

As my thoughts kept churning, they settled enough that I was able to pick out the differences in my circumstances now versus before. I knew I had my gift, but no one else did. As that realization soaked into my consciousness, my breathing started to slow. If no one knew I had it, then they couldn't demand that I use it.

But what of King Valtren? I'd been able to help him. Could I heal him completely without raising suspicion? Perhaps if I visited him daily, I could heal him a little at a time. Yet if each time I visited, he became noticeably better, surely they would connect it to me, especially since I'd told Tavric about my gift. Could I find a way to sneak back to the king's room without anyone realizing?

Unlikely. He was the king. There were guards posted everywhere.

Chapter Twelve

LYRIELLE

I went late to breakfast the next morning, partially because I wasn't ready to face anyone, and partially because I hoped to catch Tavric when he was no longer surrounded by those insisting he give them his time.

I couldn't tell him about what I'd discovered, but I knew that the morning would grate on him, just like it always did. Yesterday he'd told me I was good at comforting people, and that gave me a small sense of bravery.

I ate slowly, doing my best to be unobtrusive, and by the time I was halfway through, the crowd was already thinning.

After the last person left, I was about to say something, but then Tavric covered both of his ears and closed his eyes. His chest expanded and contracted in controlled movements and he started to rock back and forth a bit, though I had the feeling he wasn't aware of the movement. I'd never stayed long enough in the morning to see how he recovered from so much chaos, and I found it fascinating. I also had the urge to go over to him and wrap him in my arms.

That was when Prince Kavian walked in.

"We need to talk," he said to Tavric, without even waiting for acknowledgment.

Tav stopped rocking but shook his head and pinched his eyes tighter.

Prince Kavian let out a dramatic sigh and dropped into a seat close to Tavric. He waited, though it was clear he was impatient, until Tavric rubbed his hands over his face and then opened his eyes to look at Kavian. "What is it?" he asked in a nearly calm voice.

"I've invited a couple chaps from university to visit and see how we run things here. You'll talk to them this afternoon, won't you?"

Whatever calm Tavric had acquired fled, and he went nearly rigid. "No, I won't, Kavian."

"What? Why?"

"I'm already overwhelmed. I can't entertain whatever strangers my brothers drag home with them."

My brow furrowed. That seemed a bit harsh, but what did I know of brotherly squabbles or the frustrations of trying to rule a kingdom...especially while your father was dying?

"Tav, come on." Prince Kavian sounded both surprised and annoyed.

Tavric leaned his elbows on the table. "The answer is no, Kavian." His eyes flitted to me for only a moment.

Kavian noticed and looked over his shoulder, seeing me for the first time. "Of course." A scoff scratched out from the back of his throat and he got to his feet. "You can only entertain the strangers you bring home," he shot off before turning his back on his brother.

Tavric stood, anger hardening his jaw. "Kavian," he called out, but the younger prince was gone in a huff.

Tavric sighed, shook out his arms, and took his seat again. He speared a few bites of ham and put them in his mouth, which made me wonder why he didn't insist on eating before letting people speak with him. I was certain that his hunger made his discomfort worse, and now he was stuck with cold food.

After a few more bites and several gulps of what must have been tepid tea, he looked up at me.

"Good morning, Lyri."

I bowed my head out of respect. "Good morning, Your Highness."

"I hope meeting my father wasn't too disconcerting for you."

"Not at all. I just wish I could help." Which was true, but I hadn't been blessed to think of a way to help without being caught.

"Your presence helps." He gave me a smile, but it was fleeting and he was soon staring off at nothing while digging his thumb into his opposite palm. "I need to go somewhere."

"Can I show you my favorite spot in the garden?" I asked. I'd been hoping he would let me distract him.

He let out a breath, his shoulders dropping in relief. "I would love to see it," he said. After he took my advice and ate several more bites of food, we left the dining hall together.

The nervous energy that hummed in my chest made me want to walk close to Tavric. It was a combination of guilt and helplessness. Guilt over not confessing my ability and running to heal the king right away, and helplessness in knowing that I hadn't yet figured out a way to help him, even though I had wracked my brain.

So once we stepped outside, I let myself walk a little closer to Tav, our arms brushing against one another often. I longed to reach out my pinkie and try to catch his, but I wasn't that brave. Tavric was a good friend, but he was a prince, and I was just...

What was I? My lack of answer to that question was disconcerting, so I pulled my mind away from it and focused on my surroundings as we entered the garden.

The trees, hedges, and climbing flowers of the landscaped space offered a sense of privacy, and the layers of floral scents wound their way around me and made me smile. Maybe someday I would tire of the varied sights, sounds, and smells I encountered each day, but I doubted it. I was too familiar with the melancholy that came with a lack of such things.

I led Tavric deep inside the maze and to a little bench surrounded by all sorts of flowers, bursting with vibrant color and all tumbling over one another as if jockeying for position and prestige. "This is it," I said, lowering myself onto the bench.

"It's beautiful," he agreed, sitting close enough that my shoulder leaned into his upper arm. "What about it is your favorite?"

"So many flowers. So many shapes and colors. But no roses." I breathed deeply, loving the cacophony of scents.

"You dislike roses?"

"Not exactly." I looked over at him. "There were roses that climbed my tower, and I was grateful for them since they were the only flower I ever saw up close, but...I've had enough of them."

He grimaced in commiseration. "I wish I could tell you the names of the different flowers, but I'm afraid I don't know."

"I recognize a lot of them. Gregor brought me a book once that had all sorts of illustrations and information about flowers and other plants. It's one of the reasons I was so excited to explore these gardens. I was seeing things in real life that I'd only ever seen in a book, or from too far away."

His arm moved, and I suddenly felt the warmth of his fingers running over my palm and then threading with my own. "Can I show you my favorite part of the garden?" he asked.

I had been rendered speechless by the intimate touch, so I just nodded.

He pulled me to my feet and I was dismayed when he dropped my hand to pull back nearby draping vines to allow me through. He didn't take my hand again once we were on the other side, and I tried to squash my disappointment.

"What was your land like?" he asked as we ventured further into the garden. "Was it forest or desert? Flat lands? Mountains?"

"It was somewhat similar to here. Lots of trees. Hills as far as I could see, but no mountains. It was by the sea, but the water wasn't visible from my tower."

He shook his head. "It's so strange to think there is an entire land out there, hidden from view."

"Would you want to go there?" I asked, slightly alarmed by the idea.

He shook his head. "From what you've told me, I wouldn't like it at all."

We approached an arched gap in the hedge covered by hanging white flowers I recognized as wisteria. It was magical.

"Here," he said suddenly as we stepped under the archway. Instead of going straight through, however, he turned to slip through a small space between two hedges. "Careful not to let your skirt get caught," he said as he shuffled sideways through the narrow gap.

I laughed as I tried to flatten my dark green skirt to my legs. "Where are we going?" I asked.

He turned to grin back at me. "To my hideout."

"Just so you know, if I do snag my skirt, I'm telling your mother that it is your fault." I kept my eye on the cream lace that edged the sleeves, trying to keep it away from the grasping fingers of the branches.

"I'll willingly take the blame." He ducked down and disappeared through a low gap in the hedge.

I shook my head, enchanted by how like a young boy he was acting.

Then his hand appeared through the gap and he beckoned. "Come along, then," his disembodied voice called.

I took his hand and ducked through the hole. When I straightened, he pulled a leaf from my hair and turned to gesture toward the space we now found ourselves in.

"This is it," he said with satisfaction.

I loved looking around and trying to see it through his eyes. This was not a curated portion of the gardens; it looked wild and abandoned. One large, sturdy tree occupied most of the area, and it was surrounded on all sides by tall hedges. Several small bunches of flowers had grown over the hedges from the other side, but for the most part, it looked unextraordinary. "Would you hide away here often?" I asked, wondering at its significance in his life.

"Constantly."

I followed him as he circled to the other side of the tree, where a flat board was strung up horizontally by two ropes attached to a large branch above.

"Sit down," Tavric instructed, pointing to the board.

I did so, wondering at the wisdom of it. It wiggled precariously, and I had to hold on to the ropes to keep myself from falling off. "It's rather unstable, isn't it?"

He chuckled. “That’s sort of the point.”

“Why would someone want a chair that’s difficult to sit on?” I asked, scooching myself back further to steady myself.

He studied me. “Have you never encountered a swing before?”

“A swing?” I’d never heard of such a thing.

He nodded. “That’s what it’s called. You see, it’s not just for sitting.” He walked around behind me. “Are you holding on tightly?”

“Yes, why?”

“Because I’m going to show you the joy of using a swing.” He took hold of the ropes just above my own hands and slowly walked backward several steps before letting go.

“Oh,” I said in surprise as I glided forward and then swung back toward Tavric.

“I’m going to give you a little push,” he warned, and then did just that.

I laughed. “I take it back. This is a delightful chair.”

“I used to swing here constantly as a boy. It was quiet here, but not stuffy or echoey like the castle can be.”

“Did you have someone to push you?”

“No, I figured out how to swing myself.”

“Your brothers never came?”

“This was my hideout. My brothers and I have plenty of other haunts that we would escape to, but this one was mine alone. The gardener hung this swing and told only me about it, I think because he knew that sometimes even my brothers’ company was too much.”

I chewed on my lip, debating whether to broach the subject or not, but in the end, my concern and curiosity won out. “You get overwhelmed often.”

"I do," he said right away, not sounding offended by my intrusion. "I don't understand how people can concentrate or thrive or enjoy themselves when there is too much noise and too many people. Even the texture of my clothing can be bothersome."

"So it's not the socializing that bothers you?"

"Socializing is fine if it's with a small number of people I actually know. But few royal meetings or events involve only a few people. So when it's too much, I sail or I hide in the library. Once in a while, I'll come back here."

I closed my eyes as the swing arced forward once again. "Your parents don't know about this place?" I asked, wondering how it was that he could trust me with this secret.

"They never said anything, but I'm fairly certain my mother knew a lot more about what we boys got up to than she ever let on. In fact, it might have been her who asked the gardener to hang the swing. You should ask her about it some time. I'm sure she'd have stories to tell."

"I'm certain that your mother has far better things to do than tolerate me."

He caught hold of the ropes and brought the swing to a stop. "Hey," he said as he circled around to face me, holding on to the ropes and leaning down so he was at my level. "Don't do that."

I blinked up at him. "Do what?"

"Act as if you're a burden. You're not."

"I—"

"My mother has responsibilities—we all do—but that doesn't mean she is merely tolerating you. She likes you, Lyri, probably for a lot of the same reasons I like you. You're..." His eyes skimmed over my face, my hair, and my mouth—where they lingered.

My breath escaped me and I couldn't speak.

His gaze returned to my eyes. "You're extraordinary. I don't know that I could put into words how much I admire your strength and your friendliness...and your patience with me."

I shook my head. "Being around you doesn't require patience."

A smile broke over his face and the corners of his eyes crinkled. "Give it time."

"Do you have plans to become tiresome?"

His gaze dropped again to my lips. "Maybe."

My chest felt suddenly tight and my heart seemed to be pulling me forward, drawing me closer to his handsome face and kind words. "I've never thought of myself as friendly," I admitted in an attempt to keep myself from doing something utterly foolish like kissing a prince.

"How could you not? You're kind to everyone."

I shrugged. "I like people, and I like talking to them."

He gave a little quirk of his eyebrow. "Yes, and that's called being friendly." He leaned in, smiling, and brought his face so close that for one wild second I thought he was going to kiss me. My breath caught and my heart pounded, as I suddenly wanted nothing more than to feel what it would be like to share that kind of closeness with someone. Not just someone—Tavric. But then he sucked in a breath and drew back. "It's something I have no skill at." He circled around behind me again and pulled back on the swing before letting me go.

I was grateful he couldn't see my face, as I was fairly certain it was bright red.

Chapter Thirteen

TAVRIC

"Tell me why you're mad at Kavian," Dorian said as he invaded my corner of the library and took the other chair by the fire.

I scoffed and set my book aside. "Has he been tattling on me?"

His brow furrowed in confusion and concern. "Now I'm really worried. What's gotten into you?"

I scrubbed my hands through my hair. I'd been avoiding Kavian, horrified and embarrassed by his treatment of Lyri. "He was unpardonably rude to my friend and guest," I explained.

Dorian sat up and fixed his dark gaze on me. He was the closest to my age but looked the least like me. His hair was almost as golden as Lyri's. "Don't you think he might have a point?"

"No," I said with careful control.

"Our father is dying and you're playing pretend with a sea sprite."

"Now *you're* insulting Lyri?"

"You've no idea who this girl is or where she came from."

"I don't care where she came from, I care about *her*."

He spread his arms wide, as if I'd just made his point for him. "How much of your time have you wasted with this girl?"

I tensed at the accusation in his tone. With the onslaught of further responsibilities brought on by the council's concern over my father's health, I'd wanted to spend all my free time with Lyri. The way she moved through the world, unburdened by expectation or ambition, allowed me to breathe when I was around her. My brothers used to provide that same escape from society, but I certainly didn't feel that way lately. "It's not a waste of time. What I do in the small amount of time that I'm not serving our kingdom is not your concern," I said in a carefully controlled tone. I didn't want to snap at my brother, but he was testing my patience.

"Of course it's my concern, because I care about Father and this kingdom just as much as you do, and I know you have more important things to do right now. Have you forgotten who will be at our door in three days?"

"Oh, I remember. Do you remember whose fault that is?"

His jaw clenched. "I'm fairly certain you wouldn't see it as a problem if that girl weren't here."

"Stop blaming her."

"I'm not blaming her, I'm blaming *you*. Kavian says you've done nothing *but* waste time with her in the three days he's been home. I didn't have the heart to tell him that was nothing new. If you refuse to find a queen for yourself, that's fine, but there is work to be done." He pointed a finger at me as if he somehow knew more about what had been happening within these walls than I did. "There is a kingdom to be run, and Father can't do it.

Kavian and I can step in once in a while, but everyone is looking to you. We need you here."

"I am here," I bellowed, insulted and hurt that he would insinuate that I wasn't doing enough. "I've been in all the meetings, I've resolved all the disputes as best I can. Even though every clamoring, chaotic meeting makes my head pound and my palms sweat, I'm there, doing it. I answer every summons and give the council all the attention they ask for. Will you really insist on taking away the few hours of calm that I've tried to claim for myself each day?"

His expression dripped with impatience. "Her presence is not good for the kingdom, Tav. You need to send her home."

I scoffed. "You have no idea what you're asking. You have *no idea* the reasons she had for fleeing from her home in the first place. I won't send her back to be used up and spit out by those who call themselves her family." Even if I could, I wouldn't. "I can't just send her on her way. She knows precious little about the world, and I'm terrified she'll be swallowed up in it," I admitted, pressing my thumb and finger into the corners of my eyes.

Several moments passed in silence before he asked, "Are you trying to save her or control her?"

I breathed carefully through my nose before lifting my head to look up at him. "You think I want to control her?"

He narrowed his eyes at me. "Do you?"

"No," I bit out. "I want to protect her."

He studied me for long enough that I got annoyed before he finally spoke. "That's a noble thing, but the space between protection and control is narrow indeed."

His words sliced at me. Accusing but not. A reprimand, but only because I wondered if he might have been right.

I hate that he might be right.

I shook my head. "Just because I'm not kicking her out doesn't mean I'm controlling her. She makes her own decisions."

He shook his head. "I'm betting it wasn't her idea to stay here so long, suffering the whispers and judgements of staff and nobility alike. Are you keeping her as a pet? Because unless you plan to marry her tomorrow, then all you're doing is toying with her heart while you neglect your responsibilities."

"I'm *trying*, Dorian." I pounded a fist to my chest, desperate for him to understand. "I know it comes easily for you. You light up around people. Charming them seems to be a fun challenge for you. You can run off to a different kingdom and charm a princess and you love it. But me?" I pressed my palm into my heart. "I *hate* it."

He let out a short sigh. "It can't be that bad."

I swept the stack of books and papers from the little table that sat by my chair, flinging them to the floor. "It *is* that bad!" I was so tired of trying to explain it, of trying to make my family understand. I wasn't being stubborn. I never wanted to be rude, but when I was around so many people for so long, it *was* that bad. "And not just because of the people who are demanding and petty, but because everything inside of me shrivels when I'm around so many people. I just want the noise to *stop*. I want the talking and moving to *stop*. But I stay, and I do what I can, and I don't know if I have any more to give. I'm slated to be king one day. I can't change that, and I desperately want to be the ruler that this kingdom deserves, but..."

Dorian looked stunned, his eyes taking in the sight of the scattered papers and then turning to look at me with my contorted face and heaving chest. It looked like he wanted to argue, but after several more moments of staring at me as I stood, broken in front of him, he finally said, "I didn't realize."

The knot in my chest released just a little, and I blew out a breath. "You want me to get rid of her. You think she's a distraction. Well, here's the truth about Lyri: She's the only thing keeping me sane right now," I confessed. "The only reason I've been able to function is because I have her." My chest started to feel tight at the mere suggestion that she leave. "She lets me breathe. She grounds me, and I *need* that. I need *her*. I need her to keep me calm. I need... I need—"

As my own words reverberated back at me, I felt suddenly ill. I stood frozen, shocked by the truth that washed over me. For several painful moments, I didn't breathe, and then I put a palm over my mouth and stepped back, disgusted with myself.

Dorian opened his mouth to argue with me, but I cut him off with a slice of my hand. "You're right. You're right. I have no right to keep her here with me. That stops now."

I pushed past him.

"Tav, wait," he called out, but I didn't listen.

I swept from the room, my heart pounding as my mind screamed at me, berating myself for being so selfish. I needed to send her away, but not because she was a distraction. No, not at all. Because, somewhere along the way, I'd become just as selfish as her aunt. I'd started using her, not for healing my body, but for healing my soul, and if I kept her around, then Dorian would be right. I'd be keeping her as a pet. I'd be a master who used her for her ability to calm and soothe me. And what would I be giving her in return? A pat on the head and a smile to say thank you? I might not be locking her in a tower, but a gilded cage with the lure of adventure was still a cage.

LYRIELLE

Tavric's days had continued to be full and hectic since Prince Kavian's return, but he always found me in the evening. We would sit on the shore and watch the sunset, or we'd ride out in the countryside. I could have ridden my own horse, but he only ever had one horse saddled so I could ride behind him. Despite the inherent discomfort of riding two to a horse, I found that I preferred it. I'd spent so much of my life with only my aunt's presence, and having the chance to be close, both physically and emotionally, to another person was almost overwhelming, but in the best way. I wanted to be close so I could share in his energy and soak in his essence, similar to the way I craved soil and grass and earth.

I'd convinced him to take me to visit with his father one more time, and though my heart nearly pounded out of my chest, I managed a little more healing, but his condition was severe enough that it frightened me. I went the next day to see if perhaps I could sit by his bedside, but the guards looked at me with suspicion and turned me away.

Today seemed even busier for Tavric, as it was a formal audience day. The grand hall was filled with nobles, foreign dignitaries, and even a few commoners who had come to present their petitions. I was there only to watch, along with many others. The maid who'd been asked to help me had presented me with a new gown that was fancier and more complicated than my usual frocks, but she said if I was going to attend, I would want to look my best. Amilee explained further that formal audiences were a chance for nobility to see and be seen. Everyone would be sizing up those in attendance and vying for Prince Tavric's favor since the king was too ill.

I likely would have found the hubbub and pageantry amusing if Tavric's discomfort hadn't been so potent. I ached for him, knowing there was likely nothing about this situation that he enjoyed. People were always talking over one another, there was a constant din of voices, and the movement never stopped. He became more and more agitated as the minutes rolled by, and I wondered if this was how it always affected him. I kept hoping his eyes might fall on me so I could at least give him a smile, but they never turned my way.

When it was all over, I left the great hall along with everyone else, sick at heart to think that when Tavric eventually took the throne, he'd be forced into this life every day. Hopefully, if I could heal the king, that day would not come for years.

I expected Tavric to come find me, knowing that, for whatever reason, he found my presence soothing. But he didn't come, so I returned to my room and changed out of the formal clothing before going in search of him. Hopefully I could convince him to let me visit his father again.

As I wandered the corridors, peeking into any room that had its door open, the queen entered the hallway up ahead. I stepped to the side and waited for her to pass, as was expected.

"Miss Lyrielle," she said instead. "Walk with me, won't you?"

Her request was unexpected but not unwelcome, and I fell into step beside her.

"I wanted to apologize," she said, managing to startle me further. "I believe I made you uncomfortable the other morning when I told Kavian about your necklace."

"No apology necessary, but Prince Tavric told me why you were interested in it. I'm not royalty, Your Majesty." I felt the need to point it out.

"Regardless, I made you uncomfortable and that was not my intention. I like you, my dear."

A strange, lurching feeling tugged at my heart, half pain, half relief. "I like you as well, Your Majesty," I managed to whisper.

"Tavric mentioned that you'd like to find an official position, perhaps somewhere here in the palace, or in the village?"

"Oh." I blinked in surprise. Should I be hurt that Tavric wanted me to leave, or glad he was helping me do what I had set out to do? "Yes, Your Majesty. I would be very appreciative of any help you could give me."

"He said something about sewing."

"Yes, I'm good at it."

"Wonderful. You know, I do appreciate you keeping him company so many evenings. You've been good for him."

Heat rose to my cheeks. "I don't know about that."

"I do. And if you had seen him before, you would know the tremendous amount of good you've done."

I pulled back, struck by her sincerity. "I haven't..."

"Did he tell you why he's had to fill in for his father so much lately?"

I nodded.

"He'll be taking on the crown before long, I imagine"—she swallowed—"and it will be difficult. He and his father are similar in many ways, but Tavric has never been at ease among crowds. Still, I know he'll make a good ruler, just like his father." She tried to smile, but her face was strained and sadness clouded her eyes.

"I was grateful for the chance to meet King Valtren the other day. And I'm sorry for what he is suffering."

She blinked rapidly. "We all are." Then she seemed to shake off the oppressive subject, forcing a smile as she gestured down the hallway. "I'd be happy to introduce you to the head seamstress."

The seamstress? *Oh, right.* She was helping me find a position. "Thank you" was all I managed to say as my thoughts and feelings tumbled over one another. I knew I should be grateful for her help, but it felt too soon, and I couldn't help wondering where Tavric was.

I joined her in the hall, but she paused to look at me. "Unless you would prefer to work in the village. I don't want you to think that I expect you to stay here."

I wondered if that would be better, but then realized that no, I needed to stay here. If I was going to have a chance to heal the king completely, without anyone knowing, I would need to stay at the castle. "I'd like to meet the seamstress," I assured her.

She nodded, and we walked on. "Honestly, she'll likely be glad for the extra help. With the impending arrival of Princess Saria, we will need to be sure that Tavric looks his best."

Wait... What?

"We're all surprised by this turn of events, but we're happy for the potential to strengthen our alliance."

It felt like I'd been punched in the stomach. I tried to tell myself that I was misunderstanding her words, but...how else could they be understood? "A princess, Your Majesty?" A princess who was coming specifically for Tavric? *My* Tavric?

"Yes, has he not told you? Dorian's diplomatic mission was even more successful than we had hoped. Ravencairn is an ally, and it seems Tavric has caught the eye of their princess. And with the king's health so ill, I'm certain you can—"

She kept talking, but there was a ringing in my ears that prevented me from hearing the rest of what she said. My breathing came in short little gasps that I tried to keep quiet so she wouldn't realize the pain that was slicing through me with each word she spoke. Was that why the queen was shuttling me off to the servants' quarters? Because I was in the way of some grand romance? Did Tavric want me gone? Perhaps I'd misinterpreted things entirely. How was I to know the difference between politeness and friendship and...more?

As panic, betrayal, and hurt swirled inside me, my ears seemed to stop working altogether. Thankfully, whatever the queen was saying must not have required a response, because we reached the other end of the castle without me saying a word.

I was a shell of myself as I focused just enough to speak with the seamstress and answer her questions. The queen squeezed my hand one more time before departing, and I had the horrible thought that her acceptance of me had been a facade this whole time, and now she was hiding me away belowstairs so that I would not be an embarrassing complication when the princess arrived.

No wonder I hadn't seen Tavric all day. No wonder he had no need of me.

The seamstress was very kind in issuing me a uniform, and I returned to my old room to change into it and gather my own faded purple dress. I was then shown to a room that I would share with two other servants and invited to dine in the kitchen with the rest of the staff.

As I sat on the narrow bed only a third the size of the one I'd slept in for the past two weeks, with nothing to my name but my dress, my necklace, and the uniform I'd been given, I tried to tell myself that this was good. I had freedom and an occupation. That was not nothing.

It was just so much less than I'd had yesterday.

Chapter Fourteen

TAVRIC

The night left me too much time to think. Having to sit for the formal audience had been torture—especially when I refused to even look at Lyrielle for comfort—but at least it had forced me to think of something other than Lyri and how I'd been using her, how I had to stop using her. I'd attended the usual banquet in the evening, but I'd sat silent, barely even coherent as Dorian and Kavian entertained and charmed all those in attendance. I was nervous about seeing Lyri, especially in this public setting, but she hadn't come. She had planned to, but something must have happened. It was better that way—that was what I told myself. It gave me more time to plan out what I would say, how I would tell her that our time together needed to come to an end.

So I'd barely slept as guilt pounded my insides, a beat to accompany the wild hum of anxiety that the day had produced.

As a result of my restless night, my appearance was haggard as I went down to breakfast, but that would be my chance to speak with her. I'd sent word to my father's chief advisor that he should cancel the morning audience, and I felt like a failure because of it, but I refused to put off this conversation. It needed to happen before Princess Saria and her delegation arrived tomorrow.

However, Lyri was not at breakfast, and the longer I waited for her arrival, the more unnerved I became. Had she eaten before I came downstairs? Unlikely. I'd been up with the sun.

Both of my brothers came, ate, and left, neither bothering to strike up a conversation. I was pacing by the time my mother came in.

"Have you seen Lyri?" I asked without preamble.

"Not today."

"Do you know where she is? She didn't come to eat." And I knew how much Lyri appreciated the delicious variety of food each morning.

"I imagine she ate in the kitchen with the rest of the staff," she said as she spooned potatoes onto her plate.

The knot of anxiety tightened. "Why?"

Mama looked up at me, her look pitying. "Because she has secured a position as a seamstress, and that's where she will be eating from now on."

I stared at her in shock, my mouth open and my chest tight.

My mother sighed and set her plate down. "Tavric, what did you expect, darling? That you could continue to keep the company of a young foreign girl while entertaining Princess Saria?"

My lips pressed into a tight line. "I did not invite the princess here."

"But she is coming. What was I supposed to do?"

"You did this?" I asked, feeling utterly betrayed.

"Don't give me that look, Son. Lyrielle told me the very first night she was here that she wanted to find a position. And you, yourself, told me she'd been looking for positions in the village. She wants to support herself and earn her own way, and you certainly weren't in any hurry to help her, so I did."

I turned away from her, my teeth clenched as I sucked in a breath. She wasn't wrong, but she wasn't right either.

"Lyrielle is a lovely girl," she said from behind me, "but she's in no position to take on the role of your wife."

I turned back to argue with her, but she cut me off.

"And that must be the goal now," she said in a tone that brooked no argument. "Unless Caelmir returns with a cure, the way forward will include you taking on the crown, and when that happens, your first priority will be to find a worthy woman to sit by your side."

"That doesn't mean it has to be a princess." I didn't know why I was arguing. I'd already decided to stop spending time with Lyri, but this felt wrong.

"You're right, but if you're thinking of Lyrielle, consider this." She paused just long enough to ensure she had my full attention. "You said yourself that she's had little exposure to the outside world. It would be cruel to throw her into the pressures of ruling a kingdom she knows almost nothing about. You can barely handle it; how would you expect her to?"

It was like she'd sunk a knife into my side and then turned it. She was practically calling me incompetent. Even worse, she was right about Lyri. As much as I hated the idea of Lyri being gone, it was better—necessary even. I had no right to ask her to be with me, and not because ruling would overwhelm her, but because she deserved more than to be used like a healing balm for a broken king. I took a calming breath before I spoke. "I know you're right. I know I'm not good for her. I just...care about her." I wanted to say more, to justify my objections more, but the truth was that my heart was screaming at me to bring her back, but my mind knew I couldn't.

I picked at my food as my mind churned with this sharp change. I hated not having her here. And she hadn't even spoken to me before she took the position. Then again, perhaps my mother hadn't given her a choice. Did she think I wanted her gone? My heart sank at the thought. Of course she did. I couldn't let her think that her leaving meant nothing to me.

My head reminded me that I should leave her alone. She didn't need me being overprotective or inserting myself into her life. But my heart knew I had to at least say goodbye, or good luck, or something. We were friends. And friends did not part without saying *something* to one another.

So I left the dining hall and went down to the servants' wing. I was making my way to the sewing room when I saw her ahead of me.

"Lyri!" I called as I jogged to catch up with her.

She turned, and a look of pain shot across her face when she saw me, but it was quickly gone, replaced by a carefully blank expression. She sank into a deferential curtsey, which I did not like at all, with a sedate "Your Highness."

She seemed hollowed out, and I hated it. I missed the girl who had danced with me in the sand. "I...are you well?"

Her brow pulled in. "Well enough."

I nodded. That was good. "My mother told me that you've found a position."

"I have, yes."

Why was she responding so simply, so coldly? I studied her face and was not happy with the tension around her eyes and the way the corners of her mouth pulled down. "Are you certain you are well?"

"Why would I not be?" she asked without a hint of a smile.

"I don't know, you just seem...sad."

She pressed her lips together and her chin lifted in defiance. "And why would I be sad? Perhaps because you asked your mother to get rid of me?"

I sucked in a breath of horror. I'd been right to worry, then. "I never—"

"Or because I am now sewing ceremonial clothing for you to entertain a princess?" Her brow was raised high and I could see how carefully she was controlling her features.

I wanted to whip myself until I bled. How could I have been so oblivious as to not realize what this situation would look like to her? My arms ached to pull her in while my lips begged me to tell her how much I wanted her, but my own words echoed through my head. I needed her. I needed her because she fixed me, but she deserved so much more than to be used.

"There's no reason that should upset me, correct?" she asked, her tone acidic. "Because you and I were only ever friends. Right?"

No. The biggest *no* I'd ever felt, and yet I didn't say it, because the massiveness of that *no* was further proof that I shouldn't pull her back into my orbit. "I..." I had to say something, and I had to do what was best for her. So even though it felt like tearing out my own lungs to say it, I did. "My life is not my own, so as much as I've enjoyed our time together, it's probably a good thing that you've found an occupation, because—"

"You have a princess to court," she finished for me.

"That's not it." I wanted to say so much more, but I couldn't.

Her eyes were pinched as she studied me, as if waiting for me to explain myself, to take away the pain I had caused. But if I said any more, I'd no doubt blurt out my need for her, and she—compassionate creature that she was—would want to help. So I said nothing more, and finally, she shook her head. "If you'll excuse me, Your Highness." She sank into a dull curtsey and walked away.

Not chasing after her was physically painful.

I could have told her. I could have confessed that I was doing this for her, that I was trying to right a wrong. I could have told her how selfish I'd been since the moment I'd found her. And I almost had. But I knew how much she resented those who had used her for her healing power, so why would she hate me any less for using her in other ways?

I was appalled with myself for it, and I was certain it would have torn her apart to know I was no better than that worthless friend who'd brought her books only when he needed healing.

So I let her go. Even though everything in my body ached to keep her close, ease her hurt, and let her ease my own disquiet that was piling up inside of me, I let her go.

LYRIELLE

I was scaling a stone wall. Again.

This time though, it wasn't so high, and I didn't have my hair to contend with.

I'd decided that it didn't matter that Tavric had pushed me aside. In fact, it was probably better, because part of me knew that if he had realized I could heal his father, I wouldn't have been escorted to the servants' wing. If he knew I could heal his father, Tavric would have kept me close, and I hated knowing that I would have let him. I would have been happy to be nothing but a friend just for the chance to stay with him, and it would have chipped away at me, bit by bit.

Instead, I knew two things. Tavric didn't want me, and I still wanted to heal King Valtren.

So I had gone to bed in the room I shared with two other servants and waited for the castle to settle. Once my room companions were sound asleep and the noise of the castle had quieted, I went outside and made my way around the castle wall until I could look up and see the balcony that belonged to the king and queen. The height looked similar to the interior walls of my tower that I had climbed so many times, and I was confident I could do it easily.

Well, my head was confident. My body was not. After I'd tucked my skirt tightly into my waistband, my hands reached up and firmly gripped around stones while my right foot wedged into a crevice. I was ready to climb, but a wave of fear rose up, sudden and furious, stealing my breath and making me second-guess this grand plan of mine. But I was determined. The king was going to die otherwise. The healers had done all they could. He'd been given every available draught, herb, and treatment, but it wasn't enough.

So I shut my eyes, forced myself to breathe, and centered myself.

Then I fixed my eyes on the wall, adjusted my grip on the stones, and pulled myself up.

I moved slowly and deliberately, foot over foot, hand over hand. It didn't take long to reach the balcony, but my neck was slick with sweat from nerves and exertion. As I pulled myself over the railing, the clouds shifted and my dress caught the moonlight, increasing my anxiety, but I quickly stepped into the shadows and caught my breath. I waited, but there were no sounds of anyone else, no alarms raised.

A huge sigh of relief escaped me, and I allowed myself a grin. I'd made it.

Then I wondered if I would need to inform the guards or Tavric or someone else about how easily someone could reach the king this way. Perhaps after I'd healed him, I could suggest they place a guard below his balcony, but for now I shoved that thought aside and went to carefully push open the balcony doors.

The queen was asleep in a chair on the opposite side of the bed where the king lay, breathing labored and skin pale. I crossed quickly and soundlessly to the side of the bed, crouched down, and laid my hand on his chest. Then I closed my eyes and hummed softly, just enough to activate my gift, to feel the heat building up in my hand. It was strange to wield my magic this way, and yet it felt more instinctual than all the times I'd channeled my magic through my hair. I didn't push hard. I didn't concentrate on one part of his body. I just let a thin stream of magic flow from me and into him, trying to reach every corner of his form, easing pain, pulling out infection, reducing swelling. A little of everything, just enough that he might have a chance at gaining some strength, but not so much that my strength would be too depleted. That was the most precarious part. If I used too much magic, I'd be too weak to climb back down.

I longed to do more, to end his suffering in one fell swoop, but I didn't. After only a short time, I pulled back and crept out onto the balcony, then took several deep breaths to be sure I wasn't too tired, climbed over the railing, and descended once again to the ground. My arms were shaking by the time I reached the bottom, and I took several moments to rest before returning to my room.

I'd be sure to come back again tomorrow night, and the night after. The work was incomplete, but perhaps over the next week or ten days, I could bring him to full health.

TAVRIC

After failing to make things right with Lyri yesterday, I had slumped back to my library and spent the rest of the day there. I was supposed to be preparing for Princess Saria's arrival, but every time I thought of welcoming her into my home, I wanted to crawl out of my skin. It felt wrong, and I knew that had everything to do with my feelings for Lyri.

The next morning, I allowed the most important matters to be brought to me during my morning audience, which I continued to hold in the dining hall, uncomfortable with the idea of holding it in my father's study the way he always had. It would feel too much like I was replacing him, like I was surrendering to his death. Accepting it.

In the afternoon, I was deeply entrenched in my corner of the library, with nothing to show for it, when my mother burst in, looking harried and hopeful and terrified all at once.

"What's wrong?"

"Caelmir."

I shot to my feet, leaning on the desk and holding my breath.

"His ship has just docked."

I didn't wait for her, I just went. I ran and didn't stop until I skidded to a halt on the dock, where crew members were throwing lines to dock workers as they secured the ship. My lungs heaved as I scanned the deck, searching for my brother, knowing that one look at his face would tell me everything I needed to know.

And then I spotted him. He stood with his forearms tensed as he gripped the railing, his body in a would-be casual stance, but his eyes said it all. He was devastated.

I staggered back a step and then sat down there in the middle of the dock as a cold wave of nothingness washed over me.

Lack of hope is a powerful thing.

It sucks you dry, bleeding you until you're pale and withered. Nothing seems worth doing or saying and yet the world keeps moving ceaselessly around you, determined to remind you that the thing you care about most can disappear.

All three of my brothers sat with me in the dining hall after everyone else had left that evening, but there wasn't much we could do to comfort one another. "Is Mama still in with Papa?" I asked.

Dorian nodded. "I doubt she'll leave his side."

"Too afraid she'll miss the end," Caelmir commented, his tone devoid of inflection and his face drawn. He was wrecked, a shell of the vibrant man he'd been when he left. He blamed himself for his failure, and though I knew the failure didn't lie with him simply because there was no solution to be found, it was difficult not to blame him too—because I wanted to blame *someone*. I wanted a direction in which to point my anger.

Instead, I buried it with everything else that threatened to overwhelm me. "Father has been improving the last few days. Maybe—"

"Don't do that, Tav." Kavian cut me off, his voice tired and impatient. "We're all familiar with the ups and downs, but there's no denying the steep decline he's been in for the past six weeks. And he hasn't been improving. He simply hasn't been getting worse. We have to stop fooling ourselves. The kingdom is relying on this family to keep moving forward."

"We *are* moving forward," I said.

"Are you?" he challenged, his eyes bloodshot with lack of sleep. "Because it looks to me like you're trying to pretend this isn't happening. It looks like you're doing the bare minimum instead of stepping up and doing what needs to be done."

His accusation cut deeply, scraping at my guilt and stabbing at my inadequacies. "It's not that easy. It's too much for one person."

Kavian spread his arms wide. "Well, lucky for you, there is an accomplished, beautiful woman on her way to our shores who has been raised to be a queen. Not only will choosing a wife help relieve the burden of rule, but it will also reassure the entire kingdom that you have a woman beside you to ensure the line of succession."

"I—" I wanted to refute it, to give some grand reason why his suggestion was unreasonable, but if I couldn't have Lyri, did it matter who I married?

Kavian raised a brow in surprise when I said no more. "No retort?"

My face ached from the tension in it, but he was right. I had no retort.

Grief sucked at my insides, but my anger was pushing in as well. I wanted to rage at the unfairness of my position and scream at my brothers that if they thought it was so easy, they were welcome to it. But it wouldn't do any good. I'd been born to this, and though Lyri had given me a glimpse of hope that I could be something other than a servant to my country, my brothers were right.

My father was dying.

The kingdom was looking to me.

And a suitable queen would arrive on the morrow.

Chapter Fifteen

TAVRIC

I stood on the wharf, wearing only a sash across my shirt as a nod to formality. I'd tried to don the full ceremonial garb my mother had suggested, but after I'd practically ripped my jacket seams when the fit had felt too restricting, my mother had conceded that the sash over my usual shirt would be enough.

"It may even put her at ease about her own appearance after traveling a long way," she'd said.

I doubted that. It was my experience that ocean travel did not prevent royalty from showing up looking their very best, but it was kind of her to try to calm my nerves. She'd seen me unraveling over the last two days. Absorbed in my own feelings as I was, I couldn't tell whether she was looking forward to the princess's visit or not.

Diplomatically, I knew that it was a boon. But the worried looks my mother continued to shoot me spoke of her uncertainty.

So I stood on the wharf, my hands calmly clasped in front of me, my face carefully arranged to hide my disquiet as Her Highness's ship approached.

"I am sorry about this, Tav," Dorian said.

"Not now." I couldn't make him feel better about this debacle. Not right now. Not when my family was counting on me to represent the crown.

The ship moved ever so slowly into the dock, sailors throwing out lines that were caught by the marine crew. After several more minutes, it had been secured and the gangplank extended.

An official came off the boat first, looking very proud of himself, and gave me a deep bow when he stepped onto the wharf.

"Prince Tavric, thank you for your hospitality and welcoming us to your shores. May I present Her Highness, Princess Saria of Ravencairn."

He stepped aside and swept into another bow as he gestured toward the ship.

Princess Saria appeared at the top of the plank looking sure and regal as she descended the plank with the kind of grace only achievable when it's been bred into a person. She was lovely and dignified, but I could not escape the feeling that she was intruding where she was not welcome.

The pressure and expectation of the moment made my fists clench, and I could not help but long for Lyri's calming voice and touch. Why must I dread one female while craving another?

Princess Saria stopped just in front of me, and I gave a deep bow as she sank into a curtsey.

"Princess Saria," I said, holding out my hand so that she could lay her fingers gently in mine. "It is a pleasure to welcome you to Islewyn. Peace and safety be upon you as you rest on our shores."

"My kingdom's greetings to you, Prince Tavric. And thank you for the invitation." Her smile implied more than I was comfortable with.

"Yes, my brother speaks very highly of you. I'm certain he could not resist the opportunity to extend his time with you."

Her smile dimmed a bit and I chastised myself. It had been reflexive, the need to correct her and be sure she knew it was not my invitation, but I should have left it alone. No matter how many times my mind churned over the situation, I could not deny that I needed help. My father was dying, and if I had any hope of ruling effectively, I needed to have a companion at my side who could not only take some of the burden, but also be a calming influence on me. If I let Saria in, would she be able to settle me the way Lyri could? I had to hope so, even if it felt like I was ripping out my own heart by considering it.

The princess and I made our way, slowly and grandly, to the waiting carriage, conversing as we walked.

"This is such a lovely place. I can hardly believe I haven't had an opportunity to visit before now."

"I'm certain your duties keep you busy enough at home."

"Yes, of course, but this—" she said as I handed her up into the carriage. She waited for me to sit across from her before she continued, "This is part of my duties too. Making important diplomatic relationships..."

I knew her meaning, but didn't respond to it directly. I could only give a barely polite smile before turning to look out the window as we both smiled and waved to those we passed while we made our way to the castle.

LYRIELLE

We were making mourning clothing for the queen.

I'd never even heard of mourning clothes until this morning, when the head seamstress informed me that we'd be making some. Word of the king's illness had finally spread, and the entire castle felt different. There was a melancholy and uncertainty that permeated the walls and tapestries, whispering its way through halls and towers. No one said anything out loud, though. Everyone still spoke of King Valtren's strength and claimed a miracle would surely happen.

Yet, I was sewing all-black clothing for the queen.

I couldn't imagine the pain that Tavric was feeling. I knew he'd put his last hope in his brother and would be gutted by disappointment. If only I could tell him that everything would be fine. If only I could heal the king right now, all at once. If I could have done it while letting only Tavric know about my gift, I might have gone through with it, but I simply did not trust anyone else enough to take that chance, especially when no one seemed to trust me.

I had hoped that, by joining the staff, I might find acceptance and companionship, but I hadn't. The time I'd spent as a guest to the royal family had made me an object of ridicule and mistrust. The girls whose room I shared didn't speak to me, and hardly even looked at me. If it weren't for my determination to heal the king, I would have been sorely tempted to again seek work in the village.

That night, I left my room again and slipped through the darkness, just like I had the past three nights. Getting into the king's chamber was easy, almost too easy, but I was glad for the luck. I was considering healing him a little more than usual, but I had only just started when a noise in the hallway forced me to retreat. As I climbed back over the balcony, it was curious to note that though his illness was being kept at bay, and even improving bit by bit, the kingdom now believed his death was inevitable. While Caelmir's quest had given everyone hope, his failure was like a death knell. It was astounding what the absence of hope did to people.

I scaled down the side of the castle until my bare feet hit the soil and I turned to my right.

"Good evening, Lyrielle."

I nearly screamed, but clamped my mouth shut and held my breath instead, searching the darkness for the owner of the voice.

It took several moments, but I recognized the man standing casually with his hands behind his back as Harlan. That was a small relief. At least it was not a guard. "Harlan," I breathed out.

"Care to tell me what you are doing here?"

"I..."

"Because if I were suspicious by nature, and I saw a young foreigner scaling down the wall, having obviously come from the chamber of our very sick king...I might think she had something to do with his ill health."

I shook my head as my heart beat frantically. There was no good ending to this scenario. I couldn't tell him the truth of what I'd done, and there was no lie I could come up with that would justify my actions. "I would never hurt the king." My voice trembled. "And you know very well that he was ill long before I arrived."

He gave a sarcastic lift of his brow. "Oh, well, if you say so."

I wanted to run, but I knew that one shout from him would bring guards in seconds. "Take me to the prince," I blurted in desperation. "He'll understand." He was the only one who would understand, and the only one who might keep my secret.

"I will be the judge of that. Tell me what you were doing."

"I'm sorry, I can only tell the prince."

He was silent for several heartbeats, and all I could do was hope that he would take me to Tavric. I could tell Tav the truth. He would understand. He would even be happy.

"As I understand it," Harlan said with a lift of his brow, "the prince no longer wishes to indulge in your company."

Those words were like a dull knife scraping at my heart, but I swallowed down my hurt. "He will want to hear me out, I promise." My hands had started to shake along with my voice.

"Hmm." He mused over my words for so long that I feared my heart would stop from the stress of its pounding. Finally, he said, "Follow me."

My breath whooshed out in relief, and I did as he asked, trailing after him on bare feet as he silently traversed the grounds and then used a key to open a door with which I was unfamiliar. He didn't have a light with him and he lit no lantern or candle, relying only on the sparse and dim flames of the torches that lined the walls.

I expected he would take me to the prince's chamber, wherever that was, but instead we went to the library. Perhaps Tavric was up late, working there; it was not unusual for him to linger in the library for hours into the night. But when we reached the back corner where Tavric had once shown me a stack of books, and where I had confessed the truth about my gift, it was dark.

Harlan lit two lamps that were standing by, and in the flickering light, it was clear that no one else was there.

"Where is Tavric?" I asked.

He looked at me with a knowing raise of his brow. "Tavric, is it?"

I would have been embarrassed if I weren't terrified. "The prince."

"I know who you meant, Your Highness."

My chin pulled back in confusion and I turned to look behind me, thinking perhaps Tavric was there, but there was still no one.

I turned back to Harlan, whose eyes were steadily fixed on me. "Who are you talking to?"

"You."

"Then why did you say *Your Highness*?"

He suddenly stepped close to me and I flinched away from him, but he only reached out and tapped the medallion that hung around my neck.

I looked up at him, frightened by this mysterious situation. He'd said he would take me to Tavric, and instead he was spouting nonsense about my necklace. I shook my head. "It doesn't mean what you think it means. It's just an old necklace that my mother gave me," I said, my voice warbling.

"No, it's not." He turned to one of the large books that lay on the desk and flipped it open. "Have you seen this?"

I stepped forward and looked at the page he turned to, recognizing it as the one filled with illustrations of family crests that Tavric had shown me. "Yes. The prince already searched that book. There was no match."

He unceremoniously shoved the book closer to me. "Are you certain?"

A strange aggression rolled off of him, making me even more nervous, but curiosity made me study the pages he'd turned to. The illustrations were beautiful, and some of the crests even looked to be a similar style to my own crest, but—wait.

My eyes snagged on a familiar design.

"It's there," I said, pointing to the crest that looked precisely like the one stamped onto my own necklace. "Look, it's right there!" I said in excitement, jabbing my finger onto the page. It even said *The Kingdom of Branfrie* below it, even though Branfrie hadn't been a kingdom for generations. Still, this was proof that my home existed here, in this world. Or at least it was known by this world.

How had Tavric missed it?

I looked up at Harlan, hoping for answers. His eyes shone with an excitement that was almost frightening. "You came through the portal," he said.

My heart dropped and my stomach clenched. Recognizing the crest and the name of my kingdom was one thing. But speaking of a portal? "Excuse me?"

"Only those of us who came from Branfrie can see this crest."

I stopped breathing. He had said "us."

"It's not just Branfrie itself that's shrouded," he continued. "Information about our land is hidden as well. So Prince Tavric could look at this page all day long, and he would only see an empty space where this crest is drawn. Or perhaps even a different crest altogether."

The pounding of my heart made my chest ache, and it was difficult to draw breath. "You're from Branfrie?" I finally managed to ask.

He nodded.

My eyes darted about as I tried to make sense of his words. "How long have you been here?"

"Nearly eighteen years."

"But...how?"

"A dare gone wrong." His expression was suddenly shrouded with regret. "We'd heard the rumors about the castle tower our entire childhood. A powerful sorceress had lived there years before. Girls would go to learn from her, and some of them would never return. When she died, everyone said the tower was cursed, but we thought it was just a story."

I swallowed hard. He was talking about my tower, he had to be.

"So we, as lads of fifteen and sixteen, thought it would be fun to test it out. The rumors were old, after all. No one had actually disappeared in our time." His gaze stayed glued to my face, intense and disconcerting. "So we all set out to climb it, and we made it. Fools, all of us. We could have fallen at any moment, but such lads always think themselves invincible."

"Did you fall?" I couldn't help asking.

He gave a shake of his head and a shrug. "No. Just climbed down. Got nearly to the bottom and thought I'd show off, so I jumped the last bit. Only I didn't land on solid ground."

My breath was slow and heavy. "You landed in the water."

He held his hands out to his sides. "You and I understand one another."

I nodded, oddly comforted by the knowledge.

His eyes as he studied me were now more curious than suspicious. "Tell me why you were in the king's chamber."

Comfort fled. There was so little I could say. "I was helping him."

"How?"

"I had a...healing draught that I thought might work." I took a step back, feeling trapped.

His eyes reflected the low light of the lantern as he studied me, his eyes widening by degrees as his curiosity was replaced by awe. "You have magic."

I choked on air and fell back another step. "No."

"You do. You're from Branfrie. Tell me what it is."

"I don't," I insisted, my heart swelling in my throat.

He pointed a finger toward the door. "I will leave the library this minute and fetch every guard I can to tell them about your midnight escapades. You will be branded a traitor and assumed to be an assassin, unless you tell me what—"

"I was healing him!" I blurted.

His face transformed from anger to anticipation. "Healing powers."

"Yes," I choked out, my eyes burning with terror. "Please don't tell anyone."

He let out a little chuckle, perhaps from relief. "I have no wish to share your secret, believe me."

I did believe him, and yet I was less comforted by that assurance than I should have been. "Thank you," I said all the same, wondering what would happen next. Would he let me go on my way?

The light from the lantern lit his face from the side, and I stared at him, waiting for what would come next. His fingertips lightly drummed on the pages of the book as his eyes darted back and forth. He didn't seem to be focusing on anything tangible, like he was watching a complicated dance play out in front of him. Understandable, since my confession had no doubt shocked him.

I was shocked as well. Harlan was from Branfrie. I was tempted to ask if he had magic, but the way he'd reacted to my own admission made me pause. He was awed and excited by the idea of magic, so the likelihood of him having it felt low indeed.

His eyes finally cut back to me. "How does it work?" he asked. "Your healing? Do you have a talisman, potions, incantations?"

Should I lie? His intensity scared me, but I couldn't fault him for being curious. "I sing."

"Singing...yes." His eyes darted from side to side. "Very good."

Several more weighty moments passed by and I finally spoke up. "I should return to my room," I said quietly, my chest tight with the knowledge that if he wanted to keep me here, he could.

But he just glanced up, almost like he'd forgotten I was there, and then waved a hand through the air. "Of course. No doubt you are tired. Thank you for confiding in me." His eyes started mapping my face once more. "It's a real pleasure to have met someone from home." He smiled kindly, but the stark lantern light twisted it into something sinister.

I smiled in return, dropped into a curtsey, and slipped from the room. I hurried through the corridors as quickly as I dared, desperate to get back to the comfort and safety of my room but knowing it was essential not to draw attention to myself.

Once I was curled up under my blanket, my body started to shake. I'd been caught healing the king. If it had been anyone but Harlan, I likely would have been arrested.

Harlan was from Branfrie. He'd said he wouldn't share my secret, but I had no idea if I could trust his word or not.

And Tavric... I pinched my eyes shut as they burned with tears. My only friend and confidant. I missed him, and he was busy entertaining a princess.

Chapter Sixteen

TAVRIC

The applause felt as if it were pounding against my skin as the musicians bowed and then exited. I breathed a little easier once the clapping had stopped.

"That was our last entertainment for the evening," my mother said. "I do believe it's time to retire."

Relief coursed through me. Only a few more minutes, and I could close myself in my chambers and be free of the layers of noise and fabric.

"Already?" Princess Saria asked in dismay. "Can we not have another song? I'm enjoying myself immensely."

My mother looked startled. Having anyone contradict her after she'd made a statement was near unfathomable for her, and she looked uncertain about what to do. "That might be permissible, if Tavric doesn't mind."

She turned the decision over to me, and I was simultaneously grateful and horrified. I could end this here and now...if only I could find my voice.

It had been three days of this. Three days of parading around the grounds and the village with the princess on my arm. Three days of dinners and entertainment with what felt like half the kingdom present. Too much cheer, too much ale, too many people, too much noise. Too much, too much, too much. I'd been on the verge of breaking all day.

Several moments ticked by and I could feel sweat gathering at my brow.

Caelmir leaned close. "Are you well, Brother?" he asked quietly.

If only I could nod, or say yes, or respond in any way in the affirmative and have it not be a lie. But I couldn't. I couldn't speak at all, knowing that if I did anything other than maintain the iron grip that I had on my chair and my composure, I'd go flying apart. All of my effort was in controlling my expression as the seam at my shoulder started to rub my arm raw.

What could I do? I had to respond. I was the crown prince, and if I kept sitting here, silent, everyone would know how weak and unfit I was.

"On second thought," my mother said, "I'm not up for a late night. It's best we all retire." And with that, the queen turned and swept from the room, her power and authority written in each line of her gait as she left the grand hall. It was a bit of a spectacle, and one I was incredibly grateful for, as it had shifted everyone's attention away from me.

I braced myself to turn to Saria and bid her good night. It was the very least I could do. But when I turned in her direction, I found her already in conversation with Dorian.

Caelmir's hand settled abruptly on my arm and I nearly jumped. "Let's have a night cap, shall we?" he said in a jovial tone, urging me to my feet and then ushering me out of the hall.

I counted in my head. Five beats as I breathed in, five as I breathed out, forcing my mind on only that simple task until Caelmir pulled me into an empty chamber, just far enough away from the hall that the noise was barely discernible.

The moment the door was closed, I threw off his hand, then my shoulder cape, sash, and shirt, before pacing the room and shaking out my hands.

"Tav—"

"Quiet," I snapped. "Just...quiet." I put my palms over my ears and breathed deliberately, appreciating the quiet it provided. If only I had the silk coverlet from my room that I often used to wrap my body tightly. It was the fastest way for me to calm myself, even if I felt ridiculous doing it.

Well, it used to be the fastest. Lately, the quickest way had been Lyri.

After several minutes, I dropped my hands from my ears and then ran my hands through my hair, pulling on it as I tried to come back to my senses.

"I didn't know it was like this."

Caelmir's words forced me to look at him. He stood by the door, wide-eyed and worried.

I cleared my throat, fighting down my embarrassment. "You've seen it before." I'd been sensitive to *too much* since I was a child.

"Not like this," he said with conviction. "How long has it been this bad?"

That was easy to answer. "Since Papa got sick. Since I started playing the role of king." I swiped my shirt from off the floor, thinking I would put it back on, but the way the fabric scraped against my palms made me drop it again. I couldn't put it back on yet.

He looked at me, clearly wanting to say something but at a loss.

I gave a shrug. "Why do you think I prefer a ship? The wind doesn't clang. I never have to wear formal robes, and if I ever need complete silence and solitude, I can dive into the water." I paced some more.

"What do you need?" he asked.

"Lyri." I spoke before the thought had time to settle.

Caelmir pushed away from the wall. "I'll go find her."

"Don't, Cael." I put out a staying hand. "I didn't mean it."

His eyebrows pushed down to crowd his gaze. "But she could help."

"I don't want her help," I insisted.

"You just said—"

"I can't use her like medicine. Not to make you less worried, not to make me feel better. I *won't* use her." I turned and walked several steps away before turning back. "She's not a tool."

"That's not what it would be."

"I said no. I'll be fine. I have to learn to deal with this on my own. Maybe...maybe Saria can help me when we marry. Maybe she could learn to." My shoulders tensed and rolled at the thought.

If anything, my attempt at reassurance seemed to increase Caelmir's worry. "Tav, you've been ten times worse since Saria came."

"I'll get used to it. I will. I just...need to get to know her. I need to be comfortable around her."

There was a knock on the door that made me wince.

"Not now," Caelmir called out.

"It's us," came Dorian's voice through the door. "Let us in."

I opened my mouth to protest, but Caelmir opened the door, yanked them inside, and closed it swiftly.

Kavian looked me over, his brow rising in derision. "Couldn't keep your clothes on?"

"Shut your mouth, Kave." Caelmir's harsh demand surprised us all. As the youngest, he rarely tried to give orders. Kavian opened his mouth to retort, but Caelmir rolled over him. "Did you know it was this bad?"

He lifted one eyebrow. "*What was* this bad?"

Caelmir jammed a finger at me. "Him. He was falling apart in there. Did either of you notice?"

Kavian snorted. "It's quite the burden, entertaining a beautiful woman."

Caelmir shoved Kavian's shoulder, his face so stormy that Kavian finally fell silent. "You'd better shove that envy down into whatever deep, dark hole is inside you and start paying attention." Kavian stayed silent under the weight of Caelmir's glare. "He didn't even notice she was pretty. He wasn't entertaining *anyone*. He was just out there trying to endure."

It sounded so pathetic when he said it like that. "I'm fine," I insisted, willing it to be true while also wanting to prevent a fight from breaking out between my brothers.

"See," Kavian crowed. "He's fine."

"He's not fine." Dorian spoke up for the first time from where he leaned his back against the door.

Kavian looked over as if Dorian's words were a sort of betrayal. "Come on, not you—"

"He's not fine, Kave, and it's time you opened your eyes enough to see it."

I wanted to argue with them. Tell them to get out, to stop talking about me as if I weren't there. I wanted to tell them they were overreacting.

Only they weren't. I could feel the panic humming just under the surface, threatening to surge up and drown me. "There is a formal audience tomorrow. What am I going to do?"

They all looked at each other, each one at a loss for words. Finally, Kavian let out a low growl. "Maybe you should just ask the girl to marry you." He tossed the words out and they crashed to the ground between us.

Some of my panic subsided, replaced instead by anger. "The *girl*?" I asked, danger threading through my tone.

"He means Lyri," Dorian clarified, pinching the bridge of his nose.

"I know who he means," I snapped at Dorian, then turned my wrath on Kavian. "Leave her out of this."

Kavian clearly wanted to argue, but Caelmir cut him off. "I've already gone down that road, Kave. Leave it alone."

Shockingly, Kavian listened.

"I think you're right, though," Caelmir said to me as he arranged his face into an imitation of confidence. "I'm certain that if you give Saria a chance, she'll be able to help. In the meantime, one of us can sit in on the formal audience tomorrow."

"Not Kavian," I insisted, unable to trust him to actually have my back.

"I'll be there," Caelmir said. "I'll act as your ears like I used to."

LYRIELLE

I'd fallen into a routine since the princess's arrival. I kept myself to the servants' wing, going from my room to the kitchen, to the sewing room, and back again. I didn't attempt to walk the grounds or explore the garden since

I was too afraid that I would catch a glimpse of Tavric and his guest. Or, even worse, that I would run into them. So I kept my distance, but it was impossible not to overhear the chatter. There had been banquets and horseback riding. The princess and Tavric were constantly seen in company together, and everyone speculated that a betrothal would be announced soon. It made sense, after all—or so they said. If Tavric was going to be king, he needed a queen at his side.

Each bit of gossip made me die a little, as the gossamer dream of a joyful life slipped from my fingertips. I did my best to keep my head down, work hard, and close my ears. There was still a large part of me that reveled in my circumstances, happy for work and freedom, but I missed Tavric and I was still horribly hurt by his sudden dismissal of me.

Another part of me was certain that at any moment, my new life would be stolen from me. My eyes darted to the doorway probably a thousand times, wondering if Harlan would show up again, wanting more information. Or wondering if guards would show up to escort me away because he'd shared my secret.

But it wasn't Harlan who stepped into the chaotic, cramped sewing room. It was Prince Dorian.

I dropped my eyes to my work as a sinking feeling told me that he was here to speak with me, probably to ask me to leave since he likely disapproved of my friendship with his brother just like Prince Kavian did. Apparently, no one had told him that Tavric no longer wished to be my friend. That thought brought a lump to my throat, and I had to breathe through my melancholy.

"Miss Lyrielle," he said, coming right over to me. "Might I have a word?"

I looked to the head seamstress, somehow hoping she'd save me by saying I needed to keep working, but who was I kidding? A member of the royal family was requesting my presence. So I set aside the pieces of the black bodice I was constructing for Her Majesty and said, "Of course, Your Highness," before following him out into the hallway, my hands clasped together in front of me with too much force as I channelled all my discomfort into that pressure.

When we reached a door that led to the courtyard, he opened it and gestured for me to go through. Perhaps he would simply walk me all the way out the gate and tell me to keep going, but I hoped not. If nothing else, I needed much more time to finish healing the king.

He did not leave me in suspense. Once he'd looked around to see that there was no one within earshot, he turned to me. "I've come to beg for your help," he said without preamble.

I stumbled back a step. "My help? With what?" A rock sat in my stomach, the word help making me terrified that he had somehow found out about my gift. Maybe Harlan had told him. He probably had.

"My brother."

I flinched in surprise. "Tavric?"

"Yes."

"Is he sick?"

"No, but..." He shoved his hands into his hair, making a mess of it, much like his brother was wont to do. "I didn't realize the toll this entire situation was having on him. He was always quieter and liked to be alone, but I didn't realize just how uncomfortable it was for him. As he got older, he seemed to handle it better. He hid it well for a long time."

My heart slowed a little at knowing that my secret was still a secret, but then worry for Tavric slipped in. I didn't have to ask Prince Dorian what he was talking about. I'd seen it myself. "So what's different now?"

"My brother, Caelmir, returned five days ago. He's been gone for months, scouring all the closest lands for answers, or doctors, or treatments for my father's illness. We put all our hope in him, but he came back with nothing."

I nodded. "You believe your father will die soon."

"We know it," he said as anguish weighed on his expression.

Not if I had any say in the matter, but that thought was for another time. This moment was about Tavric. "Tavric is not taking the news well?"

"I think the reason he's been able to hold it together before now is because he had hope that it was temporary, that my father would rally and he would have more time before taking the throne, but now he knows..."

"It will all be on his shoulders."

"Yes, and that burden, it's...I can't even describe it. He's not himself. He can barely make it through the events of the day. He needs you."

I drew back. "Me? For what?"

"He told me you were the only one who could help. I don't understand what it is that makes him so crazy. I know things can get chaotic, but it's not just that. It's like everything is just too much. That's what he used to say every time he had to leave when we were kids. He would just say, 'It's too much.' I thought it was an excuse. But you...you helped him. He said you were the only thing keeping him sane. He needs you."

A large part of me wanted to run to him without a second's hesitation, but his dismissive words had been all too clear. "Isn't that why the princess is here?"

He huffed in frustration. "She can't help; you can. Will you come?" The way he asked—with desperation, strained patience, and a healthy dose of authority—made it impossible to refuse.

He was right; I could help. I didn't understand why, but there was something about my presence that allowed Tavric to relax. "Where must I go?"

"He's been in meetings most of the morning, but the formal audience is going to start soon. It's the hardest for him and he's already not doing well. Since he hasn't allowed himself to be around you, he's gotten so much worse. It's like I can see him cracking right in front of me, and if he cracks in front of a room full of nobility..."

"What do you want me to do?"

"Just stand where he can see you."

"During a formal audience? With all those nobles looking on, waiting to judge everyone they see?"

"I see you're familiar with them. Do they intimidate you?" He looked worried.

"Well, no. I find them rather fascinating."

That seemed to surprise him and he looked at me as if seeing me anew. "That's encouraging."

Was it? "You really believe that just standing there will do any good?"

He lifted his arms, then let them fall limp at his sides. "It's the only idea I have. Please."

"You're a member of the royal family. I'm not going to say no."

"It's not an order. I'm asking you to do this for Tavric."

I didn't answer right away, even though I'd known my answer the moment he'd brought it up. Of course I would help. I wanted to help.

As soon as I nodded, his shoulders sank in relief, and the next moment, we were in motion.

Chapter Seventeen

TAVRIC

Numbness was what I wished for. If I could sit amongst all this commotion and feel numb, that would be ideal. Instead, I was hyperaware of all the overlapping noises fighting for dominance, as well as the crush of the crowd that seemed to press ever closer. Yet I couldn't pay attention to any of that because if I didn't listen to whatever petition or issue was being put forth, then I couldn't respond, and if I didn't respond, then this audience would go on forever with nothing accomplished.

Sweat beaded my forehead and both of my hands were gripping the arms of the elaborate wooden chair as I tried to focus my energy there. The sleeves of my formal clothing draped dramatically over my hands and cascaded halfway to the floor. The weight of my ornamental robe was stifling, and the way the chain around my neck made noise every time I moved felt like it was poking at the inside of my skull. What would I do when I actually became king and I had to bear the actual weight of a crown on my head during these infernal forums?

Something would have to change. I couldn't keep doing this over and over. But for today, I had to listen.

"This is the third time I have found Baron Teagly's sheep grazing on my land."

As Lord Hough presented his dispute, I was vaguely aware of the door directly to my right opening. It must be another one of my brothers. Caelmir already sat to my left, but perhaps they thought my panic was showing through and they'd decided to double up. It was a nice thought, but it also served to amplify the fact that they needed me to do better and I didn't know how. No doubt whoever it was would take the seat to my right. There were several seats on either side of me, but I usually only allowed the seat to my left to be occupied by one of my brothers. Having more than one person whispering in my ear was detrimental.

I took a controlled breath, hoping my internal havoc was masked enough that it would not be seen by those in attendance—or make me look incompetent to the entire kingdom.

A murmur rippled through the audience, and I couldn't figure out why until the swish of skirts approached and I looked over to see Princess Saria walking calmly toward me.

She was graceful, and only a little haughty. I willed myself to be relieved at the sight of her as she walked over, offered me a small smile, stepped up onto the dais, and sank elegantly into the seat beside me, looking for all the world as though it were nothing out of the ordinary for her to take a seat at my side during a formal audience.

This was good. This was precisely what needed to happen. Caelmir had been at my side, acting as my second set of ears. If the noise ever got to be too much and I was unable to focus on whomever was presenting their case, Caelmir could lean in and give me an idea of what to say. It worked, but only if we used it sparingly. I couldn't be seen whispering to my brother every time I needed to speak. But if Princess Saria could sit at my side as my equal...

I hated the idea, even though I knew it was the most practical.

She seemed completely at ease sitting beside me, and I tried to let some of my own tension go. But when she reached over to lay her hand on my arm, no warmth seeped into me. My fingers gripped the armrest even tighter and my breath felt trapped in my lungs.

I could see from my peripheral vision that while she sat close, she was facing forward, maintaining her royal bearing and decorum while I debated whether or not I could extricate my arm from her touch without causing a scene.

LYRIELLE

Prince Dorian led me to a spot in the grand hall near the front of the assembly, close to the raised dais, but off to the side. The moment my eyes landed on Tavric's face, my lungs heaved in relief. At least for a moment.

In the next moment, my gaze landed on the delicate feminine hand resting on Tavric's arm, and I wanted to sink into the earth and let it suffocate me.

Was this a cruel joke? Did Dorian wish for me to see this cozy scene with Tavric and the princess sitting close, side by side, and looking for all the world as though they were already the king and queen of the land? Perhaps it was his way of showing me that any ludicrous dream I might have of a future with Tavric was not only impractical, but already burned to ashes.

I turned away. "I can't do this," I muttered and tried to walk toward the archway we'd just come through, but the prince caught my arm.

"Please," he hissed. "He needs you."

I whipped around to glare at him, my face strained in agony. "He doesn't need me. He has *her*." The perfect match, born and bred for this duty and this world.

"Watch. Just watch him," he begged. "The longer she sits beside him, the worse it's getting. Look."

I didn't want to. I didn't want to see any more. But I did it anyway.

TAVRIC

Lyri was here. I wasn't certain when Dorian brought her in, but the moment I caught sight of her, there was an easing in my chest. The contrast between my response to her and my response to Princess Saria was astounding, and it made me dismiss any idea of pursuing a strategic match with the princess.

Lyri looked sad and uncertain, but she was still here. I didn't deserve her kindness. I didn't deserve her at all. What had possessed her to come here when I had so coldly dismissed her?

As the afternoon progressed, I was able to look to Lyri once in a while, and each time, her bolstering smile reduced my stress just enough to keep me from fleeing the room. She allowed me to survive.

When it was all over, I was incredibly grateful that the king was expected to leave before anyone else, and that I had a private door right off the dais that exited the grand hall. I needed to get out of this room, take off this suffocating costume, and just be alone.

Well, maybe not alone. What I really wanted was for Lyri to be with me, maybe even with her arms wrapped around me, but that wasn't an option. I reminded myself a hundred times that she wasn't a tool for me to use. Just because she could fix me didn't mean it was acceptable for me to ask it. She'd done enough. The only reason I'd made it through that audience while knowing my father was dying a few floors away was because she'd been there.

I briskly walked from the dais with my head held high, resisting the urge to look back over my shoulder for one more look at her. I heard Princess Saria call my name, but I continued through the doors and into the safety of the corridor beyond. Once I was out of the grand hall, I dropped my regal posture, ready to tear the oppressive costume from my body.

Unfortunately, Saria followed. "Prince Tavric, do slow down and speak to me," she called out in exasperation, clearly impatient and expecting me to obey.

I turned on her, and the cheeky smile that had adorned her face quickly slipped when she saw my expression. "No, Princess, I will not. You know nothing about who I am or what I need in this moment, so I must ask you to depart and not harass me any longer."

I didn't bother to wait for a response, but turned and hurried toward my chambers, taking off chains and rings and handing them off to my valet as my feet carried me at a frenzied pace through the corridors. Stephan was used to it. He knew how uncomfortable all the accoutrements made me, and we only made it to the antechamber of my rooms before he made quick work of helping me out of the heavy ornamental robes, leaving me in my trousers and linen shirt. "Now go," I said, breathing heavily. I just needed some time in the quiet of my own room to get my panic and discomfort under control.

The door shut behind Stephan, and I sat on the closest chair and dug my palms into the tops of my thighs, then pushed them toward my knees. The exertion on my hands and the pressure on my legs gave the panic somewhere to go, and the almost painful sensation gave me something physical to focus on.

A knock sounded on my door.

"Away!" I shouted.

The door opened anyway.

I got up, ready to scream at whomever dared to enter my room when I'd clearly refused them entrance, but when Lyri was pushed abruptly through the doorway, the anger died in my chest.

She stumbled a bit as the door closed after her. She looked at me, then at the door, then back at me.

Just seeing her was a relief, but it wasn't enough. I wanted so much more from her than just a glance at her beautiful face or a few minutes of her reassuring presence. Finally, I found my voice. "What are you doing here?"

"Prince Dorian thinks I can help."

I shook my head but couldn't form the words to deny it. I was pressing my hands together, my breathing barely controlled. Lyri was too observant, so telling her that I was fine would be a waste and a lie.

She hesitated near the door for only a few moments before her mouth set in a decisive line. Then she was across the room in a flash, and instead of stopping in front of me, she practically crashed into me, wrapping her arms around my torso and squeezing while I latched onto her in return.

Her entire body was pressed to mine, and something about the pressure grounded me.

"Breathe with me," she whispered, and I obeyed.

For such a small woman, her strength was impressive and profound. In less time than it had ever taken before, my breathing and my heart slowed, and I regained my composure. I could have pulled back, but once the discomfort was gone, I realized just how good it felt to be wrapped around Lyri. Not because she was helping me, but because she was precious to me.

I drew back just enough that I could look into her eyes and drink in her features. *What would it be like to kiss her?* my head wondered. *Heaven*, my heart replied. For once they were in agreement, and I had the sudden desperate urge to tilt her chin up and press my mouth to hers. I leaned in, but caught myself. I couldn't do that. She was comforting me. I couldn't take advantage of that by turning it into more. So instead I pulled her close again and just held her. I blinked back tears as the pleasure of holding her combined with the bitter ache of not being able to make her mine.

"Dorian dragged you into this?" I finally asked. I should be angry at him for disregarding my wishes, but my relief was too profound.

She pulled back just enough that she could look up at me, her eyes swimming with uncertainty. "Why is she here?" she asked in a tiny voice.

I pinched my eyes shut, wanting to kick myself. Of course she was upset about Saria. "It wasn't my idea. Dorian was there, in Ravencairn. He was interested in her, but then she decided to come here. I guess because...because..."

"Because she thought you'd be king soon, and she saw an opportunity?"

Her words slapped me across the face, not because they were cruel or biting—they weren't—but because they rang with such truth. How had I not seen it? Saria wanted to be queen. I was going to be a king. And yet...was I any better for considering a union with her for the exact same reason? I was going to be king. I needed a queen.

I was no better than she.

In fact, I was worse, because right in front of me was a woman whom I loved and who obviously cared deeply for me. "I didn't know what to do," I admitted, my whole body feeling heavy, as if it wanted to surrender to either sleep or death right in that moment. "You saw...you saw how I fell apart."

"Yes."

"I can't do it, Lyri. I'm...incapable of ruling on my own. I thought..." There seemed no excuse for the fact that I'd honestly considered marrying the princess, but I wanted to explain, and I hoped she would understand, if only a little. "Saria knows how things work. She's been raised to be a queen. I thought she could help."

My body went suddenly cold as Lyri stepped abruptly out of my embrace, her face blanketed with such pain and torment that it physically hurt me to see it.

"Why didn't you ask *me* to help you?" Her mouth trembled as she asked it.

"I couldn't." The words were pathetic, unworthy of either her or me.

"You needed help, and you didn't ask me. But you asked *her*?" Her voice cracked and her eyes filled with tears as she took another step back. "You prefer her over me?"

"Of course not."

"Then why?"

"I don't want to use you."

"What are you talking about? It's not using me."

"It is," I insisted, determined to tell her the truth, determined to do what was right, instead of what I wanted. "I *needed* you, and I came to you day after day so that you could fix me," I spat in disgust. "How is that different from the way the villagers used you for your gift?"

She tilted her head, quiet for several moments before answering. "Is that what you think?"

"It's what I know!"

"Well, you're wrong. You never used me."

"Yes, I did. I *needed* you."

"And I needed you!"

My head told me that those words should have made me feel used, and yet my heart latched onto them, proud that she would see me in such a way, and more than willing to fill that role. We both stared at one another, our breathing labored.

"I don't have very much experience with...friendship," she said in a much calmer tone. "But I think that what we had was friendship, wasn't it?"

"Of course." Even if I wanted so much more from her.

She nodded. "And that included being together and laughing together, talking about hard things and happy things. I shared my burdens with you and you were honest with me. You listened to me." She pressed a hand to her heart as if my simple act of listening had been some great gift. "Tavric, the people who came to my tower only wanted to take from me. With the exception of Gregor, they didn't want to know me. They didn't want to hear what was on my mind or in my heart. They didn't care if I was sad, so they never bothered to make me smile.

You think you've taken from me, and you have, but I was more than willing to give, and you gave me just as much in return. Do you regret giving me so much?"

"I didn't give anything."

She took two steps and put her small hands on either side of my neck, forcing me to look at her. "You gave me *everything*," she said with a sternness that surprised me. "You asked me not just what I needed, but what I wanted, and then you just...gave it—with no thought of what I could give you in return. You gave me earth and flower and ocean. You taught me to dance. You gave me companionship and kindness." Moving her hands from my neck, she instead shoved at my chest in frustration. "How can you say that's nothing when those things are exactly what I've craved for years?"

Her words made sense, but I was afraid to really believe them. "I just don't want to hurt you more."

She grabbed the front of my shirt. "Then stop pushing me away," she begged, emotion suddenly choking her voice.

The great iron gate I'd been using to lock away all my inconvenient longing for her broke open, unlocked by her pleading eyes. And as we stood there, so close, breathing each others' air, I made a decision.

I covered her small hands with mine and tugged them gently from my shirt, then moved them up and around me, reveling in the feel of her fingers resting against the back of my neck.

Her eyes widened a bit, and I appreciated the small gasp of surprise that made her lips pop open.

"Is this better?" I asked as I threaded my own hands around her waist.

She gave a silent and quick nod of her head.

The words *I love you* clung to my tongue and pushed at the back of my teeth, but I swallowed them down. *Not yet*, my mind prompted. I wanted so much to confess my feelings, to kiss her, but instead I rested my temple against hers and closed my eyes. “I want you and I need you, but I’m scared I won’t be good for you,” I admitted.

“You are.” She angled her face so that her lips were wonderfully, torturously close to mine. “You’re the best thing that’s ever happened to me.” The words fanned over my own mouth.

Kissing her suddenly became a necessity. In that moment, it was no longer a choice; it was simply what *must* be done. So I did. I pressed a gentle kiss to her lips, worried that too much would overwhelm her, but as soon as I pulled back, she chased after me, reclaiming the kiss and pulling me closer.

I kissed her again, slow and sweet, feeling my whole body sigh into her as I let go of my worry and allowed myself to love her. Because that was the truth of the matter—I loved her.

Pulling back again, I skimmed the backs of my fingers down her cheek, swimming in the realization of just how much I loved this woman and everything that meant. I’d known her for so little time, and my head wanted to argue that loving her could not happen so fast, but my heart was sure.

She smiled up at me, clearly content with this new development.

“I missed you,” I confessed in a bare whisper. “It was only a few days, but I couldn’t really breathe without you, my love.” The endearment slipped past my throat without my permission.

She snuggled closer and buried her face in my neck, breathing me in like I’d seen her do with the soil outside.

"Tell me what you've been doing these past days. I want to know everything."

She stiffened and I ran my own words through my head. What had I said?

Chapter Eighteen

LYRIELLE

I'd been sewing mourning clothing for his mother. That was what I'd been doing.

I wanted to tell him everything, especially about Harlan and the revelation about his origins. Actually, what I really wanted was to go back to kissing him. I wanted to talk about this new feeling between us and just take a moment to be. I wanted to revel in the fact that he'd called me his love. But all that black fabric I'd been sewing needed to be addressed first. Tavric was drowning under the weight of the throne, and there was one very important thing that I could do to relieve him of that burden.

"I'll happily tell you about my days, but will you take me to see your father first?"

Confusion pinched his eyes. "Why?"

"Please, Tav?"

My use of his nickname softened him immediately. "Very well." He took my hand and led me to the door, still in his trousers and shirt. No vest or jacket. It was a stark contrast to the formal costume he'd worn earlier. I greatly preferred him this way.

He didn't drop my hand as we traversed the hallway. "You can check in on my father. It's time I did the same anyway. But once you've seen him, I want to know everything that is on your mind." He cut his eyes over to me.

"You can know it all." I wanted nothing more, but it was time for me to heal Tav's father.

We reached the door to the king and queen's chamber and Tavric stopped, taking a moment to collect himself. Then he nodded to the guard, who opened the door.

The room still held the oppressive weight of illness and hopelessness. The queen lay fully clothed beside the king, her hand holding his and her face pressed into his shoulder.

Tavric stepped over to the doctor, who was close at hand. "Is she sleeping?" he asked.

"Yes, and she should not be woken if it can be avoided."

"Of course," Tav agreed.

"She was up most of the night worrying about him." The doctor pressed his lips, his brow furrowed. "He is not doing well, Your Highness."

Tavric swallowed but nodded. "Will you leave us for a moment?"

The doctor bowed his head and left immediately.

That was good. I didn't want anyone but Tavric to see this.

Instead of walking straight over to the king's bed, he hesitated. I could see the toll that seeing his father this way took on him, and I hated myself a little for letting his pain go on for so long.

"Do you ever wish you'd known about my power when you pulled me from the sea?" I asked in a guilty whisper.

"Why would I wish that?"

"If my hair hadn't been cut, I could have healed your father."

"If I hadn't cut your hair, you would have drowned," he stated.

"So you've never thought about it?" I found that hard to believe.

He gave me a grim smile. "Of course I thought about it when you first told me about your gift, but it was more like a fanciful thought than a real lament. The idea that he could be healed by magic is such a foreign one, and your gift was gone long before I knew anything about it."

"What about now? What if I still had my gift?"

"What ifs are useless. I'm grateful I met you, and that has nothing to do with your powers." His eyes slid in the direction of his father, sadness pulling at the corners of his eyes. "Besides, he's been doing better lately. My brothers think I'm foolish to hope, but I can't help it. There's still a chance he'll pull through."

I swallowed hard and tamped down my nerves. "He will."

He nodded, but a heavy hopelessness tugged at the corners of his eyes. "I truly hope so."

"No, Tavric. I mean…" I pulled my hand from his and walked over to stand at the king's side, then reached out my hand to take King Valtren's hand, placing my other hand on his chest before looking back at Tavric. "He will," I promised.

Closing my eyes, I started to sing. Heat rushed to my hands, and I allowed the full strength of my magic to gently flow into the king's body. This time, I didn't hold back. I didn't heal a little here and a little there. Instead, I urged the healing magic to saturate his lungs, to strengthen his heart, to burn off any infection.

It was arduous work. There was so much that needed repair, and I was determined to heal him fully and completely. I willed more magic to pour from my hands, repairing damaged tissue—not because it was expected of me, but because I wanted to.

TAVRIC

I was entranced once again by her song. It was so beautiful, but on top of that, the way she held my father's hand with such tenderness and strength brought a surge of affection and gratitude into my chest for this marvelous woman who had somehow found her way into my life.

Emotion washed over me as I watched, my eyes transfixed on her lashes as they rested on the curve of her cheeks, fascinated by the way her lips moved as the soft cushion of her voice filled the air. It was incredible, the way the air seemed to clear and lighten just by the sound of her voice.

Then my eyes went to her hand that rested on my father's chest, right over his heart, and I stopped breathing.

There was a glow under her palm. I squinted, trying to make sense of what I was seeing, and stepped closer. It was there, I was sure of it. Pale golden light was emanating from underneath her hand.

Was she...?

As my father pulled in a full deep breath, the truth hit me. Lyri was healing my father.

She could still heal? When and how? For how long?

Tentative joy surged within me as my father's face became less pale. I still couldn't breathe. She was doing it. Lyri was healing my father. Perhaps he would live.

Perhaps she would be able to save him. A terrifying rush of hope bloomed within me.

I looked at Lyri's face, overwhelmed with gratitude and wanting to drink in her beauty and sweetness, but instead my heart sank.

It was like all the color that had been infused into my father's skin was being slowly drained from Lyri's. She looked pale, almost gray, and her whole body looked like she was being dragged down.

"Lyri, stop," I said, reaching out to touch her shoulder but worried that I'd cause more harm than good if I acted too rashly. Perhaps it was normal and nothing to worry about.

She ignored me and kept singing.

But then her voice wavered, becoming weak and breathy.

I wrapped my arms around her and pulled her away from my father. Her song cut off and she immediately went limp in my arms. I sank to the ground beside my father's bed with her draped across my lap, wondering what had gone wrong. She'd never said anything about her healing taking a physical toll on her. Had she just kept that to herself? Or were things different since I'd cut her hair? I had no idea. I didn't know how magic worked!

I pushed her hair back and cupped her cheek. "Lyri?"

Thankfully, her eyes fluttered open and managed to focus on me. "I was healing him," she breathed out, her eyes blinking slowly.

"Yes, but at what cost?" Her skin was cold and her limp weight was heavy in my arms. It was terrifying. "It was too much for you."

"It was worth it," she murmured, and then her eyes drifted closed.

Panic surged through me. “Lyri!” I shook her a little, my panic rising to cloud my vision. “No, no, no. Lyri, wake up!”

When she still didn’t respond, I ignored my labored breathing and shifted her until I was able to stand with her in my arms. “Help!” I shouted. “I need help in here.”

“What’s going on?” my mother asked as she sat up, eyes still clouded with sleep, but I didn’t have time to answer.

Several guards, a doctor, and a nurse all poured into the room.

“Check on my father,” I ordered the doctor. “And you, come here,” I said to the nurse as I moved Lyri out of the way and laid her on the floor. “She collapsed and I don’t know what’s wrong with her.”

The nurse spared only one glance toward the king before focusing her attention on Lyri. My focus was split between the frantic energy surrounding my father’s bed and the desperate fear that Lyri’s collapse caused in me.

Not knowing what was wrong with her was eating away at my insides, and there was nothing I could do to help.

Was it her magic? Did it always drain her like this?

The nurse was efficient and professional, and after several minutes, she looked down on Lyri in confusion. “I cannot find anything wrong with her, Your Highness.”

“Nothing?”

She shook her head. “Her heartbeat is strong, her breathing regular. She has no injuries, swelling, or rashes. I believe if we wait, she will wake on her own.”

Relief washed through me. “Very well. Tend to the king.”

She hurried away, and just as my panic started to rise again, someone knelt beside me.

“I’m here, Your Highness.”

I looked up, relieved to see Harlan at my side. "I don't know how to help her, Harlan." I looked over my shoulder at the bed. "And my father..." I wanted to check on him, to see for myself if his condition had really changed, but Lyri... I looked back at her, watching her chest rise and fall. The nurse had said there was nothing wrong with her. Was it just fatigue from healing?

"Go check on the king," Harlan urged me. "I'll watch over her."

I looked back at the bed, where my mother and the doctors all surrounded my father. My mother's shouts of confusion and worry tore at me.

"Go." He rested a hand on my arm and fixed his gaze to mine. "She'll be all right for a moment."

I hated doing it, but I carefully shifted her head from my arm to his, beckoned by my mother's frantic cries. "I'll only be a moment."

"I know."

I stood, giving Lyri one last lingering look, noticing that her face seemed perhaps a little less pale, and then ran over to my father's side, pushing my way in between a doctor and a guard until I was able to see him for myself.

Chapter Nineteen

LYRIELLE

A heaviness weighed me down, and my whole body was uncomfortable. I heard the sound of footsteps close at hand, and something or someone was holding me. I moaned, trying to open my eyes and ask what was happening.

"Shh, go back to sleep," someone said, and since that was exactly what I wanted to do, I allowed that encouragement to relax me enough to fall back into oblivion.

When I roused next, I was rocking back and forth, and the lapping of water reached my ears. It was soothing, reminding me of the day Tavric had taken me to the island. But...was I on the water now? I pulled my heavy eyes open for just a moment but shut them quickly when the light was too bright, forcing myself to listen and think.

The sound was definitely water. And the snapping of fabric must have been a sail. Had Tavric taken me on a boat? No, Tavric was with the princess now. Or, no, not anymore. I'd helped him and he'd kissed me. Then I'd healed his father, and then...

What happened after I'd healed his father? *Had* I healed his father? I'd tried. I'd thrown all my strength into healing him, but had it been enough?

Why couldn't I remember?

Slick fear coated my skin and the inside of my mouth, and I forced my eyes open again. I was staring at the bottom of the boat, so I turned my head and was met with a wide expanse of blue sky, interrupted by the white sail, swollen with wind as it pulled the boat along.

It took incredible effort, but I managed to push myself up on my elbow, giving myself a view of the man who sat at the other end of the boat, holding the steering oar.

"Harlan…what's happening? What are you doing?" I asked, frustrated when the effort of holding myself up was too much and I had to lie down again.

"We're just taking a sail, Your Highness."

He was turned away from me, so I couldn't see his face, but his tone sounded like he was…laughing?

The wind was strong, and it felt as though we were going much faster than Tavric and I had gone that day we went to the island, which was terrifying when I had no idea where we were going or why. Harlan's lack of answers or concern compounded my fear.

"Why am I so weak?" I asked, terrified by how similar I felt to the times Aunt Ethel had given me calming potions. "Did you…did you give me a sleeping draught or…"

"It wasn't my doing. I just took advantage of the situation."

"What situation?"

"You passed out when you tried to heal the king."

I supposed that made sense. Healing always took a toll. I just hadn't been prepared for how large this toll would be. I looked up at the cloudless sky extending in every direction.

Endless, fathomless, terrifying.

"Don't worry, Princess," he said. "You'll be right as rain soon enough, I'm sure."

"I already told you, I'm not royalty," I reminded him, frustrated by my continued confusion over this whole situation.

His eyes cut over to me and then back to the horizon. "Your mother gifted you the royal crest of Branfrie. No doubt it was passed down from mother to daughter until it got to you."

"Even if that's true, it doesn't make me royalty. You know there hasn't been royalty in Branfrie for generations."

His eyes settled on me this time and he tilted his head. "Either way, you being a descendent of the old royals makes you special."

"I was an orphan and a captive in Branfrie. Nothing about me is special," I said as anger and fear choked my voice. "Why am I here, Harlan?"

"Do you realize that if the High Court had discovered that an actual descendent of the royal family also had powers as coveted as yours, they would have either killed or enslaved you?"

He asked the question casually, as if it weren't rewriting my entire childhood. Was that what Aunt Ethel had feared? If I truly was a descendent of the old royals who had ruled our land for hundreds of years... I supposed my magic could have made me a threat, at least in the eyes of the High Court.

But why was he pointing it out now? I was sure I didn't want to know. "I was essentially enslaved anyway," I told him.

"That's probably best. You'll be used to it."

My heart pounded in my throat. "Used to what?"

He looked over at me, a grin pulling his face into a cruel mask. "The High Court pays a substantial reward for any magic wielder delivered to them."

Fear washed over me as his words and his smug expression tilted my world.

"And when I give you to them," he continued, "they'll give me more money than I could spend in a decade."

Tears streamed from my eyes while my mouth hung open, gasping for tiny bits of breath that my lungs didn't want to permit. He was taking me back to Branfrie.

"Please don't."

He just smiled and looked off at the horizon.

I breathed carefully, swallowing down my terror. "You're Tavric's friend." Surely that meant something. "You're a good person." Did he feel no remorse?

"You don't know anything about me. And friends come and go, my dear. Earning the confidence of a prince served me well."

"How did you do it?"

"I worked on plenty of merchant ships in Branfrie, so when I came here, I already knew how to sail. The prince loves being on the ocean." He shrugged as though that explained it.

"And you'd betray him in such a way?"

I could only see a slice of his profile, but it was clear there was no sympathy or remorse in his expression. "Yes." When he didn't elaborate, the heavy silence saturated the air once more.

The wind was making me cold, but there was nothing with which to cover myself, so I just lay there, helpless and trembling. Healing had never made me so weak. I'd been so focused on letting my magic work through the king's entire body that I hadn't noticed how depleted I was until Tavric pulled me away. But then I'd been hit with a weakness and exhaustion like I'd never felt before. Maybe the king had been sicker than anyone I'd healed before. Maybe my magic wasn't as strong now that my hair was cut.

Maybe, I thought as I stared up at the man who planned to deliver me to those who would enslave me, *it didn't matter.*

TAVRIC

Lyri was gone.

My father was sitting up in his bed, awake and alert but very hungry. My mother hadn't stopped sobbing. My brothers had shown up, asking questions and demanding answers, but I'd pushed them off, knowing I had to care for Lyri.

My sweet Lyri who had just saved my father's life. Lyri, who was terrified that her gift would be discovered and used. I had to protect her. I had to be certain that she recovered from whatever had made her collapse. Surely it was just exhaustion. Healing a person had to be tiring, right? That just made sense.

But when I'd turned to search for her, she was nowhere to be found. My brow furrowed, and I pulled away from my family's grasping hands and loud questions, looking around the room, waiting for Harlan to appear or for Lyri's bright hair to catch my eye.

"Where is she?" I asked the room at large.

"Who, Your Highness?" a guard inquired.

"Miss Lyrielle. She was here." I pointed at the ground. "She was ill. Harlan was watching over her. Where is she?" My voice rose as disquiet permeated my chest and weighed on my lungs.

"He carried her out, Highness. I assume he went to find a place to lay her down."

I was out the door in a trice. The guard's words made sense; I wanted Lyri to be comfortable. But...I'd told Harlan to stay put, hadn't I? Maybe not. He'd said he'd watch over her. Maybe with all the chaos surrounding my father, he'd deemed it best to take her somewhere quiet.

My feet pounded against the stone floor as I hurried down the corridor, dipping in and out of shadow and sunlight. I asked everyone I passed if they'd seen Lyri or Harlan. A few had and pointed me in the direction of her old room. Maybe he'd gone there?

My father was going to live, I was sure of it, yet I couldn't feel the exultation of that knowledge because Lyri's absence had caused a deep-seated worry to burrow into my gut.

I burst through the door of the guest room Lyri used to occupy, hope rising, anxious to see her lying peacefully on the bed.

The room was empty. Why was the room empty? What possible reason could Harlan have had to take her anywhere else?

This time I ran down the corridor. I thought maybe I'd find her in whatever chamber she now occupied in the servants' wing, but as I continued to make inquiries, it was clear that Harlan and Lyri were no longer in the castle.

He was gone, and he'd taken Lyri with him.

Why?

There could be no good reason, no benevolent answer to that question. The cutting and blatant truth was that something was very wrong. He must have discovered her secret, but why steal her away?

"He went that way, Highness," the guard at the gate said, pointing to the path that led down to the ocean. "Thought it was strange, but he said all the castle doctors were needed for the king, so he was taking her to the village."

I ran again. Legs pumping, chest heaving, I scrambled down the rocky pathway to the little beach until I skidded to a stop on the dock where my skiff was meant to be. It was gone.

Harlan had taken my boat. Why, why, why, why, why?

It didn't matter why. I retraced my steps and ran hard until I reached the main port. I shouted commands and demands at a few dock workers until I was situated in another skiff, shoving off from shore. A larger boat might have been faster, but it took longer to prep. I didn't have time to gather a crew, and I didn't trust anyone else with Lyri's secret.

I had no idea where Harlan would have taken her, but I knew that Lyri's deepest fear was that she'd be taken back to Branfrie, so I did the only thing I could think to do. I pointed my boat in the direction of the spot where I'd first pulled my little siren from the ocean.

I didn't know the exact place where I'd found her, but if I could get to the general area quickly enough, maybe I could catch up to Harlan.

And then I could kill him.

The wind blew in my face, the sail snapped, and my hand ached where I gripped the steering oar. Was there any way I would actually find them? It seemed impossible, but impossible wasn't an option. If I lost Lyri...

I kept sailing, fueled by fear and betrayal, my heart twisted so tightly in my chest that I felt it ripping at the seams. When the position of the sun and the shoreline told me I was close to my destination, I looked around, fiercely hoping to see another small boat bobbing close by. I turned and looked and then turned and looked again. I sailed a little farther, my breathing becoming more ragged by the second, then I stood precariously on the bench and studied the horizon, hoping for a glimpse of *anything*.

There was nothing.

I stepped off and sat down on the bench hard. I was afraid to go too much farther in case I overshot their position, but how could I possibly know where to go?

A splash to my right drew my attention, and when I looked to locate the source, shock rocked my whole body.

A woman's head and shoulders showed just above the water.

What was it with women being suddenly dropping into my ocean? Had she come from Branfrie like Lyri had, or was she...

My eyes dropped from her face to look beneath the surface of the water. The water was clear and her silver tail reflected the sunlight, making it glitter in the current. My jaw flapped, useless. She was a mermaid, but not the one who had saved me months ago. Melody had distinct red hair and bright green eyes. This creature had black hair, and her eyes were a startling blue. Her hands, arms, and shoulders were bare, but I noticed that the silver scales of her fin extended up her abdomen and covered her chest, trailing off at her clavicles.

"What is your name, Prince?" she asked, the words almost a song.

"Tavric," I choked out, blinking hard to see if the ethereal image would vanish.

"My name is Saskia. Are you looking for the girl?" she asked.

I stared wide-eyed for several moments before her question slotted into place and hope surged. "Yes," I blurted, leaning on the edge of the boat, anxious for more information. "Did you see her?"

"A man took her. He's looking for the portal."

Having my worst fears confirmed sent a blast of horror through my whole body and I felt suddenly weak. "Where? Where?! You must show me!"

She backed away a little, and I realized I'd been shouting.

I tried to calm myself, but it was impossible. "Please. Will you help me?"

"Yes, but you will not be fast enough in your boat. Do you trust me?"

I hardly had a choice. "Yes."

"Then come. I will take you to them. They are still searching."

LYRIELLE

We'd been sailing a long time, and yet my strength was returning far too slowly. I shouldn't have been surprised. I was desperately hungry and thirsty. Aunt Ethel may have held me prisoner, but she'd always fed me, especially if it had been a taxing day of healing. My body had never been pushed to this limit, and it frightened me to feel so wrung-out for so long. I couldn't fight if I had no strength.

There was a puddle of tears beneath my head, but Harlan had ignored every sob and all my begging. So when he spoke, it startled me. "Sing, Lyrielle."

The request confused me. He wasn't hurt, so what use was my singing? "Why?"

"We need to open the portal."

"I don't know how," I snapped. *How dare he demand anything of me right now.*

"Don't be dim. The portal operates on magic. You have magic. *Sing*," he commanded.

I shook my head, frantic. "I can't go back there." My breathing was speeding up, getting out of control. "I won't sing."

He lunged toward me, causing the boat to rock. My head slammed into the bench behind me, but my cry of pain was cut short when Harlan grabbed hold of my chin, his cold eyes boring into mine. "You will, or I will throw you overboard with your hands tied."

His cold glare and sharp threat washed me in terror.

"You can't swim, can you?" he asked with a raised brow.

No, I couldn't.

"And you're too weak to even sit up, so I can't imagine you have much strength to fight in the first place. So if you want to live, you'll have to open the portal to save your own life."

New tears streamed down my face, joining the rest.

His grip on my face intensified and he gave my head a shake, screaming in my face. "Sing!"

I tried to obey, but fear choked my voice. He grabbed hold of me and dragged me up against the side of the boat, lifting me enough that he could shove my upper body over the edge. I gripped the boat weakly, crying out in fear, trying to lean back into the boat, but his large hand held the back of my head, keeping it bent over the water. "Sing."

I did so, singing over my own sobs, making up the words and the lamenting melody as I went.

Selfish. How can you be so selfish?
How can my life mean nothing?
My choice is a corpse upon the ground
My wants a shipwreck on the ocean floor.

"Keep singing," he demanded as he let me go and returned to his seat to take the steering oar in hand. He searched our surroundings, studying the air around us and the water below. He raised his hand to shade his eyes and then adjusted the oar.

I kept singing as he turned the boat this way and that, hoping with everything in me that this wouldn't work, that he wouldn't find what he was looking for.

But all too soon, I heard him say, "I see it" in whispered awe.

Those words were a blade to my heart, and I summoned all my strength to lift my head and look out over the water. It was still a ways off, but the golden glow at the surface of the water was unmistakable.

"Keep singing!" he screamed as we sailed swiftly toward the portal.

You offer a choice that's no choice at all
Fill my lungs with sea water
And welcome death
Or be sold, imprisoned, enslaved
You are no man, you are no man, you are no man.

On a different day and in a different world, the swirling magic that seemed to rise up from just below the surface would have left me entranced. It didn't spread very far; the glow was only as wide as a wine barrel, but I could feel the power of it pulling on me, like it envied my magic and must claim it for its own.

Harlan lowered the sail and used an oar to maneuver us alongside the shimmering light. Then he grabbed a rucksack I hadn't noticed before and strapped it to his back.

TAVRIC

Holding on to a mermaid's shoulders while being pulled through the water at shocking speeds was an experience I'd have to marvel at later. Right now, I was focused on the sailboat on the horizon, especially when the sail lowered.

"They're stopping," I choked out past the salt spray in my face. "Did they find it?"

"Take a breath, we're going under," Saskia said without any further explanation.

I managed to gulp a breath before she pulled us beneath the surface. My arms ached from trying to keep a grip on her slick shoulders, especially when we seemed to start going even faster, but I was grateful for the pain. It meant progress.

She brought us to an abrupt stop, still underwater, and my eyes popped open—then went wide as I saw a pillar of glowing...magic. That's what it was; it had to be. Harlan had found the portal she had mentioned. It bubbled and sparkled at the surface and then faded as it reached down into the depths.

Saskia yanked on my arms again and we soon broke the surface of the water. The boat sat close by, bobbing back and forth. Harlan stood in it, throwing some sort of pack on his back.

"Why did you stop? I have to get to her," I urged, haunted by the sound of Lyri's singing as it warbled over the water.

"I can't get any closer, or I risk being sucked into the portal. I'm sorry, Prince. You're on your own. Go." With that, Saskia gave me a shove in the direction of the boat, and I didn't waste time wondering about the why or how; I just started swimming, my arms cutting through the water as Lyri's singing stopped.

"Please, don't do this," she begged. "Please."

"Keep singing or I'll slit your throat here and now."

I swam furiously, my blood boiling with anger, my heart torn open in fear. I was getting closer. If I could just get in that boat and get a hold of Lyri...

The disjointed sound of her singing filled my ears as I reached for the boat. I looked up in time to see Harlan cradling Lyri's small form, and then they disappeared over the other side, right on top of where the water glowed gold with magic.

"No!" I shouted and dove under the boat, straight toward the light.

Chapter Twenty

LYRIELLE

Air hit my face and I sucked in a deep breath, my arms sweeping out to keep myself afloat before I realized that it wasn't just my head above water. The water was gone, and my clothing was damp but not dripping. Though the darkness around me was profound, I was now lying on what I assumed was a stone floor, trying desperately to catch my breath and slow my heart.

The portal had worked.

"Where are we?" I heard from beside me. It was Harlan's voice. We'd both made it through. But through to where?

I weakly crawled away from the sound of his voice but didn't make it far before he grabbed my ankle and yanked me toward him. I fought him with what little strength I had until something hard and sharp pressed to my throat and I froze.

"Do you feel that?" Harlan asked in a terrifying hiss. "That's what a knife feels like when it's pressed to your neck. Do not trifle with me."

More tears leaked out of my eyes. "I can't even stand."

"We'll see about that." He pulled away, then groped around until he got hold of my arms and hauled me to my feet. I did what I could to stand on my own, but I still slumped against him.

"Where are we?" Harlan repeated as he shuffled a few steps.

"I don't know. I can't—" My foot hit a hard object and there was the clang of something metal as it fell and rolled across the floor.

My heart turned over. I'd heard that sound before. It was the noise my candlestick would make when I accidentally kicked it over because there was no light in this place.

My body started to shake. I knew exactly where we were.

"We're in the tower," I said, my voice only a rough whisper of trepidation. I'd wondered if we might end up at the tower, but my mind had conjured images of landing in my old living space, surrounded by books, or perhaps ending up at the base of the tower where I would have landed if the portal hadn't taken me the first time. It had never occurred to me that I would end up in this dark place.

"How do you know?"

"This is where she kept me when I was disobedient or ungrateful. She would say I needed solitude and put me up here."

"Who?"

"My aunt."

"Where's the door?"

"I think forward and then to our right, but it might be locked. She always locked it," I babbled as he continued to shuffle forward.

"Was it the healing that knocked you out?" he asked, sounding annoyed. No doubt he wanted me mobile so that I could walk myself to the seat of the High Court.

"Yes. It's always taxing, and the king was much sicker than anyone I've ever healed."

"When will you get your strength back?"

"I need food and water, and even then, I don't know how long it will take."

He stopped, and I heard him groping around in the dark, then the metallic scrape of a latch.

I was surprised when it opened. Aunt Ethel must have locked it only when she'd put me in there for solitude.

Harlan anchored me to his side and dragged me down the steps. "You lived here with your aunt?"

"Yes."

"So there's food here."

He made quick work of the stairs, not caring when my arm bumped and scraped against the stone wall of the stairwell. We reached the small landing where the door led to my home, and I had no time to take in the conflicting turmoil of the moment before he flung the door open and pushed me through it.

A startled cry brought my attention to the far side of the room, where Aunt Ethel had her back against the wall, looking stunned and speechless.

A part of me felt like I should have the urge to run to her, to ask her to keep me safe from Harlan, yet that urge was absent. My aunt was not any safer than he was, and my heart tore just a little more at that thought.

Ethel's gaze fixed on me. "Lyrielle," she breathed in astonishment, a hand pressed to her heart. "Oh, Lyrielle, you're back. I'm so relieved." She slumped against the wall as though overcome with emotion. "I've been so worried about you. What happened? Where have you been?"

She took a step toward me, and as much as I wanted to recoil, I didn't have the energy, and Harlan had an iron grip on me as he slammed the door shut.

"She needs food," he said without preamble and walked us over to the small table, where he deposited me in a chair.

I clung to the edges of the table so that I would stay upright as an eerie silence filled the space. I looked up to see my aunt's face contorted in rage and dismay. "Her hair," she gasped in horror, her frame trembling. "What have you done to her? Who are you?"

"Who I am doesn't matter. All you need to know is that you don't want to cross me. She's weak and needs food. Get it for her, now."

"But her hair!"

Harlan took one menacing step toward her and she fell back. "Food. Now," he said with dark authority.

Ethel swallowed, the defiance in her eyes only slightly overpowered by the fear. "Fine," she conceded and went to the kitchen, grabbing bowls and cutting her eyes over to me and Harlan in turns. "Are you going to tell me what happened to your hair?" she asked bitterly as she crossed to the fire, which had a pot hanging over it.

"No," I replied, leaning my forearms heavily on the tabletop. "I don't owe you any explanation."

Her nostrils flared, and the bowl of stew in her hands trembled with rage. "Then you'll get nothing from me," she spat.

Perhaps she'd forgotten that she didn't have control of this situation, or perhaps denying me everything I wanted was too ingrained for her to stop. Either way, when Harlan stalked toward her, she seemed surprised, and when he snatched the bowl out of her hands, she flinched. Perhaps I should have felt bad for her. I didn't.

Harlan slammed the bowl down in front of me, and this time, I was the one to flinch away. "Eat," he ordered.

I did so, picking up the bowl and drinking the stew's broth from the edge since I didn't have a spoon.

He turned back to Ethel. "She needs water, too."

Ethel sneered in contempt but went to fetch water. "Why is she so weak, anyway?"

"You'd be proud of your little niece. She saved a king's life."

Ethel looked confused. "You cut her hair after she saved your king?"

He snorted. "Her hair was cut long before today."

Ethel's arms dropped to her sides and her face lifted into stunned surprise. "But…" she stammered.

"What?" he bit out.

"She can't heal without her hair."

He turned to me, his brow raised in surprise as he looked me over. "Is that why your hair was so long when we found you?"

I nodded, seeing no reason to lie, and dumped another mouthful of stew onto my tongue. The tiny bit of food I'd eaten was already making me feel better. Not much better, but enough that I felt sure I would recover soon enough.

"Hmm," Harlan mused before turning to face my aunt. "Well, it seems your girl doesn't need her hair to heal after all." Harlan pulled out the chair opposite me and threw himself into it, putting his back to Ethel like she was of no consequence. The way he crossed his arms over his chest made his upper arms bulge, and he still held his knife. I supposed, to someone like him, Ethel *was* of no consequence.

Ethel stood frozen, her eyes suddenly less angry and more greedy as she studied me and sized up Harlan.

"What are you going to do with her?" she asked as she retrieved two cups from a shelf.

"Take her to the High Court, of course."

Aunt Ethel stiffened. "You can't do that."

"Watch me," he said while looking at me.

"The people here need her," Ethel cried. "They've been suffering ever since she left."

"She needs water," he reiterated.

Out of the corner of my eye, I saw Ethel fill the two cups with water and then add several drops of potion to one of them. I tried to keep my face passive. If she gave me that cup, I wouldn't be able to drink it, no matter how thirsty I was. But if she gave it to Harlan...my heart raced with hope. If she put him to sleep, I could leave. If I flung myself off the balcony, would that take me back to Islewyn? Was I brave enough to do such a thing? Or foolish enough? I might have to wait until my full strength returned and then attempt to climb to the ground again. But I could do that. If Harlan slept long enough, I could make my escape.

I carefully tracked Aunt Ethel's movements, keeping my eye on the cup that had the added magic.

She set it in front of Harlan and gave me the other.

I grabbed mine up and took a sip, just to be sure there was no taste of magic, then I quickly drained it.

Harlan eyed the cup Ethel had set before him, then turned his derisive eyes on her. "So you do have some manners," he said as he snatched it up and swallowed half the cup in one gulp. "Don't worry. We'll be on our way soon enough," he assured her.

Then he coughed.

I took another bite of stew, wondering how long it would take for him to fall asleep.

Then he coughed again and the table shook violently.

I looked up to see Harlan clutching at his throat, looking at me with huge eyes. He reached for me and I lurched to my feet, stumbling away from him. "What's happening?" I asked, terrified by the purple color crawling up his neck and spreading over his face.

He pushed out of his seat and stumbled toward me, backing me up until I was on the balcony, determined to avoid his grasping hands as he fell to his knees.

The door leading to the stairs crashed open, and my heart soared when I recognized Tavric's towering form. His eyes swept the room and immediately fixed on me as he ran full tilt past Ethel and jumped over Harlan, who writhed on the floor. He swept me up into his arms just as my legs buckled.

"I have you now," he whispered. "I have you."

Tavric was here. I didn't know how, but he was holding me up, protecting me, and claiming me. That support was all the permission I needed to fall apart. In the safety of his arms, the events of the last few hours caught up with me and I dissolved into a sobbing mess, wailing into his chest as he held me together and whispered reassurances in my ear.

I didn't know what would come next. Part of me knew we were far from out of danger, but the bigger part of me knew that as long as Tavric was with me, we would figure it out.

"Harlan took me," I sobbed.

"I know, love."

"He was going to turn me over to the High Court for reward money."

A breath hissed past his teeth and his grip on me tightened. "Not anymore. He's dead, Lyri. You're safe now."

What? Dead! I hadn't wanted him to *die*. Surely Tavric was mistaken. He'd probably just never seen a sleeping potion work before. But even as I thought it, I knew that Harlan's violent reaction wasn't how sleeping potions worked.

I looked up into Tavric's eyes and gave myself one moment to soak in his comfort before I turned my head to look at Harlan's prone body. His face was an unnatural, mottled purple, and he lay on his stomach, eyes open and lifeless.

My whole frame started to shake as I looked over at my aunt, who stood looking stubbornly fierce and unrepentant. "You killed him?" I asked in a bare whisper.

"Of course I did," she stated without remorse. "He was going to take you away. Now get away from that man," she demanded.

My grip on Tav tightened. "No," I cried as Ethel took a step closer.

"Don't," he said, his tone dangerous as he turned us so that his back was almost to her, placing himself as a barrier between Ethel and me. "Don't touch her."

From the safety of Tavric's arms, I peeked out at Ethel, who looked incensed. "Watch yourself, young man. You don't know—"

"I know everything I need to know," he said, releasing me so that he could face Ethel and tuck me behind him. "I know Lyri. I know what you put her through."

She ignored Tav and looked to me, softening her features into an imitation of tenderness. "We'll be just fine, Lyrielle. You've still got your magic. You can still help people, and that's what matters. They need you, my dear."

I blinked at her, astonished. "Why would I ever stay with you?" I asked. "You never saw any value in me. You only saw value in my magic, just like everyone else in this village. Why would I *ever* want to be around people who care nothing for me?"

The tenderness slipped from her face, replaced by stony determination. "You foolish girl," she said bitterly. "You were revered."

"My *hair* was revered."

"It's the same thing."

A bitter guffaw burst from my lungs. "It's not. And if you cared about me at all, you would know that."

"You would disrespect the memory of *my dear sister*—"

"She was *my mother*!" I shouted, stepping out from behind Tavric. "And he was my father! You don't own all the grief of my parents' deaths. And you don't own me, so you don't get to decide how I use my gift."

Her eyes blazed. "You aren't leaving here."

"Yes, I am," I said with an intensity that made Ethel step back.

Tav wrapped an arm around my waist from behind and dropped a kiss on top of my head. "Let's go," he murmured.

But before we could take more than a step, Ethel bent and picked up Harlan's knife, pointing it at us. "You aren't going anywhere!" she screamed and then charged at us.

I froze in fear, but Tavric pulled me behind him again and backed us away from her. Ethel swiped at Tavric with the knife. I screamed and he jumped back to avoid it, but there was nowhere to go on the small balcony and the backs of my thighs hit the banister. Ethel swung the knife again and Tavric leaned away from it, pushing further into me, and I lost my balance. His weight was too much, and my strength was too little.

Chapter Twenty-One

TAVRIC

I barely had time to register the pain of Ethel's knife slicing through my arm before I stumbled into Lyri and fell back into nothing but air.

Even worse, Lyri was falling with me.

I'd had her. She'd been safe in my arms for only a precious few moments, but then...

What had I done?

I'd killed us both. And in those few moments of free fall, all I could do was try to get a hold of Lyri while I lamented my own stupidity. She deserved better.

The impact came, but instead of pain and nothingness, I found myself submerged in water. The tower room was gone, replaced instead by the ocean that held us in its embrace. Luckily, I had the wherewithal to keep hold of Lyri, and I kicked hard toward the sunlight shining through the water.

Our heads broke the surface and Lyri coughed and gasped. My head whipped around, searching for danger, but there was nothing but swells rocking us back and forth, so I brought my attention to sweet Lyri. I cradled her cheek in my palm, frantically searching every inch of her face to reassure myself that she was alive. "You're all right. You're all right," I babbled, and then bound her up in both of my arms. My legs churned beneath the surface to keep us afloat as I clung to her. "I'm so sorry. I'm so sorry I couldn't get to you sooner. I came through the portal with you, but he had the knife, and you had no strength."

Her breathing was still panicked and wheezing as she held on to me with shaking arms. "We're back," she muttered amidst rasping coughs.

"Just breathe slowly," I told her, trying to pull my mind from the torment just enough that I could help her. "We're safe now." I leaned back so I could look at her, keeping my arm firmly anchored around her waist. "Are you hurt?"

"Harlan is dead," she choked out, the horror in her voice matching the horror in her eyes.

"I know, love. I'm so sorry...for everything. Now, please, are you hurt?" I didn't think she knew just how vital that question was to my well-being.

"No, I don't think so." She was starting to calm, her breathing becoming less harried and her eyes less frantic. Then she started to wilt.

"You're still fatigued," I said as her body sagged against mine. "You healed my father, Lyri," I said with wonder and thanks.

"Did I?" she asked as she rested her head against my temple. "Is he well?"

"Yes, love. He's going to live because of you."

"Good, good...but are we?"

"Are we what?"

"Are we going to live? We're in the middle of the ocean, Tav."

A shot of terror pulsed through me. She had a point. But I pushed my worry aside. "We just have to find the boat. It should be close by." Though how far it had drifted was anyone's guess. I strained to look around, and pain lashed across my abdomen. Air hissed past my teeth as I winced.

Lyri pulled back, suddenly alert. "What's wrong?"

"It's nothing," I lied.

She looked down and pushed back so she could see my torso beneath the waves. My shirt was shredded. "You're bleeding!"

I was, yes. Ethel's knife had not only cut my arm, but had sliced across my ribs. "It's not deep. I'll live," I gritted out, exerting myself to keep us both afloat as the pain set in. It was a good thing I'd spent so much of my life in the ocean and treading water was as easy as standing.

"Hold still," she said, reaching for it.

"No!" I said, catching her hand before she could touch the wound. "If you sing, it will open the portal. We have to get away from it first."

"But you're bleeding!" I could see her spiraling into a pit of fear.

I cupped her cheek and made her look at me.

"I won't risk us going back to that tower. Hold on to the back of my shirt. I'll swim us away and then...I'll let you heal me." I hated saying those words. I hated the thought of using her in that way, especially when she was still not recovered from saving my father.

"Fine," she conceded, no doubt realizing that a little cut was not worth a potential trip back through the portal.

She maneuvered around to my back, and I marveled at the trust she put in me. She looped her hands under my shoulders so that she wouldn't choke me, and I had to hope she had enough strength to hold on.

My mind flashed through everything that had just happened. We'd fallen from Lyri's tower. The portal had brought us back here. Harlan had betrayed me in every way imaginable and was now dead. Lyri's aunt was a more terrible human being than even I had imagined and was utterly unworthy of Lyri.

To be fair, I was unworthy as well, but at least I knew how incredible she was—and it had nothing to do with her magic.

I swam hard, pulling us through the water. With every movement, I gritted my teeth and choked down a groan, breathing through the pain.

"That's far enough," she insisted, and I felt her grip slip.

I stopped and turned so that I could hold her up. "I'll be fine. I don't want you to waste your strength."

"You won't be fine, and neither will I!" She grabbed hold of my chin and forced me to look at her. "I can't swim, Tav, and that means I need you. I need you to be strong enough to get us to the boat and sail us to shore, and that means you need me to heal you. So stop being stubborn and let me work!" The way her eyes sparked with fiery frustration made me love her just a little bit more.

"You'll be even weaker," I pointed out, terrified that she might lose consciousness again.

"It doesn't matter."

"Of course it matters." I craned my neck around to look for the boat. "Where is it? AGH!" A searing pain ripped through my torso as she shoved a hand over my wound and sang.

Just let me heal you.

Please, I have to know you are well.

The sensation of her healing power rushing through me took my breath away. It was like nothing I'd ever experienced—a sweet agony as my flesh knit itself back together, and then the euphoria of relief when the pain was gone.

She stopped singing, and I breathed in wonder. "Wow," I sighed. "That was extraordinary." I put a hand to my ribs and found that there was no searing pain, no pinching, not even an ache. Even more extraordinary, my arm had been healed as well. I brought Lyri into the circle of my arms and hugged her, then pulled back and looked in her eyes, grateful that she did not look any weaker or more tired than she had before. "Thank you, sweetheart." I placed a gentle kiss on her mouth.

When I pulled back, she was crying. "Thank you for coming for me."

"I always will."

She nodded. "But I don't want to do anything like that again. Ever."

"Never." It was all I could say because the fear was still too fresh. I'd been so close to losing her. Then I looked around again, still not seeing the boat, and realized I still might lose her. There was no boat, no ship, no help in sight.

But there might be help out of sight, I realized. How did one summon a mermaid? I did the only thing that came to mind. I put my face into the water and yelled, "Help!"

"What are you doing?" Lyri asked as I lifted my head from the water.

"A mermaid helped me earlier. Perhaps one of them will help again." I could hear my own lack of confidence.

Her eyes were huge. "A mermaid?"

"Yes. She helped me to find you and the portal."

"She... But... I thought you had to have magic to go through the portal. An actual mermaid really helped you to—"

A head appeared above the water and I jerked away, startled, pulling Lyri with me.

"Peace, Prince," the young lady said with calm surety as sunlight glinted off her blonde hair. "We're here to help."

"You're a mermaid." Lyri stated the obvious, awed as we both gaped at the mermaid, mesmerized by the glow of her pale pink tail that beat back and forth close to my own legs. I doubted I would ever get used to magic, no matter its form.

The mermaid smiled. "Of course. My name is Neeah, and I'm glad to see you well, miss," she said to Lyri.

"Me?" Lyri blinked in confusion.

"Yes, you." The mermaid glided closer to Lyri and put a hand out to support her, making it easier for me to stay afloat. "When you first came through the portal, we would have helped you, but you were fortunate enough to be dropped practically on top of a ship." Her eyes sparkled as she said it.

"I don't understand," Lyri breathed.

Saskia appeared beside Neeah, startling Lyri again. "We all came from Branfrie," Saskia told her.

"All?" Lyri gaped.

"Yes, all. There are many of us who were made for these waters."

I looked at Lyri. "You didn't tell me there were mermaids in Branfrie," I said.

"There aren't," Lyri responded.

Saskia smiled. "She's right. There aren't. We're made here."

What was she talking about? "Made here?"

Saskia nodded. "When we are dropped in these waters, we cannot survive as humans."

I nodded. Of course they couldn't.

"But if you surrender to the ocean," Neeah continued, "your magic will save you. The portal doesn't want us to die. It put us here so that we could thrive in our own world."

"So if I hadn't been found...I would have turned into a mermaid?" Lyri asked.

"That's right."

My head was spinning, and Lyri looked even more off-balance than I did with the onslaught of information.

"We try to give everyone a choice though," Saskia assured us.

"What kind of choice?" Lyri asked.

"If ever we find someone like you—someone like us—we tell them this: If you want to stay with us, all you have to do is breathe in the water and your magic will do the rest. I'll pull you under, and we'll be your family. But if you don't want to stay with us, I'll take you to land." She tilted her head at me. "But I'm guessing you don't need the choice."

Lyri smiled, allowing Neeah to support one arm while the other was wound tightly around my shoulders. Despite her fatigue, she was trying awkwardly to help us stay afloat by kicking her legs. I wasn't sure if it was helping or hindering, but I loved that she was trying. I needed to teach her to swim, and soon.

"I'm staying on land," she said.

Neeah sighed, looking at us as if we were the most remarkable thing. "You found love. Isn't it divine?"

Saskia rolled her eyes but smiled. "We can take you to your boat, if you'd like."

I let out a breath of relief, glad that the mermaids wouldn't have to swim us all the way back to shore. "Thank you, yes."

Neeah offered both hands to Lyri, who reluctantly let go of me.

"Please stay close by," I said to Neeah, unable to bear the idea of being too far from Lyri, and she nodded like she understood.

"And you take my hands," Saskia said as she faced me and held out her hands.

I wondered why she wished to pull me this way instead of having me hold her shoulders like last time, but I decided to trust that a creature of the ocean would know better than I would in this scenario, so I grabbed onto her wrists and she held onto mine.

The moment her grip was firm, she started propelling herself backwards. I half expected my head to be dragged through the water, but something about the way she moved kept our shoulders out of the water as we cut across the surface, Neeah and Lyri moving alongside us in like manner.

It was...exhilarating, much more pleasant than my first trip through the water, since this moment wasn't plagued with worry over Lyri. At least, not much worry. I did wonder how she was faring.

That question was answered when a light chuckle reached my ears, and I relaxed. Lyrielle was doing just fine.

Saskia looked over at Lyri and then back at me, a storm in her eyes. "The man who took her...will he be coming back through the portal?" she asked, concern tugging at the corners of her eyes.

I shook my head, glad that Lyri couldn't hear this conversation. "He's dead."

After several seconds, she nodded calmly. "One of my sisters saved him, you know. Years ago when he came through the portal. He didn't have magic, so she helped him to shore."

"I thought he was my friend," I murmured, then we both lapsed into silence.

My skiff came into view over the bobbing waves, and the rush of relief that coursed through my entire body when I reached out and took hold of the pitch-covered wood was overwhelming. That relief doubled when Lyri was brought up alongside me and I was able to wrap her up in my arms again. "Thank you," I breathed out my gratitude to the mermaids as the reality of what our fate might have been struck me. "Thank you so much. I don't know how... Thank you."

"We were happy to help." Neeah said. "Milin told us about you."

My brow furrowed. "Milin?"

"You met her a couple of months ago, I believe."

Of course. Melody. "Red hair?"

Neeah grinned and nodded. "We wish both of you joy, and you will always know us as friends."

"Thank you." Lyri suddenly let go of me so she could throw her arms around Neeah, who looked stunned, but then closed her eyes and embraced her in return.

Lyri turned to Saskia and gave her a hug as well. That was my Lyri, embracing everyone around her.

The mermaids were kind enough to counterbalance the boat as I struggled to climb in and then reached down to hoist Lyri in with me.

Tired but smiling, Lyri leaned over the side of the boat to bid them farewell. "May I come visit you sometimes?"

"Of course, Princess," Saskia responded.

Lyri let out a strained laugh. "I'm not a princess."

Saskia gave a little shrug. "You are to some." She smiled and then dove beneath the water, followed quickly by Neeah.

Lyri turned to me, looking baffled and bedraggled. "What do you suppose they meant by that?"

I'd been about to raise the sail, but instead I took in the sight of Lyri, with her drenched golden hair, bright eyes, and sweet face, and I knew I couldn't wait any longer to speak up.

"I'm not certain what *they* meant." I carefully maneuvered over to her, kneeling in front of where she sat on the bench and took her hands in mine. "But one thing that I know with absolute certainty is that I want you to be *my* princess." Her chest rose as she sucked in a long breath and held it, her eyes wide as I ran a finger over her cheek. "I want you in my heart, in every piece of my life, and beside me when it's time for me to take the throne, which will hopefully be a very long time from now."

She finally let her breath go in a stuttering wave, and then swallowed. "Tav, are you asking me to marry you?"

I chuckled. "Yes, and not very well, it seems."

"I..." A breeze rose up and goosebumps peppered her arms.

I looked around the bottom of the boat, hoping to find something to wrap around her, but there was nothing. "We must get back to shore," I said, and started to move away from her, but she grabbed my arms and forced my attention back to her.

I swallowed at the uncertainty in her eyes. I'd give her time to consider my words, because even though every bit of me ached for her, the last thing I wanted was to pressure her into such a monumental decision.

LYRIELLE

My eyes drank him in as I tried to convince myself that this moment was real. So much of my life had been consumed with pushing aside my own wants, too afraid to hope for someone to love me because that reality was so far out of my reach. Yet, this man knelt before me, drenched, and with hair dripping water down his face, which was soft with patience. "Do you mean it?" I had to ask.

"Of course," he breathed out. "How could I not?"

"Because I'm not…anything. Despite the crest on my necklace, I'm not royalty." I thought of all the missteps I'd made in the castle. "And I still don't know all the rules about when to stand and when to bow and when to talk."

He framed my face with his hands and looked deep into my eyes. "You are the most naturally regal person I've ever met. Crowds don't ruffle you. Stares don't intimidate you. You aren't arrogant, and you genuinely like being around people."

His words calmed my angst almost immediately. I loved being around people.

"But more importantly, you are kind and good, and you make me laugh. And against all odds, I think I've actually been good for you as well." There was the smallest bit of doubt in his eyes.

"More than good," I assured him, wondering how he could be anything less than confident.

"So when I say I want to marry you, I mean it with every piece of me." He swallowed down the emotion that had crept into his voice. "However," he said as he rubbed his hands over my chilled arms. "You are only allowed to say yes if you truly want it. Not because it's what I want. Not because you think you have no other options. Not because you believe I or my mother or the kingdom needs you. It can only be because you want me as much as I want you."

I scooted forward and wrapped my arms around him, creating a little circle of warmth and raking my fingers into the hair at the back of his neck. "What if I want you more?" I asked as I took in the utter sincerity in his eyes.

"Impossible," he whispered and then fit his lips to mine, tightening his arms around my waist as the waves rocked us gently from side to side.

I marveled at the give and take of our shared affection, and I marveled at the idea that we could have this always, that such profound connection and intimacy could be a consistent part of my life.

I pulled back as tears welled. "I love you."

He smiled as his thumb brushed over the curve of my jaw. "And I love you. Does that mean you'll marry me?"

"Of course I'm going to marry you, but you must promise me one thing."

"Name it."

"We must have babies."

He grinned, then pressed a small kiss to my lips. "My love," he whispered against my mouth, "we will have lots and lots of babies."

Chapter Twenty-Two

TAVRIC

Lyri and I were walking down to the shore, her hand wound tightly around my arm so that I could ensure her balance. She said that she felt fine, but it was difficult to forget how fragile she'd looked just a day before. I was still reeling from the events of yesterday.

Harlan, my most trusted friend other than my brothers, had betrayed me in the bitterest way, and I was finding it impossible to reconcile the Harlan I thought I'd known with the reality of who he'd become.

Lyri was endlessly optimistic, but I knew that the things she'd suffered were lurking in all the moments when she would go still and silent.

It had surprised me when she suggested we come down to the cove. I would have assumed she'd want to avoid the ocean, but she'd insisted, and I had a strong suspicion that she was doing it for my sake. She was helping me escape the castle, which was buzzing with the news of my father's recovery.

Granted, very few people knew just how much he had recovered. After we'd returned last evening, Lyrielle and I had been pulled into the chaos of my family, who had been frantic when I'd disappeared. We'd had a long time to talk as we rowed back to shore and had decided to confide in them. They were astonished at the story we had to tell, and when she insisted on treating him again to be certain that all vestiges of his illness were gone, Lyri became the immediate favorite of my entire family. Papa was alive because of her.

My family knew the truth, but we all agreed that no one else would. Everyone else would be told that Caelmir had returned with a medicine, that it had been given to the king with no improvement, and that we had all thought it had failed until he'd made a sudden recovery. Still, my mother planned to keep him in their room for several days, both to give his body a chance to truly regain his strength, as well as to give the impression that he was recovering more slowly than he was.

Everyone was elated. My father was beloved by nearly all his subjects, and news of his recovery had caused a joyous uproar throughout the entire castle.

That is, everyone was elated except for Princess Saria. She had not appreciated the way I'd left her behind after the formal meeting, and she'd liked it even less when I disappeared all afternoon. When Lyri and I had shown up, drenched and holding hands, it had been the final straw. The princess had given me one frigid glare and then gone to pack her things. She was sailing out this morning, and it was all very awkward, stilted, and diplomatic.

Thus Lyri had convinced me to bring a picnic down to the shore. For having met only a short time ago, she certainly knew me well.

I set down the basket of food and spread a blanket a little ways from the dock. "Admit it," I teased. "You like eating on the sand better than in my fancy dining hall."

I took her hand and she lowered herself with an effortless grace onto the blanket. "I like eating anywhere. Your cooks make magnificent food."

"I'll be certain to pass along your compliments."

"Oh, I've already told them a number of times. Amilee even convinced one of them to teach me how to make those little cakes that I love so much."

I was momentarily stunned, but quickly shook it off. "And yet, you don't see yourself as friendly."

She gave me a smirk. "I'm certainly not a favorite among the staff, but I'm determined to win over some of them." She opened the basket to dig through its contents, and I had the pleasure of watching my future bride find enjoyment in simple things.

We ate, reclining there on the beach, and I let myself enjoy it all. My father was well, Lyri was here with me, the crown would not fall to me for many more years, and the ocean looked serene and inviting.

"Tavric?" she asked after we'd had our fill and were lying in the sun.

"Yes, my love?"

"Will you take me sailing?"

I sat up, surprised by the request, and turned fully toward her. "Are you certain?"

"There are few things I've enjoyed more than sailing with you," she said as her eyes dipped to my lips. "And I don't want what happened yesterday to ruin that."

I looked away, anger bubbling up. "Is it terrible that I'm glad he died?"

"If it is, we're both terrible."

I turned back to look at her, blinking to keep my furious tears at bay. "You must let me teach you to swim," I insisted.

"Agreed."

"In fact, I can't believe how remiss I've been in teaching you. You nearly died the moment we met because you could not swim. It was stupid of me not to teach you right away when we live so close to the water, and maybe if you'd had that skill, then...then..."

She looked at me with such tender understanding and patience as I babbled, and when I ran out of words, she simply leaned in and said, "Tavric?"

My disquiet seeped out of me at the sound of her sweet voice speaking my name. "Yes, Lyri?"

"Will you take me sailing?" she asked again, and I almost chuckled.

"Of course," I said, as if there were ever a question. I'd do anything for her.

"Thank you." She pressed a quick kiss to my cheek, then jumped up and ran toward the dock, laughing.

I chased after her, catching up when she was halfway down the length of wooden planks. I caught her around her waist from behind, picking her up and spinning her around. She laughed more, her hands clinging to my arm. Part of me thought maybe this was a fever dream. I couldn't possibly be allowed to be this happy, could I? But when I set her down and she turned in my arms, she felt all too real.

She tipped her head back and smiled up at me, and I tightened my grip on her waist, loving the way her body molded to mine. She invigorated and soothed me all at once. I bent down, brushing my lips against hers, and was gratified when she sighed into me like she'd been waiting for me to kiss her for too long. I pressed my lips to hers more firmly, moving my hand to cradle her jaw so I could kiss her exactly how I wanted to. If I had my way, I'd spend the rest of my days doing exactly this.

When I pulled back, she blinked her eyes open in a haze and lifted her lips in the sweetest smile before nestling her head under my chin. "I didn't know life could be like this," she quietly confessed.

"I'm not sure I did either." Had I ever imagined that one person could fill me up so completely? No. I'd hoped for love and companionship, but the way Lyri and I fit together was so much more profound than that, and I truly hoped that I could always make her feel safe and cherished.

I squeezed her again and pulled back to press one more gentle kiss to her mouth. "Now, it's time to sail." We crossed to the boat, and I stepped in before helping her to board as well. After she sat down, I noticed her shiver. "I'll grab the blanket for you," I said and jumped from the boat once more.

I jogged back to our blanket, closed up the basket of food with a grin, and then walked back toward Lyrielle, who sat in the boat, leaning on one hand and gazing at me with such adoration that I nearly stumbled over my own feet.

I hurried down the dock, anxious to go sailing with my favorite person.

Epilogue

TAVRIC

It took my sweet Lyri years to overcome her guilt over not healing everyone who might need it, but I just kept reminding her about the way the people of Eldmere had turned out. How they had relied on her so heavily that they forgot the value of herbs and salves. How they took their health for granted and put themselves in danger for sport.

As a compromise, she started working with the castle doctor even before we married, learning how to heal without her magic. She had an instinct for it, and before too long, she was as proficient as her teacher. If, on occasion, she used her magic to nudge a patient into better health, then that was all the better. She learned to give of herself in moderation, and we were able to keep the truth of her abilities a secret.

Lyrielle was known as the healer princess, not because of her magic, but because of her compassion, empathy, intuition, and knowledge.

And it wasn't just sickness and injury that she treated. I marveled every day at the way she saw into the soul of a person, most especially those closest to her. The way she saw my struggles and eased them without any strain or judgement was profound.

Though I no longer had the duties of my father weighing on me, I still had my own responsibilities, which increased year after year.

Soon after we married, she had asked me why I allowed so many people to clamor for my attention at once. I told her that was how my father did it, how it had always been. She'd tilted her head and said simply, "Then we can change it."

After talking with me at length about what things specifically caused me to feel overwhelmed, she essentially trained my advisor to be a guard dog and a gatekeeper. I dealt with only one person at a time, unless my father was absent and I had to hold a formal audience, and even then, she applied strict rules. Only one person could address me at a time, and all spectators must remain quiet and respectful, or they would be asked to leave. This cut down on a good portion of the drama, which then cut down on the number of people interested in watching the proceedings, in turn cutting out much of the noise and chaos.

I often had the impulse to resist her help to avoid feeling as if I were using her, but the more time I spent with her, the more I realized she loved it. Seeing a problem and finding a solution gave her peace and satisfaction—so long as those solutions weren't demanded of her.

When I explained the way certain textures against my skin could make me uncomfortable and distracted, she herself modified my ceremonial clothing. She ensured that the fabric touching my skin was comfortable, that everything ornamenting the cloth was sewn into place so it wouldn't make noise, and she even sewed little sandbags into the shoulders to add a comfortable, calming weight to them.

She also made new clothing for herself, despite the dozens of dresses that had been gifted to her by my mother. When I asked why, she cut her eyes over to me and then looked back at the material while a blush climbed her cheeks. "If you think I have any interest in wearing clothing that you'll be uncomfortable touching, you are greatly mistaken."

I was shocked for a moment, then realized that yes, the fabric she'd chosen, as well as the few embellishments, were all textures that didn't bother me. A lump formed in my throat even as my heart raced. I couldn't help but walk over, bend down, take her face in my hands, and press a gentle kiss to her mouth. "You are brilliant," I said after drawing back.

She just smiled, shrugged, and went back to sewing.

And as for me, I delighted in giving Lyri everything she wanted. She accompanied me on any and all diplomatic missions so I could show her as much of the world as possible. I reveled in teaching her every dance I knew and then hiring a dance instructor to show us even more. I took her sailing often and we swam in the cove of the island where I'd first taught her to dance and then later taught her to swim. I also built her her very own swing, and I put it where I could see it from the library window.

That was where she was now, swinging in the garden, reveling in an activity that she hadn't experienced until after she'd appeared in my ocean. Her shoes and stockings had been tossed aside, and she was letting her bare toes skim the grass below her as she swung back and forth.

After several minutes of staring out at my wife, I decided it was useless to pretend I was still working, and I went down to find her. She grinned when she caught sight of me and stilled her legs, causing the swing to slow.

"I was hoping I could tempt you away from your duties," she called out with an unrepentant smirk.

"You, my princess, are the worst and best sort of distraction." I caught the swing and dragged it to a stop, then stepped close enough that our legs tangled together and Lyri had to tip her head back to look up at me. I kissed her smiling mouth, reveling in the calm that washed over me.

When I drew back, I smoothed my hands over her rounded belly. "How is my little one?" I asked.

"Too big, but she loves to swing."

I felt a nudge against my hand as the baby agreed with her mother's assessment. "Our baby is a girl today?"

Lyri's mouth twisted to the side. "I think so. Then again, I've thought it was a boy plenty of times." She looked down at her rounded midsection. "I keep being certain I'm right, but then a few days later..."

I chuckled. "I know, darling. I think you're just impatient."

"I want to hold her," she whispered. "I want her to fall asleep on my chest. I want to feel her warmth and weight curled against me."

"We will," I assured her. "Soon enough we will." I stepped back and took her hands, pulling her to her feet. "Until then," I said as I wrapped my arms around her, "I will take all the chances I can to hold *you*."

She immediately relaxed into me and let out a sigh. "That sounds lovely."

I rested my head on top of her head and let my eyes drift closed. "The loveliest."

The End

To My Readers

If you would like a FREE short story, as well as access to bonus material, including a bonus epilogue for Lyri and Tav, please go to my website and sign up for my newsletter. Annetteklarsen.com/extras

Thank you for reading! If you enjoyed *Tangled Sails*, please recommend it to others!

All the advertising in the world cannot compare to real people recommending it to their friends. Please take a minute to leave a review (a sentence or two is great) for other potential readers on Amazon, Goodreads, or anywhere else. Word of mouth is essential, so if you enjoyed reading Lyri and Tav's story, tell a friend! Take a photo of the book and post it on social media. Tag me. I'd love to see my readers out in the world!

You can also follow me on Instagram (@AnnetteKLarsen) or Facebook (authoraklarsen).

Happy reading!

Annette K. Larsen

About the author

I love words. I always have. In songs, in poems, in books, in movies—words move me. In my younger years, I dabbled in writing as a therapy and an escape, but I never expected it to become more than that. While deep in the depths of mommying several small children, I took seven years to write my first book, *Just Ella*. During that time, I taught myself how to write a novel through a whole lot of trial and error. Not the most time-efficient method, but it gave me an education I wouldn't have received from a class or a how-to book. Something about the struggle of writing without a formula or rules worked for me. I wrote for me. I wrote from my heart space, and I think that's the reason that *Just Ella* has found room in so many of my readers' heart spaces.

I write clean romance because I love it. I love the discovery of new love. I love the relationship building that's done with looks, words, brushing fingers, and tentative kisses. Jane Eyre is the hero of my youth and taught me that being true to yourself and clinging to your convictions will be hard, but it will bring you more genuine happiness than giving up on yourself ever can.

I've lived in Utah, Arizona, Missouri, and Virginia, but my heart is now firmly ensconced in Idaho, where we've built a home and a community.

I love chocolate, waterfalls, pretty teacups, the sight and sound of ocean waves, and most especially my husband and my five beastlings. I love books that leave me with a sigh of contentment, and I aspire to write stories that do the same for my readers.

Acknowledgements

Thank you to Kayla Eshbaugh for coming up with the concept for this series. I fully intended to take a break from fairytale retellings after I released *Paths Unknown*, but your idea was so intriguing that I had to join. I'm sad that life got in the way of you participating in this collaboration.

Thank you to all my fellow Displaced Fairytale authors for all your time, effort and support. It was lovely working with all of you.

Thank you, Kimberly Pearl, for alpha reading for me and telling me the hard truths about just how much work my initial draft needed.

Thank you, as always, to my editor, Jana Miller, for all of your correction and direction. This was a rough one, but working with you to find solutions always feels so doable. You truly are brilliant.

Thank you to my proofreader, Bethany for catching the many typos created by all my edits.

Thank you, Cameron, my love, my everything, for all your love and support. Thank you for building a life with me where I can pursue this craft.

I love you all! Now go read a good book.

Peter Pan Reimagined
By Annette K. Larsen

Prologue

Before

I KNEW NO WORDS would change my situation as I watched my uncle making final checks and preparations on the coach that would carry me away.

"Your life will be much better when you are the wife of Captain Huckley," my mother said as she fussed with some hairs that had come loose from the knot at the back of my head. It seemed they wished to escape just as much as I did.

"But I don't want to get married." My voice was flat.

"We've waited as long as we could, Wendolyn," Mother cajoled. "But your uncle is adamant. We are fortunate that he was willing to take us in in the first place, but to allow you to stay here even after a wealthy man has offered for you? You are lucky he has been so patient. You've had these years to grow up, to learn how to run a household."

I inwardly scoffed at that. I had learned to run a household long before Captain Huckley took notice of me. I'd done it for years. We had been wealthy once, but I barely remembered it. I had been only nine years old when Papa was arrested for treason. My mother and I were shocked, completely blindsided, but the magistrate's words to us as my father had been hauled away were clear. Father and a group of merchants and townspeople had been working to overthrow the reign of the sovereign duke. My father roundly denied any involvement, but every member of the faction pointed to him as the leader, the man intended to seize control and rule Winberg. He'd been incarcerated and we'd been stripped of all our property. We'd had no choice but to go begging to my mother's sister. She and her husband had taken us in, and for the past seven years had fed, clothed and sheltered us, though they were not particularly well off. In exchange I worked alongside my aunt, running and fetching, organizing and planning. They kept up appearances by allowing me a few new dresses to wear to public events so that I could catch a man's eye. Then they could be rid of me.

It had worked.

I was only fourteen when Captain Huckley came to Norsing on business and attended a local gathering in which I had been allowed to participate. He'd been attentive and flattering, but he was also decidedly old. It never occurred to me that his flattery was an attempt at flirtation until he approached my uncle to make his interest known. Uncle Horace was ecstatic at the offer.

Captain Huckley was a merchant with a fleet of ships. He was not of the noble class, but his abundant wealth made up for that. A betrothal agreement had been struck. I remembered looking to my mother over and over, waiting for her to speak up for me, to object, to tell them no. Or simply to ask my opinion about whether or not I wanted to marry a man a full twenty years older than me. She never had. Instead, when the contract was officially drawn up, I was compelled to sign it as Uncle Horace loomed over me. They hadn't even allowed me to read it.

So now, only four days after my sixteenth birthday, I was being sent off to my future husband. My trunks were packed and strapped to the hired coach. I was to travel alone to Captain Huckley's house a half day's journey from here. My uncle had spared only a maid to accompany me, in order to keep everything proper. Neither my aunt and uncle nor my mother would attend my wedding. I would simply arrive, be escorted to the church, bound to a man who terrified me, and then expected to be a dutiful wife.

I knew how to run a household. I did not know how to be a wife. I did not want to know.

Uncle Horace gave the driver a nod and looked to me. My mother took that as her cue and took my hands in hers. "Now," she said in a stiff voice. "Hold your head high. Remember who you are. Who are you?" she asked in a whisper that my uncle would not hear.

"Lady Wendolyn Cecilia Stoffard," I answered. It was something my mother had asked me many times over the years. Her way of reminding me that I came from something better and deserved more, but all it really accomplished was to remind me of all I had lost, all my father had taken from us because of ambition.

"That's right," my mother affirmed, then kissed my head and ushered me into the coach where I sat across from my maid, Annabelle. I tried to believe that my mother was doing what she thought was best, but the lack of light in her eyes told me that she had simply given up. She stood back, letting the footman latch the door. If only she would say something, do something so that I would know she cared—not about status or survival, but about me.

My aunt cared so little for me that she wasn't even there to bid me farewell. I didn't bother looking to my uncle for pity or remorse. It was too easy to see what he gained from this. One less mouth to feed and a handsome "investment" into his financial holdings. Uncle Horace was desperate to protect himself. If only my mother had been as desperate to protect me.

And I would need protecting.

Mother refused to give any heed to the rumors. The many wives the captain had had. The way they'd all died. But I heard them, and I knew in my heart of hearts that they were true. My marriage was a death sentence.

"Goodbye, Wendolyn!" my mother called as the coachman climbed up onto the seat.

I turned to look at her, and at my uncle as he stood a little behind her, but I didn't say anything. Bidding them a good anything would have been a lie. So I simply stared until the coach rolled forward, pulling me from their view.

As we clattered down the rutted drive, past the overgrown gardens, I pulled the hem of my cloak into my lap, pressing it between my fingers to reassure myself that they were there. Annabelle's hand covered mine, giving me hope that not all was lost. She and I had been carefully hoarding coins over the past two years, and we had worked together to sew them into my cloak hem, between the layers of fabric. Six gold pieces and nineteen silver. They were our only possible means of salvation, and I had to hope they would be enough.

Chapter 1

Nine Years Later

Despite the dirt and dust, the stables held a sort of magical glow in the morning, made even more magical by the rapt attention of the children gathered around me for a story. Whenever Her Highness went riding, I would come here to entertain the stable master's children and any others who wished to listen while I waited for her return. "And with one wave of her hand, the pixie Annabelle sprinkled her sparkling, golden dust over the fair maiden, and together they flew away from the evil captain."

"They flew?" five-year-old Lindy asked in a whisper, her eyes wide with the magic of the story. I'd only been here at Sutton Manor for three weeks, but I'd already gained a small audience.

"Yes," I assured her. "For when you have freedom and joy, all you need is just a bit of magic to make your heart so light that it lifts you right off the ground."

"Where did they go?" she asked.

I grinned down at her from my seat on the barrel in the corner of the stables. "The Never Kingdom," I answered. "A magical place ruled by a fairy princess with the kindest heart and the most beautiful smile. A place where the maiden would never be forced to grow up and marry that awful, old captain with the maimed hand and the blackened heart."

"What happened to his hand?" Ansel asked, almost as enchanted by the story as his younger sister.

"A sea monster chewed on it when he was marauding across the seas!"

The stable master's children gasped at my dramatic declaration.

"What did the pixie and the maiden do next?" Lindy asked.

"They had to go their separate ways. The pixie had other young girls who needed her help. But they will always be friends, even if they can't be together."

Lindy smiled in contentment, but Ansel crossed his arms, looking at me with his mouth screwed up to one side. "I thought these stories were supposed to have a prince that saves the girl."

I laughed at his criticism. "Many do. Would you like me to tell you a story about a dashing hero next time?"

"Yes. And there should be swords," he stated as a matter of fact. "Like Falstone," he said, pointing toward the door of the stables. "He's good with a sword."

I looked over my shoulder and spotted Princess Marilee's personal guard, Falstone, there in the doorway. The sun cut in behind him, throwing his shadow onto the packed dirt floor. He was observing quietly the way he always did, his gaze skimming over me the way it always did as he took in the stables, the grooms, the loft overhead.

I resisted the urge to sigh. Falstone would make a fine hero for my stories. He had never given me reason to doubt his motives because he'd never acknowledged me as anything other than a lady's maid to Princess Marilee.

I remembered all too well my internal upheaval when Marilee was trying to choose which of her father's guards to keep as her own. It had been disconcerting to have so many new people to deal with. New men. I had done my best to stand tall and not let my intimidation show, but it had been terrifying, especially when Falstone had seen me. Because he hadn't just looked at me.

That first time we'd met, when he'd walked into the drawing room of Bridgefield with the other soldiers, his eyes had landed on me and done a full assessment. I knew as his scrutinizing gaze swept over me that he saw more than I would wish. He saw *everything*. And for one terrifying moment, I had felt the need to run, far and fast. But then the moment was gone, and once his examination was complete, he moved on. It was as if that one assessment had told him everything he needed to know about me and he was thus free to continue on his way without spending any more time or energy on me.

Since then, he'd not spared me more than a glance unless we were conversing specifically about Marilee.

It had been a relief while at the same time my skin bristled at the slight. But relief won out in the end. After narrowly escaping being sold to Captain Huckley, my need for safety would always win out.

Falstone's gaze fell on me once more where I sat in the stables and I realized that I'd been staring at him, his stance strong and silhouetted by the bright sunlight behind him. I jerked my eyes away, wondering why he was standing there anyway. Was Marilee back from her ride? Wasn't it his job to guard Her Highness?

A bark sounded and Rogue bounded through the doorway, quickly honing in on my tiny circle of children and loping over to receive pats and praise before circling around them and herding them toward the door amid the sound of their giggles.

"It must be time to get back to work." I chuckled as the children squealed in delight. Rogue seemed to consider the little ones to be his personal responsibility. He'd likely try to tuck them all in their beds if anyone would allow it.

Lindy and Ansel ran to their father, Pryce, allowing the stable master to scoop them up for a moment before he sent them out to find their mother. Oliver retrieved his pitch fork and returned to the business of cleaning stalls. At eleven, he was becoming a dedicated stable boy, but he couldn't seem to resist the urge to pause for one of my stories.

I stayed perched on my barrel, watching as Marilee came in as I knew she would. Rogue never strayed far from his owner. Sir James was quick to follow, leading both of their horses by their halters.

"Explain to me again why you are allowed to drench me, but I cannot retaliate." Sir James's smile was wry as he looked to his wife. The princess's new husband was nearly as devoted to Marilee as Rogue was. I noticed the wrinkles in his shirt where he'd likely had to wring it out. By contrast, Marilee's riding habit was entirely dry.

"I told you it wasn't my doing," she said with a not-quite-innocent smile.

"You cannot blame everything on sprites and elves."

"Fairies," Marilee corrected, sounding completely serious.

I grinned. Sir James just shook his head and tried to hide a smile.

Marilee's riding habit was bright, her smile brighter, and I happily soaked in the evidence of her happiness as she and Sir James handed their mounts over to the grooms and headed back out into the sunshine. I'd give them a few moments and then follow. Marilee would need help changing out of her riding habit.

I made my way to the stable doors and leaned my shoulder into the post as I took in my fairy-tale life. Some would think me strange for describing it in such a way. What servant in their right mind would view their life as charmed?

Me, that's who. Everything I'd told the children about that fair maiden's escape was true. Exaggerated, yes. But true. Annabelle and I had bribed the coachman to take us to the town of Tethurn instead of Huckley's residence.

We'd found positions in the same house, working side by side as maids. Life in service had been difficult, more difficult than I had imagined, despite all the work I'd done in my uncle's house. Still, I was determined and work didn't scare me. Though I was a servant instead of a noblewoman, I had gained the one thing that I truly longed for—freedom from men who would control me.

And I *was* free. Especially now that I worked for Princess Marilee and Sir James. Sutton Manor was my home. The place where I was safe, and loved, and free. The place where I was never afraid, never controlled, never abused. This was my Never Kingdom...

You can find Hooked on Amazon...

Also by Annette K. Larsen

Books of Dalthia series:
Refusing Mia (Mia and Archer)
Just Ella (Ariella and Gavin)
Missing Lily (Lylin and Rhys)
Saving Marilee (Marilee and James)
Painting Rain (Lorraina and West)
Keeping Kinley (Kinley and Rylan)

Dalthia Companion Novella
To Betray a King (Faelyn and Bram)
Part of The Shattered Tales Multi-author series

The Hidden Gift (Tales of Winberg prequel)
Part of The Christmas Chronicles Multi-author series
Tales Of Winberg series:
Hooked (Cecily and Falstone)
Cloaked in Scarlet (Emeline and Hunter)
The Swindler's Daughter (Miriam and Rowan)
The Starling and the Hatter (Elise and Hatcher)
Waking Roslyn (Roslyn and John)
Paths Unknown (Ansel and Gretchen)

Contemporary:
If I Could Stay
All Our Broken Pieces
All That Stands Between Us
Songs for Libby
You can find all my books on Amazon.

www.ingramcontent.com/pod-product-compliance
Lightning Source LLC
La Vergne TN
LVHW091035080826
845145LV00002B/507